HILL OF
DEAD HORSES

SARAH BIRDSALL

⌇⋀⋁⋀⋁ Epicenter Press Inc.
Alaska Book Adventures™
KENMORE, WA

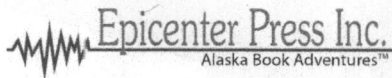

Epicenter Press Inc.
Alaska Book Adventures™

6524 NE 181st St., Suite 2, Kenmore, WA 98028

Epicenter Press is a regional press publishing nonfiction books about the arts, history, environment, and diverse cultures and lifestyles of Alaska and the Pacific Northwest. For more information, visit www.EpicenterPress.com

Cover image: Sidney Hamilton Photograph Collection,
Anchorage Museum, B1976.082.304
Interior design: Melissa Vail Coffman

Library of Congress Control Number: 2024939762

ISBN: 978-1-684922-48-2 (Trade Paperback)
ISBN: 978-1-684922-49-9 (Ebook)

*To the people of the Northern Susitna Valley
and all those who have known the wild beauty at mile 248.5
of the Alaska Railroad, with or without a grand hotel,
and to anyone who ever lost a loved one to opioid addiction.*

*Dead Horse Hill received its name when a
team of horses became frightened at seeing
a bear, ran away and plunged to their death
from the top of a steep hill.*

NELLIE NEAL LAWING, *Alaska Nellie*

CHAPTER ONE

EMILY WELLS
1985

WE DIDN'T KNOW ABOUT THE HORSES, Thomas and I, back when we'd first arrived, but in the years since I have imagined them over and over: a black wet night, a grizzly bear in the dark, the stomping of the hooves and the screaming of the horses and the roaring of the bear. The day we stepped off the train, the only thing Thomas and I knew was that we thought Alaska would save us—the pure water, the clean air, the mountains and miles of trees—and miles of distance between us and San Francisco, the parties and the friends who encouraged us, the families who were shamed by us, the drugs and alcohol that consumed us. We walked away as if by leaving, the people we were stayed behind and carried on as we once did, while the new versions of ourselves slipped off into a new life in a new land. But it doesn't work like that, does it? And of course, being who we were, we picked a spot already contaminated, a place of dead horses with ashes of destruction deep in the ground—ashes, and worse.

FALL 1974

"THOMAS, WHAT'S THIS?" I ASKED, LOOKING unhappily at the length of whiteish something that appeared in the post hole I was digging. We were on a hill—our hill, as Thomas called it—located a mile from the Alaska Railroad line that brought us here. Thomas was working on his own hole, diagonally across an imagined floor space from where I worked on mine. Thomas had this theory that it would be better to dig opposing corners first, run a string between them, then do the same with the other corners so we would end up with a perfect X that would equal a perfect rectangle. I wanted to do it the other way, the two front post holes then the back, but really, neither of us knew what we were doing and relied on drawings in an old book on cabin building. Even on the hill, the black flies, which had appeared as soon as the mosquitoes started to thin out, were terrible.

"Rock?" Thomas asked, pounding the step of his shovel with the bottom of his boot.

"No—a stick, I think. It's across the hole and I can't get it to budge."

Thomas put his shovel down and walked over the grassy rock-riddled high-country ground to my corner. He knelt beside my hole, his lanky frame folding like the hinged measuring stick we brought with us instead of a proper measuring tape. I watched his face as he evaluated the situation, his dark blond waves plastered away from his forehead by sweat and bug dope, the beginnings of a beard sprouting from his round boyish cheeks, dirt on the end of his nose. There was a clear sparkle in his blue eyes that made me think yes; yes. We did the right thing.

His brow furrowed. He reached down into the hole.

"Maybe you shouldn't touch it," I said, and his arm shot back up.

"Why?"

"I don't know. We don't know what it is."

He shrugged. "Rock, wood, or bone I suppose."

"Bone," I said, giving voice to the thought that crept into my mind from someplace unwanted.

"Well, if it's a bone," he said, "it's gotta be an animal's. Moose, caribou, bear. They're all out here." He made a sweeping gesture with his arm.

I pulled in a breath and looked at the view in front of us. The hills tumbled down to the railroad tracks and the river, between which was the ghost of what once was an elegant wilderness hotel that burned to the ground in 1957. The hotel had served as a stopping place between Seward and Fairbanks during the days of the slow-moving steam trains and was once known as the "palace in the wilderness." From our hill, there was no sign of the ruin that bordered the rails that followed the river, but it bothered me that it was there, the remnants of a past that felt disconnected to the wilderness around us. There'd been a tennis court, a swimming pool, a small walking bridge across the massive glacial river. Alaska's elite, if there really was such a thing, rode the train up from Seward and Anchorage or down from Fairbanks with their skis, their snowshoes, their fishing rods, and their wallets, stopping on their way through hundreds of Alaska miles, or coming specifically to experience the uniqueness of "luxury" lodgings in the wild. Across the river from where the hotel had been, a huge ridge rose abruptly, like a massive wall.

Behind us hills continued to roll, the land rising and dipping, with the occasional rocky face and thick patches of brush and clumps of tangled alders that resembled, from a distance, a scraggly, haphazard beard. Pointy little spruce trees decorated the landscape like bristle-brush Christmas trees, with random white birch trees reaching upward, stern silent sentries.

A short distance in front of me, and as ever-present as an unwanted neighbor, was the steep face of the hill, and directly beneath it a fiercely tumbling stream twisted and flowed. I would later learn this stream was called Deadhorse Creek and the gash in the land it ran through was Deadhorse Canyon, of which the steep side of our hill was part. The past was closer to us than I had first imagined.

"It's probably a stick, Emily," Thomas said, knowing how my mind worked. "It's got nothing to do with that old hotel. A caribou bone, at the most." He reached again into the hole, his arm disappearing up to his armpit. "You really went deep," he said.

"Wasn't I supposed to?"

"Yeah—I guess. We'll have to check the book."

If only I'd stopped, let the hole be deep enough a few shovelfuls ago. Then we would never have found the bone.

Thomas's eyes roamed the gray sky as he felt away in the dark. "It does seem like it's a bone," he said.

"Couldn't we just re-bury it?" I asked. "I mean, if the hole is deeper than it needs to be, shouldn't we—maybe—cover it back up?"

His hand was working under there, loosening the soil, and I could tell by his face that he'd gotten his stubborn on, that now he had to know. He bit his lower lip as he worked, face turned to the sky, and I thought, Thomas, Thomas. I could not love him more than I did at that moment, my lost boy. *We'll be okay.*

He pulled it free and brought it up, that thing, no—not a thing, a piece of a person. I could see it right away, from the days before Thomas when I studied to be a nurse. I felt that knowledge in my heart, my knees, and in the pit of my stomach. What had we found?

"Wolf?" he said, proudly holding it up. "Caribou?"

I stepped up beside him, tentatively touched it, and quickly pulled back my hand.

"What's wrong?" Shadows circled across Thomas's face, shadows that I had no means to swipe away. "No—it can't be. Not way out here!"

"It really looks like it, Thomas. A tibia." God—where was the rest of it? I quickly added, trying to soften the blow, "I can't be sure."

He sat down on the wild ground, dying grasses and twisted twiggy bushes dotted with hard sharp rocks, placing the bone as far from him as his arm could reach, and rubbed the hand that had held it back and forth on a little patch of green moss. I lowered myself between him and the bone, grabbed his moving hand and held it tight in both of mine—his beautiful hand, with his fine, slender fingers and graceful bones, with the scars across the palm—scars that weren't there when we first met, in a Sacramento club where he was the singer in the band that was playing, a once-local band back home for a brief stop during a state-wide tour. I was out with friends, not knowing my life would turn, not knowing the beautiful rag-doll singer would come to the bar near where I sat when the band went on break, and that after downing two out of three shots of tequila he would turn to me and smile, then drop to the floor like a falling tree.

I sprang to his side. "I'm a nurse!" I had yelled to the press of people. It was almost true. "Give us room!" What we needed. Then and now.

All the room in the world is what we thought we had, on this land we staked out ourselves on this hill in the wilderness that loomed above the site where that grand hotel had once sat incongruously between that great glacial river and these hills where caribou roamed, all gone now except the railroad stop and the name: Findlay, the same as my Thomas—Thomas Findlay—and the same name as that bloody band, "Findlay," that had gone on without him. As my eyes wandered to the bone on the dead flattened grasses beside me, careful so Thomas wouldn't see me looking at it, I wondered if the hotel were really gone. In that moment, the two of us surrounded by raw wild beauty and not another human soul in sight, the bone and the ghost of the hotel seemed to be compressing the very air around us, and I heard those old words come back to me, *Give us room.*

HARRY HARBOUR
FALL 1974

A SMALL CONFESSION, SINCE I'M GOING TO tell this story and I should be honest about it. It's about whether or not I was a player here. I'll say I wasn't, as much as I longed to be. Until the end. Then I guess I was a factor—not a player. The unexpected thing that comes flying across the stage toward the end of the final act. The unplanned unwanted unimaginable thing that upended my life and changed who I was forever yet didn't make me a part of the story. A witness first, a random factor second. That's all I ever was. Even now I feel like an intruder, attempting to relay what I know. And I don't like to remember what happened. I tell myself it's because of her that I can't forget, that she's the reason I keep going over it again and again, though I know it's also because of me and what I did. In a story that wasn't even mine.

IN 1927 I WAS A SMALL time/small town (Anchorage was more small town than not) Alaska boy who was awestruck at the miraculous wonder of the Alaska Railroad's Findlay Hotel, a "northland palace" as it was described in the old advertisements. I'd never seen anything so grand and never would again. It was mysterious and mesmerizing, I think in part because of the setting: you had this place with forty-two rooms and growing, a golf course, a tennis court, a swimming pool, a dining room that served "Prime Ribs of Beef Au Jus," indoor toilets, and hot water baths. Then there was that mighty river at its backside, and the grizzlies on the hills that rose into the wild on the other side of the railroad tracks. It was all a big contradiction, such a hotel in such a place. Jackson Keats knew that, it was on his face each and every time he came down from those hills, his hair dark and wild and his eyes as black as the coal that fueled the trains. Striding onto the platform, people staring, his big wolf-like husky beside him.

"Jackson! Can't take that dog in there!"

The mail that came on the trains was what brought him down. I wondered always what he waited for, who it was he was hoping would write.

I was twenty-one. Jackson Keats wasn't much older than I was, yet there seemed to be decades between us.

He showed up, of course, the day Sonja Antonov got off the train on a clear and crisp September day—or I should say Sophia Petersen, though I did not know that then. What I did know was that I was anxious for that train to get in, not knowing that Fate was riding along beside it, so I could send my "Aunt" Cora on her merry way.

FALL 1927

"YOU'VE RUINED THE PLACE, HARRY," CORA said as she and I sat in the dining room waiting to load the gear for her Fairbanks moose hunt onto the train. Because the train wasn't going any farther than Findlay until the next morning—it was spending the night just like the passengers—Cora's plan was to toss her stuff into the baggage car and get herself gone, start walking north and let the train pick her up tomorrow. She was ready to "get some air" as she put it, and I was counting the minutes until Cora'd get on with it and get on her way.

"*I* have?"

"Well, you're up here aren't you and you're taking a paycheck from these people."

"You mean the Alaska Railroad, Aunt Cora." Cora wasn't really my aunt—or anyone's aunt for that matter. I called her that because she knew my parents and had known me since I was born. Alaska, despite its vast landscape, was like one big small town someone once said, and sometimes when she came to Anchorage Cora would stay with us and bring hunks of moose meat or dead animal skins and she and my parents would laugh and talk long into the night. Up here most people called her Crazy Cora, or simply the

Crazy One, though no one thought she actually *was* crazy. She was a wild woman with a gun (well, lots of guns) and had done things most men wouldn't even attempt, like chase a grizzly bear with a knife when her gun was out of reach and walk alone from Seward to Girdwood, some sixty lonely wild miles. Cora had been here long before the hotel, back when the place was a railroad camp called Deadhorse Hill because of those poor horses that fell off one of the many hills when a bear came along and scared them into bolting to their deaths. Most people didn't know that, or that she had the run of the railroad's roadhouse here back then and killed lots of animals, but then got pushed out when the railroad built the hotel. She came back once in a while to check on things, and to spit in the face of it.

"Yes, the damned railroad," Cora said and heaved a sigh. We were sitting at a table by a window, drinking tea. Cora wore trousers, tall lace up boots, a flannel shirt, and a plaid wool jacket. She had a hat made from a marten she'd killed that sat on the table between us, its face and its little paws all there, with black beads where the eyes used to be. "How many of the railroad men—including your father, young man— did I give shelter to over the years? Cook them breakfast, pack their lunches, send them on their way so they could lay another mile or two of track? I helped them in the building of this god-damned railroad. And they thank me with this: a mass of civilization in the middle of my wilderness."

"Well, like you said, Cora, you helped build the railroad."

She gave me that look, like she was imagining seeing me through the sights on her rifle. "I wanted people to be able to get out here and see all this—to get off the train anywhere they wanted between Seward and Fairbanks with a backpack and a good gun and just see and experience Alaska." She said it in a way that didn't leave room for disagreement.

"And stay at your roadhouse," I added.

Her mouth twitched, as if suppressing a snarl. "That's not the point."

"Hmm."

"You know damned well what I'm talking about, Harry. Majestic wilderness with a train coming through and a rough old roadhouse here and there are one thing. This thing, and all that comes with it, is another."

"Well, all I can say is, you come here enough for hating it so much." I said that, though I knew what she meant, and I knew what Findlay—Deadhorse Hill as it was in her time—meant to her.

I heard a whistle in the distance. Thank God the train was coming. I wouldn't have to worry about Cora until she came back down on her way home to Seward. My connection to the Crazy One didn't serve me well with the higher ups on the hotel staff.

"Train's coming, Cora. We'd best get out there." I stood and waited while she took her time finishing her tea. When the train finally pulled up to the platform she pushed back her chair, grabbed her hat and slammed it onto her head. I walked out with her and tried to help her load her gear into the baggage car, but she would have none of it. "Don't you touch my rifle," she said as she hoisted up her duffle. I pulled my hands away from the gun case and let her take care of it. "Wish us luck on the hunt," she said. "Probably have better luck up here though I imagine they'd hate to see blood and guts all over that pretty golf course." She patted her gun case as it slipped inside the baggage car, turned, and looked at me. "You sure you won't come? You wouldn't want to waste a good train ticket now, would you?" Cora had bought me a train ticket to Fairbanks in the hope that I would join her, stubbornly ignoring the fact that I could get a railroad pass to anywhere on the rail line anytime I wanted, provided I could get the time off for traveling. "All right— well, I'm heading out," she said to my lack of response. "See you on the return, Harry. We can start planning the caribou hunt—and you're not going to weasel your way out of that one."

"See you, Cora." The wind blew off the river and there was a slight nip in it. We all knew winter was on its way as fall in Alaska never amounts to much. There would probably be snow in the hills by the time Cora dragged me into them for that damned caribou hunt which I could not seem to escape.

Herman, who worked the baggage car, told Cora they'd see her tomorrow and she strode off down the side of the tracks, a backpack with her camping gear and a .22 rifle to shoot her dinner her only company. She had loved it when she lived here. I knew that. I stayed watching her until the train emptied and Herman slid the door of the car closed. Crazy Cora. You could say they don't make them like her anymore; I'd say they never did make them like her to begin with. There was ever only one Cora Allen.

I turned, and on came the moment that changed my life for the rest of it. The new arrivals on the platform were finding their way into the hotel lobby, giddy and excited to be here, all their gear in tow, suitcases of clothes and lengthy cases with fishing rods. Before long some of them would be on the walkway crossing the river and heading for Findlay Ridge, or out on the tennis court or the golf course, trying to get some fun in before dinnertime. My favorite thing had always been watching the old guys get out their fishing poles and wander down to the river in the evening. I thought I could feel what they were feeling in those moments, that life was still good. Here was a river in front of them, a warm bed and a hot bath behind them, nature and comfort miraculously combined.

I was watching the flow of people move toward the big open doors of the hotel when I saw her. It was obvious she wasn't a guest, dressed as she was in a long thin skirt and an oversized sweater with that crown of gold braids on her head. That pretty face, fair skinned and blue eyed, as fragile as one of my mother's porcelain figures that lived an unmoving life on a shelf above our old fireplace. I wondered who she was and why she was dressed the way she was, like an old woman when obviously she was nothing of the sort. She looked around worriedly, that soft little mouth slightly open, and I began to walk toward her. That's when Jackson Keats and his big old wolfdog strode on to the platform. I would think about that moment a lot over the years: Jackson walking toward me, me walking toward her, the three of us there, in that moment. Then, being the good hotel employee that I was, I had to say it— "Jackson! Can't take that dog in there!"—trying to sound gruff. He ignored me as usual and continued on, though not before noticing the young woman in the old woman's clothes. A flash of something crossed both their faces, which I caught like a glimpse of a leaf in the wind and promptly forgot.

I should have known. The moment I saw the look on her face, right as Jackson and his dog walked on to the platform, I should've known something...maybe not everything, but something: the way her face went white, and the shadow of fear that fell across it at the sight of him, the expression of haunted confusion on Jackson's face as he brushed past me and went into the hotel.

I watched him go, and figured I'd let someone else yell at him about the dog. He showed up every week or so to see if he had any mail, and from what I heard from Sheila, who worked in the little area called the "post office," he never had anything. I turned back toward my purpose, the strangely dressed, pretty girl on the platform. "Excuse me, miss, can I help you at all?" She seemed not to hear me and was looking toward the hotel entrance where Jackson disappeared. "It's all right," I said, thinking I knew what she was thinking. "It's a big dog but it's just a dog. Won't hurt anybody." She looked at me as if just realizing I was there.

"Oh," she said. "Perhaps you may help me, please. I am to go to the laundry." She had an accent, something European I thought, and her voice was very quiet.

"I do know where the laundry is," I said, smiling. "I guess I'm the lucky fella who gets to take you there!" She gave me no response. I suddenly saw myself as she might—gawky and goofy. I looked down at the platform and tried again. "I mean, I can show you where it is, if you'd like." I looked up and met her eyes, and that stricken look on her face eased a little and she gave me the faintest nod.

"Thank you," she said.

"I can get your bags," I said, and turned to what was left of the pile that had come out of the baggage car. Only one thing remained—a small brown tattered bag, patched here and there with pieces of bright fabric. It looked nearly empty. Before I could reach it, she stepped past me and snatched it up. "Is that all you brought?" I asked. Of course it came out the wrong way. Sometimes things got left on the train. I had to ask.

She nodded. "This is all."

"All right then," I said. I longed to offer her my arm, or gently take her elbow, like someone might do in a book. Instead I stood there, longing to say something, longing to do something, longing to be someone other than who I was. Then Nellie June from the laundry stomped onto the platform, her apron on and her thin dishwater-blond hair pulled back from her sweaty face, and I lost my chance at anything.

JACKSON KEATS
FALL 1927

SOPHIA. IT HAD TO BE HER; I would not be mistaken. Why was she here? Our last day, on the cold wet windy beach, her hard little fists beating my chest. No no no no no! When I passed her on the platform our eyes locked with a sharp jolt. I kept walking, though my heart had fallen into the pit of my stomach. Someone was yelling at me: the hotel boy. I didn't stop. Snow followed me; the guests in the hotel did not seem to mind. He is a beautiful dog. His real name is Snowy Day, because he is the color of the sky when it snows. He knows how to behave.

I waited for the mail. I stood against the wall and trembled all over. I prayed that Sophia would disappear, that when I returned to the platform there would be no trace of her. As I waited, people smiled at Snow as they walked by, then would look at me to smile at the master of the pretty dog. They would quickly look away. As if I were the one who was part wolf.

When my name was called by the young lady who sorted the mail I thought, Am I dreaming today? First here was Sophia on the plat-form. Now for the first time my name gets called at the mail. My hand shook as I took the letter, the writing on it as familiar to me as the movement of air in my lungs. I tore it open and read. I nearly fell as the words slammed across the miles at me: You can come home. Sophia Petersen is dead.

JACKSON KEATS CRESTED A STEEP HILL and only then did he stop, Snowy Day coming up beside him. He was sweating and the black flies circled where he stood. He allowed himself to look back at the hotel, small and distant now and far below, and fell suddenly to his knees in the sharp, brittle brush of fall.

Sophia!

Her ghost, there on the platform? He had thought so, even before reading the poisonous letter from his father. But the hotel boy had seen her, too. Perhaps it was some other young woman, and he had placed Sophia's face onto hers. Or perhaps Sophia's ghost had created the illusion, to torment him. He had heard of such stories, the faces of the dead momentarily on the faces of the living.

Sophia Petersen is dead.

His father was not a man to make mistakes—not, at any rate, on matters of fact. He said Sophia Petersen was dead. Then she must be dead.

"No!" Jackson yelled suddenly into the endless air, the endless nothingness around him. Snowy Day startled and looked around, as if he had done something, or as if something were about to be done to his master and him.

If she had only believed in him, if she had only trusted him…

But she had. That black cloud he had been running from for the two years since he left the island wrapped itself around him in a tight grip. He hadn't believed her. In the end, he was the one who didn't trust.

A drowning, that's what his father said. They searched and searched for her, the villagers, and found nothing. The sea had swallowed her. But the young woman on the platform. He let his heart lift. If there was a chance . . . Nothing made sense. A ghost: that made more sense than the other possibilities. If the village believed Sophia was dead, she must be dead.

No! The knowledge ripped its way through him, like a wild animal trapped inside his chest, all tooth and claw, shredding. It tore its way from one end of him to the other, and he raged against the earth he fell upon, his hands quickly scratched and bloody, Snowy Day standing at some distance now, watching.

No.

At last he stopped, and now could not move. He lay on the ground and Snowy Day came up and lay beside him. Gradually, he could taste the earth in his open mouth, feel the pulse of his heart against it. He moved his eyes and there were Snow's two eyes, blue like the very September sky above them, locking on to his. Silently Jackson pulled himself up, and he and Snowy Day finished the long walk home, pushing open the rough wooden door on the small low-roofed cabin as the last of the light disappeared from the sky.

IN THE HOURS THAT FOLLOWED, JACKSON SAT in his only chair by his small hand-hewn table, his father's letter there in front of him. The darkness deepened and Jackson embraced it, the letter glowing faintly in the blackness. He could not stop his thoughts, and he let them run, felt a safety in the dark, as if within it the thoughts were thin, without substance, and would dissipate when the light broke over the hills. So tonight he remembered, and let the thoughts take him where they would.

The day on the hill that overlooked the cemetery, three years ago. The crooked crosses, pale dead grasses swaying in the wind. The threatening gray of the coming sky; they had no jackets; they would get wet; how Sophia laughed at that...

"We have been wet our whole lives, don't you think?"

Together they looked out past the cemetery, past the shore, past the rolling water to that mysterious horizon. "There are places where it doesn't rain so much," he had said. Sophia's face grew as distant as the horizon itself as she nodded. He knew then they shared the same dream, to leave the village, to leave the island, to go where the sun sparkled on the sea.

"Someday, Sophia, we could go."

Her face turning to his. The only sun he would ever need. He placed his lips on hers, knowing it was harmful to do so, that it would taint her more than him, that God saw everything, knew everything. For a moment they were swept away, as if the wind lifted them from the earth itself.

Another day, gray and wet and cold. A year later, shortly after the death of Sophia's mother. The same spot above the cemetery—the cemetery where her mother would not be buried, Sophia like a burning flame beside him, the heat from her anger swirling in the wind.

"Let us be married, Sophia. Father Mikhail would approve. There is no reason now. We could take care of Peter together. Your brother would be my brother, Sophia."

Jackson's father would welcome them into their home. They would make a new family, the four of them. For so long, it had been Jackson and his father and an emptiness in the house where his mother had once been.

"We cannot."

"There is no reason, Sophia."

"You know nothing, Jackson—nothing!"

"Then tell me what I don't know!"

Sophia rose from the ground and ran down the hill.

Jackson would not let it be.

He wondered now who mourned for her in that village of hate. Peter, surely; he initially forgot about the boy. What would become of him now?

He knew that whatever happened to Sophia, she would fight for Peter with her dying breath.

She went out on the water at night, Jackson, when the village was asleep and the weather was very bad. Perhaps they were hungry, and she was trying to catch some fish for their breakfast.

Father Mikhail has suggested perhaps she took her own life.

He knew Sophia would not desert Peter, even though he is older now—what, eight? —than he had been. When Jackson left the island, the boy had been only six.

Of course if we do find her, we will not be able to bury her in the cemetery.

Jackson fought the urge to tear up the letter. His father had not always belonged to the church; his father had been a young man once, a fisherman/adventurer who staked a claim for land on the island. Then he met Jackson's mother in the Russian Orthodox village, and they became one.

With shaking hands, Jackson lit the kerosene lamp on the table. He tore off the empty bottom of his father's letter, found his pen, and began to write.

Papa—

At last I hear from you. Am I so much of a leper that you could not write to me until you had such news as that you sent? Or do you think now you have the cure, right? Sophia was the disease and her death—her death—

I thought I saw her today. Here, in this far off distant place. Standing right in front of me. But your letter says this could not be.

He knew what his father hoped: that with Sophia gone, Jackson would be forgiven and could slip back into the village as if nothing had happened. Jackson could see this, see how this would be what the village would want, too. They would pour their pious forgiveness over him, and in that way erase all they would not do for Sophia. The church would be happy once again. His father would be happy once again.

A drop fell upon the page. He heard it as it hit, the cabin was so quiet. As he glanced up toward the ceiling, he felt how his whole face was wet. He touched a bearded cheek and looked back down at the page, knowing. There was no leak in his roof, no leak in the sky above it. The leak was inside of him. And he was the leaking boat in which Sophia did not survive.

SOPHIA PETERSEN
FALL 1927

HOW COULD HE BE HERE, HOW—THIS *ghost that he had become, now here, living and breathing, in the very place I came to, to be where no one knows me, where no one knows anything about me. And here, the very splinter in the center of my wound, here. If I had the money, I would leave now, today, or as soon as the train would go. To where? I know of nowhere else.*

Except the village where I come from, where I am now dead. It frightens me every time I think of it. I am dead. Sophia Petersen is no more; she joins her mother in the heavenly promised land. Or she doesn't. Many would think that. For me, or for my mother? Or for us both. Because my words were infected with fly larvae that grew into maggots that fell from my tongue into the ears of others. What would they say, now that I am dead?

On the platform, the noise of the train, so hungry I felt I would faint, and wished for it almost: to lose all consciousness, to have it all out of my control, whether I fell forward toward the young brown eyed man who approached me or fell backward onto the hard surface of the now unmoving train. Then Jackson was there, the sound of his foot on the platform like the death-knell I had run from, and I felt it all again—everything that once was, and everything that was no more.

THIS IS HOW I DIED.
I will start this journal there, on this day of September 17, 1927,

the day when I became Sophia again, brought back into a state of being the instant Jackson's eyes flashed onto mine. I am known again, and while that very fact may become the true end of me, I find a relief in it, like God has found me at last and insists Sophia Petersen exists. For how long, I do not know. Once again my fate is in Jackson's hands. It was my choice the first time. Him being here, now, how could I have foreseen such a thing?

However, I know how that is. It is not too wondrous. Very simple, in fact. A stranger in the village, whom Jackson and I heard in the grocery, telling the clerk about this grand hotel to the north where the train pulls up right in front of the doors.

"It's in the middle of the wilderness," the stranger had said, "along a massive glacial river. The hills rise up all around and they're loaded with moose and bears and caribou. I'd wager there's nothing like it on the planet. Findlay—that's what it's called. Named after some California fella."

"How is the weather there?" Jackson had asked, and I suppressed a giggle.

"As the Irish would say, grand. Grand like the hotel itself."

"Sounds like a place," Jackson said. We left the grocery and went down to the docks and talked about it for the rest of the day, the grand hotel in the great wilderness to the north, and later we forgot about it...or so it seemed.

So much, so much between that day and now. The day I died was not the beginning; nor, it seems, was it the end. As I crawled, beaten and bloody along the windy beach in the darkness, the water from the rising tide reaching its arms toward me and nipping at my side, I thought it could be, that indeed perhaps it should be. However, the animal instinct to survive stirred in me and pushed me forward until I found the old, deserted boat we had used for years now, the one that leaked and was not safe, but was on this night far safer than the shore. I found it, untied it from a tangle of driftwood, and pulled my battered body up into it. I rested for a moment on its cold hard bottom. I found the paddle

Peter and I had made together, and as the water lapped in the darkness around me, I pushed with the paddle until the old boat was free from the shore. I thought, I would just let the ocean take me; of course there was nowhere I could go that was close enough and far enough at once.

The will to live gripped me again, and as I sat in the little boat, rocking and recovering, I heard the ocean say to me, "You can live, Sophia, if you die," and I knew what the words meant, and I imagined myself—free of Sophia Petersen and the whole village that stood against her—in some distant place, alive yet not alive at once, and in that state somehow perhaps I could find a way to help Peter, or to at least know that he was well. He would grieve for me, but he would be spared, and he would be cared for. He would be free from the truth that makes my fingers tremble as I hold the pen and which I know I should not write upon these pages.

In the past, my journals had always been my friends. Where are they now? Will they be found and burned? I no longer kept one, after my mother's death. The story of my life had turned in a way I did not want to memorialize, though I feel it now, wanting to be told. Perhaps in the end I will have to burn these words myself, in the fireplace of this great place. This place like a castle, something from a dream. Yet it lives in the same reality as the rainy island I come from, as the village that would not ever have me, though for so long I did not know why. Even after that great unveiling of truth, I did not truly know—anything. Yet that first distribution alone was enough to set in motion my great undoing.

"Sophia you mustn't, you mustn't ever . . . you mustn't, mustn't, mustn't."

My mother lay on her deathbed, the room rank with her diseased flesh, the unwashed sheets, the vomit in the bowl. Just us, Peter asleep, and Father Mikhail finally back to his more comfortable lodgings in the village, though it felt as if he would stay until the end in his determination not to leave my mother and me alone together. The kerosene lamp burned too high, the flame licking the glass globe, the wick in need of trimming and coating the globe with black soot.

Burn it to the ground.

That thought came to me in that moment, holding my dying mother's boney hand, the weight of her secrets transferred now to me. Take the lantern and throw it on to the floor, free my mother from the stink of her bed, free myself from the awful knowledge she had given me. How—how could I possibly carry that with me, like a living thing buried inside my chest, pounding against my bones, crying to get out? The lantern could free us, free us all. But I could not do that to Peter, and at that time I could not do that to Jackson.

I have stepped back further than intended on these pages on this first evening in my new lodgings. I am warm, I am comfortable, and I have been fed. My ribs feel much improved, though my bruises have not faded, all hidden save for the yellow ovals on my throat which I cover with an old bandana—Jackson's, which I'd kept in my skirt pocket despite the feelings for him that had turned so painful. I'd remembered the bandana the night I died and pressed it against a cut on my forehead as it wept streams of blood. No sooner had I surmised I would survive the beating than I felt the water deepening in the bottom of the boat. I bailed it with the rusty can we kept in there for that purpose, and knew that when the tide turned I would be lost to the open sea. That is when the idea came to me, and I began to paddle against the wind through the darkness to the point of the bay.

Paddle, bail, paddle, bail, that is what I did, and soon I could make out the jagged silhouettes of the trees on the point. I knew I had to jump into the water before reaching the shore and the thought terrified me. My skirt, thin and worn as it was, along with my old leather boots, might work together to pull me down. My ribs throbbed with pain and I wasn't sure I could swim. The temperature of the water would allow me no hesitation, no mistakes. It would take me as quickly as anything. Yet I knew I must try. I told myself, if I can survive this night, then I can survive tomorrow, and perhaps after tomorrow, I could survive another day. I stood on the rickety rowing seat and jumped, spinning down into the ice-cold water of the bay.

It swallowed me. The freezing cold wrapped its claws around me. I would survive, or I would die. But Father Mikhail would not be the one who decides.

CHAPTER TWO

EMILY WELLS
FALL 1974

"WHAT DO WE DO NOW?" THOMAS whispered, later in the tent, his words inside the nylon walls akin to the soft shush of wind that brushed past. I had already told him, again and again: flag down the Sunday train, ride to the village, contact the Alaska State Troopers. Put the bone back where we found it, so they could see it where it had been.

"They'll tear up the hill," Thomas said, continuing to whisper, words I'd heard throughout the day. "It'll be wrecked, ruined, and what happens if they don't get to it until next spring? What are we supposed to do? We have to build our cabin, Em. We have to get on that. We have to get it done."

"You don't have to whisper, Thomas," I said, turning my face toward his. "There's no one around to hear." We were on our camping pads under a pile of sleeping bags. Though the light outside was fading, it was much too early for sleep. We should be out by the fire, drinking tea and singing songs. Smoking the last of the pot. I'd hoped he'd go to sleep if we went into the tent, and tomorrow we could figure this out.

"Are you sure you can't tell how old it is?"

"Thomas, I'm not an archeologist."

"How hard can it be?"

"Hard, Thomas. That's why there are bone experts."

"Maybe there's an archeologist in the village," he said, his voice lifting hopefully. "If we could just find a way to prove it's an old bone, like a really old bone." His hand searched for mine under the sleeping bags, found it and squeezed. I thought about letting that slide, letting him hang on to that hope for a time, and maybe he would fall asleep; however, I could hear him, in the morning, accusation in his voice: *How come you didn't tell me?*

I pulled in a deep breath and released it as quietly as I could. "Thomas," I said gently, "if it's an old bone the hill would probably become an archeology site."

Thomas' face turned sharply toward mine. "What?"

"Well, that's what happens when old bones are found."

"Are you sure?"

"Pretty sure." I'd taken anthropology, after all. The thought lingered in my brain and had come from somewhere.

"But you're not totally sure," he said.

"No."

"If you're right that means there'd be archeologists swarming all over our hill and digging holes everywhere."

"Something like that."

"And those are the options, then, police or archeologists. Crime scene or dig site."

"Alaska State Troopers," I corrected. I couldn't help myself. "Sorry," I said. "I knew what you meant." I had seen the flash of pain on his face. His father used to berate him daily. *Damn kid can't get anything right.*

He swallowed, and I watched the bob of his Adam's apple. I turned toward him and worked my head onto his slender shoulder where I could feel the rise and fall of his slim chest and touch the long scar near his clavicle. He was here. His heart was still beating. That was all that mattered. Everything else was inconsequential. "It'll be okay," I said. The wind had picked up, and the sides of the tent billowed and puffed.

"What are we supposed to *do*, Emily?"

"We'll figure it out." I kissed the side of his neck, where life flowed through his veins with each beat of his heart. "We have time. There's no phone, there's no way to send a message to anyone, and it's days before the Sunday train."

"We could walk out."

"You want to walk twenty miles?"

"Twenty-two," he said, and I felt his face shift into a smile.

"Twenty-two," I said, so glad to be corrected. "Yes."

"We could build a raft and float down the river."

"And drown on the way," I said, trying to keep it light. I felt us drifting toward the edge of things we did not like to talk about… couldn't talk about, though should.

"You're right," he said. "No drowning for us."

"Train," I said, steering us back on course. Already I saw him face-down on the bottom of the pool. His own thoughts didn't go there, I was quite sure; he remembered nothing of it, and it remained in his brain as something someone told him, not something he had lived. "That gives us a few days to think about it."

"I don't want to move the cabin site, Em." He had been so sure, right from the buggy, rainy day we'd arrived to stake our piece of open-to-entry land. He'd seen the hill from the flat area near the river where the train let us off, one hill among many rising into the wild—not the biggest, not the prettiest, not the farthest, not the closest. He saw it and marched off into the thick and dense chest-high brush and knotted stretches of boney alder. I followed as best I could, scratched by branches and bitten by bugs while tall green ferns wrapped around my legs. The land rose slowly at first then swiftly, and soon we were far above from where we had started. Thomas found that hill, as if a map had been drawn in his mind or as if a beacon calling his name was planted in its center. *Here. Right here.* And we'd pulled off our heavy packs, the muscles in our legs shaky and spent, and let them fall onto the varied and uneven ground.

Likewise, Thomas had been set on Findlay from the beginning, from when we'd first decided we had to leave California behind. Thomas' name was Thomas Findlay Brown, the Findlay coming from his mother's side where he was distantly linked to the long-ago California Representative Charles Findlay, for whom this stop along the Alaska Railroad and once thriving community was named. As soon as he was old enough, Thomas dropped the Brown and legally changed his name to Thomas Findlay, saying his mother had raised him and all his father had done was beat him before he'd left them. A police officer; his father was a respected police officer. Thomas could not get over it. So when he saw Findlay on the map of Alaska, and he remembered that distant family connection, that was all there was to it. Findlay was where we were meant to be.

"I don't want to live on top of a grave," I said now. We had ten acres. There were other places we could build. Our camp was down at the base of our hill, and I found a comfort in being closer to more trees than were in the higher areas. They would help shield us from the wind, which in winter would be cruel up on the hill. In contrast, Thomas wanted to be able to see; he didn't like the mystery of the thick forest, he didn't like the swarms of bugs or the wondering what might be there, lurking in the dense brush. I felt the trees offered privacy, protection; Thomas had liked the stage, to be up above, to be exposed, to be elevated away from his fight with the world, from the messy tangle below.

We let the rising wind take over, whipping around outside the tent, beating against the thin orange walls. Eventually Thomas eased, his breathing slow and steady, and I lay awake a long time with my head on his shoulder, my arm now snugly across his chest, listening to the music of his body, the wave-like *shhh* of his breathing, the rhythmic swish and bump of his miraculous heart. It was nearly dark now, and I knew if I didn't pee I would regret it later when the full thick of dark descended on the campsite and anything, *anything* could be out there unseen and mere yards away. I stopped myself. Not *anything*. No people. There were no people here. I could move freely in the night and only had to fear the bears. I was, however, feeling the return of the dark. I had loved the constant light of summer and had felt safer than I had in a long time. Now I felt the fear gnawing at the edge of every shadow. My secret fear. My secret. While Thomas lauded how beautiful it was, the moon and the stars from this point of the turning earth, I concentrated on the distance we had put between ourselves and California and whoever had—

This was about Thomas. This was his rescue, not mine. And if he was saved, eventually I would be, too.

Carefully I slipped away from Thomas, paused a moment to stare at his beautiful face in the soft light, a curl falling across his forehead covering the small scar there, the scruffy fuzz that would never pass for a beard sprouting on his face. My lost boy. Would he be found here?

I slowly unzipped the tent, just enough to crawl outside. I looked around as I walked several yards, my feet bare and cold, pulled down my long johns and squatted. The only time I was ever jealous of men was when doing this; they could urinate standing up, clothed and protected, while we women had to bear our bottoms to the world and the mosquitoes and hope our piss didn't find our feet.

When I stood again my eyes went to the hill, where somewhere past the grainy outline of the edge, the cabin site and the hole where we'd found the bone sat shrouded in twilight amid a whispering silence. My heart jolted. Something moved in the almost dark. I narrowed my eyes and strained to see. The shape shifted and solidified in silhouette: a wolf, maybe, or someone's very big dog. We had no near neighbors. At least none that we knew of. We had checked, and I had double checked. The closest person lived

four miles south down the tracks, someone named Raymie something. Thomas had talked with him one time on the train: our age,
shorter than Thomas and broader, with an open, expressive face
and generous smile. Thomas had liked him instantly; Thomas liked
most people instantly. I was pretty sure this Raymie had no dog; he
got off at his stop alone, and I had watched him heft his backpack
up onto his shoulders and walk into the woods as the train began
to move again. So what I was seeing now was a wolf, most likely,
near our cabin site, not far from the hole that revealed the bone.
Did he smell it there, sense its presence? It wasn't there anymore, I
reminded myself. The bone was here with us, in the camp despite
Thomas' protest, wrapped in my wool shawl which was the only
appropriate thing, and tucked safely in the bottom of my pack.

I could tell the wolf-like creature was looking down at the camp,
at me. I nearly called for Thomas then it turned and folded away
into the dark, and I quickly crawled back into the tent and pulled
the zipper closed.

HARRY HARBOUR
FALL 1974

I'D STAYED ON WITH THE RAILROAD, when I left the hotel after
everything happened and Cora rightly said, "You can't stay here,
Harry. You'll either go mad or you'll spill your guts. You did the
right thing—let that be your solace, turn your back on this place
and get on with your life. Deadhorse. I don't believe in curses, but
there's a bad wind blows through that place now and again, and
we got caught up in it. Like the ghosts of those poor dead horses,
charging through."

I thought of those words in 1945 when a boiler explosion
destroyed the powerhouse at Findlay, and again when '57 came
around and we got word the hotel burned to the ground, taking
three souls with it—two little girls in one room and a lone woman
and her dog in another. I was down in Seward at the time, working

that part of the line. Cora'd wanted me to help run her roadhouse there, and though I lived on the premises and helped when I could I worked the trains, starting off in the baggage car and sometimes working the freights. I could ride for free, and sometimes I'd volunteer to take an extra shift or two on the northern end of things so I could ride past the place and make sure it was still there. Cora passed two months after the hotel burned, her heart failing while she was out hiking up a 4,000 foot-plus mountain at the ungodly age of 85, and I transferred out of Seward and worked my way into a conductor's uniform. Now I pass by there all the time and watched over the years as Findlay faded into nothing except ghosts and a few old doorknobs lost in the weeds.

FALL 1927

ONE OF MY DUTIES AT THE hotel was to check on the guests roaming the grounds in the evening, make sure no one had too much to drink—on the sly of course, as it was Prohibition— and was heading for the suspension bridge. No one had fallen off though I thought it was probably a matter of time. That bridge was something that looked like it belonged in an adventure film, even though in 1927 films were scarce in Alaska, and Anchorage had yet to build its grand movie theatre on 4th Avenue. It looked like a good place for a sword fight or a killer grizzly trapping its prey or, my favorite suspension bridge fantasy, a fair damsel hanging by a thread over the rushing gray glacier water of that deadly river.

The evening of Sonja Antonov's arrival, I was talking with an old gent along the riverbank as he cast his rod into the swirling gray. Really, smaller streams were better fishing, but it was more than a little late in the day to take a jaunt to one of the nearby waterways. The old guy didn't seem to mind that he wasn't catching anything. He was happy as hell just to be there, in the crisp air of a September evening, the river murmuring along its way and the occasional flock of ducks crossing overhead.

The old gent was telling me about how he'd always wanted to live in the wild. Life and responsibilities kept interfering, and he got stuck in Anchorage because of his job and all the mouths he had to feed (six kids, I'm guessing that would tie anyone down) until it was too late to do such a thing. I could already see how that could happen. I thought of my own father and hoped he didn't feel the same, "promoted" to an office job with the railroad, which he said he liked, though places like Findlay and all the other beautiful spots along the rail line weren't part of his working week anymore. Anytime I went home to visit he'd ask me the same series of questions: what sort of weather you having, seen any wildlife up in the hills lately, how's that mountain looking, from up there on the ridge? I could feel he missed it, though not the back-breaking work of fixing track and clearing out snow slides. The big excitement was when they were laying the track for the first time; of course, he was a lot younger then. That's when he and Cora became pals, back in those days when this place was called Deadhorse Hill and Cora had her roadhouse.

The old gent was still talking when I noticed someone standing in the middle of the suspension bridge. I recognized the long skirt from the young lady who got off the train a few hours earlier. Her hair was now free and was whipping around in the wind that came rushing down the river's path, longer than anything I'd seen on any of the young ladies I'd known in my life. What was she doing there? From what I could tell, her hands were fiercely gripping the cable. She wasn't moving. Was she frozen in fear? Was she thinking of jumping and was now in the middle of a before-suicide prayer? I couldn't figure it out, and my alarm bells were ringing. I excused myself from the old gent and agreed to meet up with him shortly by one of the fireplaces in the lobby. I made my way to the bridge. Before I could get there she was on the move, heading toward the other side. What was she thinking? It was going to be dark soon, the bears were still a factor, and she was a stranger here and didn't know her way around. I hurried after her. She scampered up the ridge trail on the other side as if she was part mountain goat and disappeared before I was even halfway across.

I found her, though, a while later when I finally caught up to her; that trail was some torture chamber if there ever was one. The ridge was huge and about as majestic as a ridge could be; the area's Alaska Native people, back in the days before the flu epidemic decreased their population and white men changed their way of life, hunted caribou on this ridge and in these hills. They called the ridge K'esugi, which meant "the ancient one." The presence of the ridge was always there, looming over the hotel from the other side of the river, a watchful judge and constant reminder of our intrusion in this country.

I wouldn't ever say such to Cora. She'd feast on that idea.

My legs burned and my heart thundered, and I couldn't breathe fast enough. Thank God she hadn't gone far and found a viewing spot a short way up this particular side. She was sitting on the ground, staring back across the river at the hills that rose beyond the hotel. The full trail was five miles long and led to one of the most stunning views of the Alaska Range anyone could ever imagine, like a row of white giants you could reach out and touch, though of course, even from there they were miles and miles away. The wind could blow something wicked across that ridge, on every part of it, as it was on that day. I thought how she must be cold, in her skirt and that old sweater and no hat or anything, though I wasn't exactly dressed to be up there, either. As I walked toward her, I thought how I would take off my wool shirt and drape it over her shoulders. Maybe she'd lean back against me a bit, and that beautiful hair of hers would fly up into my face.

I guess I was young and stupid, and spent an inordinate amount of time—or so I'd been told—reading classic novels like those of Charles Dickens or studying Shakespeare's plays, the latter of which especially always made my heart sing. Anyway, when she realized someone was coming, she shot to her feet, grabbed all that glorious hair and twisted it up somehow on the back of her head. I realized too late I'd broken the moment for her, and I had no choice except to finish walking up to her, which I did and said, "Hello."

She smiled a little and looked at the ground. "Hello."

"Nice evening," I said. "I imagine the range is pretty—" I hesitated; sometimes the Alaska Range defied all words and I wanted to convey how really stunning it was— "*splendid* right now." I hoped that would do the trick; I always felt my words fell short. She would have seen the range as she rode the train.

She glanced at me and said nothing, her eyes going back to those other hills, the deep gash of Deadhorse Canyon where Deadhorse Creek tumbled through, like a painful scar across the face of the landscape.

"That's a good view, too," I said, awkward as could be. Below us and across that wide gray water sat the hotel and the little row of cottages where those railroad employees who were lucky enough to get one lived—mostly folks who were married or had families. I being young and single was always tossed around in terms of living quarters. I'd spent the summer before this last in a canvas tent "bunkhouse" with the bellhops, and this past summer I was in a bunkhouse with wooden walls, again with the bellhops. Now that things had slowed down and staff was thinning out I was back to my "winter room" as I called it, all the way down the end of the long hall on the main level, in the back of the hotel that reached toward the river. The room kept me within easy reach of anybody who needed an extra pair of hands as I was always on-call for that; however, the view of the river from my window was worth every pounding on my door. This evening the lights were on in the hotel, glowing in the descending twilight, and one by one the windows of the little row of cottages were themselves filling with warm yellow radiance.

"The world is so big here," she said. I felt a start run through me. She didn't look at me; it was as if she were talking to herself and I didn't exist. "Very different from where I come from. There the land is small and the sea is big. Here the land is everywhere, like a sea of hills."

I tried to see it as she did, and for a moment imagined the two of us on a little boat together, riding a sea of hills.

The darkness was growing fast now, as it would do that time of year after a spring and summer of more daylight than anybody would ever need, and it was a shiver of cold rushing through me that made me remember my other fantasy from just moments ago. "Let me give you my shirt," I said. "It's getting cold up here."

"I am fine," she said. "But thank you very much."

"You must be cold. I know I am."

A smile played around the soft corners of her mouth as she kept her eyes on the distant hills. "Then why would you give me your shirt?" she asked.

The question surprised me. Of course it was a logical question, but I had already formed it in my mind that she was timid and shy and as fragile as a tundra flower in a cold wind. Challenging, joking, whatever it was, was not on my expectations list. Her eyes had slid into the corners of their sockets, looking right at me now, looming above that mouth that was almost smiling. There was nothing I could do except smile myself and say, "You got me there." And I knew I was a goner.

JACKSON KEATS
FALL 1927

SOPHIA PETERSEN WAS THE ILLEGITIMATE DAUGHTER of a whore. That was the consensus in the village, though some would say Sophia's mother was taken against her will by a fisherman passing through. Others would say it was her will; nevertheless, the outcome was the same however Sophia was conceived, and she and her mother lived on the outskirts of the village in every way. If not for Father Mikhail it is likely they would have been completely shunned; Father Mikhail was merciful and draped them with his protection. They were allowed in the church, they were allowed in the shops, and eventually Sophia was allowed in the school. However, Father Mikhail was not physically present in the school, and while no one dared bully her, she was properly avoided, mocked, and whispered about—even by Jackson, at first. The older he became, however, the more aware he was of his own misplacement in the village—his father was not of those people— and he began to see the quiet and determined blond haired girl as similar to himself: tolerated, yet on the edge of not.

There was a day, many years ago when they were children, when Sophia walked with her arms full of books. It had been raining and the road to the school was covered in mud. Two boys threw rocks at Jackson and he chased them, trying to get a hold of them before they disappeared into the protection of the school. Though surely Sophia had heard them coming up behind her, she kept on her way and did not move her head to look at them. One of the boys slipped and fell into her as he passed, quickly righted himself and scurried away. Jackson was almost upon him when he stopped and looked at the girl on the ground. He let the boys go.

"I will be in trouble," she said, when he knelt to help her with the books. She wiped at the books with the kerchief from her hair, and Jackson took off his wool shirt and used that as well. Even if they cleaned the books, she could not go into the school with the back of her skirt covered in mud.

"He did not mean to," Jackson said, defending the boy. "He was running from me and slipped."

Her eyes locked onto his. "It does not matter. It will make no difference."

Jackson knew what she said was true. "Come," he said, and held out his hand to her. "Father Mikhail will help." Father Mikhail and Jackson's father were friends; the priest would be welcoming, Jackson was sure, if he knocked upon his door.

A long moment passed in which the girl did not respond. She stared vacantly at the school she could not now enter, then she looked at the muddy books. Jackson was about to give up and leave when she looked at him warily and placed her own wet and muddy hand in his and let him pull her up and off the dirty street.

Father Mikhail greeted them with a friendly smile, exactly as Jackson had thought. "What brings you here today, friend Jackson?" the priest asked, and Jackson explained what had happened. "It is for little Sophia's sake, that you come to me today?" the priest asked, as he welcomed them into his living quarters adjacent to the church. "We will see what we can do." He called for his housekeeper, Mrs. Nicholai, a plump, red-cheeked woman whose ice blue eyes were wide and round and glanced always quickly at Father Mikhail as if the sight of him might burn her irises should she look at him for more than a flash of a second. Father Mikhail instructed her to clean up Sophia as best as she could and do the same for the library books. The housekeeper led Sophia from the room, and the girl looked back over her shoulder at Jackson before disappearing down a narrow hall.

"Mrs. Nicholai will see to her," Father Mikhail said, "and you, my young friend, must get yourself to school." Jackson soon found himself on the other side of the now-closed door.

Later that day, when Sophia came to school, a person could hardly tell she had fallen into the mud. She had a note for the teacher and so did not get into trouble for being late (unlike Jackson). Jackson did not know how the books fared; he guessed that Father Mikhail would fix that problem as well. He thought Sophia should be happy. Then later in the day he saw her blinking back her tears.

What did those tears mean? Jackson did not know. As they grew older, he fell in love with Sophia. When she turned against Father Mikhail, he felt as if ice he thought solid had broken beneath his feet. He chose to believe her. A short time later he chose not to.

Which way was right, he wondered now, in his chair at the table in which he'd passed the night. For him, though, neither: each choice cost him everything, because the choice to believe Sophia had come first.

"He lay with her —he *lay* with her! And he won't allow her in the cemetery! She was his slave, Jackson. His slave!" This was how she had first told him, words he knew would only bring trouble to them both.

"He is a priest, Sophia. He has shown your mother every kindness, he—"

"You know nothing, Jackson! Nothing!"

"I know what I see! I have seen his kindness to all three of you with my own eyes!"

"Then tell me if you see this." She stood before him and removed her outer clothes. Her ribs, red and blue. Marks on her stomach, her shoulders, her sides, places where they would not be seen.

Stop, Jackson told himself now; stop. It was all madness. It was all lies. The young man who had assaulted Sophia confessed; it was Ilian Nicholai, the youngest of Mrs. Nicholai's sons, an odd young man. No one was surprised. Ilian was lashed for it, and Father Mikhail took no action against Sophia.

"She is distraught over the loss of her mother," he'd said. "We must let her recover so she can care for her brother."

But before Ilian's confession, Jackson had stood with Sophia in the church, in front of God and everybody, as she pointed her finger at the priest. "I know what you did to her! I know! And I know what you have done to me!" She'd pulled her sleeve up her arm to show some of the bruises.

Father Mikhail said, "Sophia, you know I have not done that."

"I know you did! As sure as the things you did to my mother!"

"I have not touched you, Sophia, and you know that."

Peter was pulling at her skirt. There were tears in the boy's eyes. Jackson grabbed them both and rushed them out of the church. Sophia broke free of his grip and ran off, toward the ocean, and Jackson held Peter's hand and walked the boy home, the sound of his father's voice shouting his name following him down the wet road.

Then came the confession, the lashing, Father Mikhail's forgiveness and the shunning of both Jackson and Sophia. And Sophia's shunning of Jackson, after he begged her to confess her own lie.

"You must confess, Sophia! You must! It is the only way. The only way for us."

"Tell a lie to fix a lie?"

"Sophia, you know what the truth is!"

"I do, Jackson, I do. That is the problem. The truth. I know it now."

JACKSON ROSE FROM THE TABLE, THE GHOSTS of the night clutching at his throat. Snowy Day watched him from where he lay on the bear rug by the cold stove. Jackson ladled some water from the bucket, a mugful for him and a bowl for Snow. He found a reasonably clean piece of paper and fashioned it into an envelope for his letter to his father. He drank more water and opened the door to the outside to let the dog wander where he would. Snow never went far except if there was a dead salmon to be found, and here they were miles from the river. Miles from the hotel. After sealing the letter with melted wax, he joined the dog on the rolling hill with the grasses and rocks and a slim scattering of trees. The rose-gold sun of morning was kissing its way across the tall peaks of the Alaska Range. The ground was stiff and cold with frost and as Jackson sat down near Snowy Day he aimlessly plucked hard, cold crowberries out from a patch of tundra moss and placed them in his mouth. The body needed food, no matter the weight that filled it. He realized he mustn't linger long—he must go down to the hotel again, buy postage for his letter and get it onto the train. If he did not do it today, he knew he would never send the letter, and it would join the stack of unsent letters in the tin under his rough wooden cot: letters to his father, and letters to Sophia Petersen.

SOPHIA PETERSEN
FALL 1927

I HEARD HIM BEFORE I SAW HIM, Jackson, his voice somewhere

near, in the early morning when Nellie June and I had gone outside before the work was to begin.

"Who is the girl who got off the train yesterday? Who is she!" Jackson was yelling.

"Jesus Christ Jackson! I mean, what the hell?" I recognized the voice of Harry.

Earlier in the morning Nellie June had woken me like this: "Come on, get out of bed if you want breakfast! I don't know how they do things in whatever country you come from—here we get up and get going. If you miss breakfast, you miss breakfast!"

I was in a dark, bottomless sleep and did not want to come back. The bed they had given me was soft and warm. My stomach was full from the supper I was given the night before. And for once I did not dream.

"What country?" I'd wanted to say. "I am from the same country as you. I am from the Territory of Alaska, which is part of the United States of America. It is the only place I have ever been."

I said nothing and obediently rose. In the basement kitchen I was handed a bowl of oatmeal by a skeletal woman named Mrs. Grant and sat near Nellie June at a long narrow wooden table. There was sugar and cream; I was careful not to take too much. There were other ladies who chatted and introduced themselves to me, ladies who worked in the dining room and the kitchen and some who cleaned the rooms, and there were men at one end of the table—railroad men—who grunted hellos as they shoveled their breakfasts into their mouths. There was toasted bread, too, for anyone who wanted it, and there was fried bacon that made my mouth water and made me want to vomit at once. Because Nellie June did not take any, I didn't dare touch it. The men ate it by the handful.

They must have been the same men in the basement men's reading room last night. I could hear them from where I slept, in a small room with Nellie June that was once a storage room. The basement was a world of men—the laundry workers and Mrs.

Grant's kitchen aside—and because housing was limited we stayed in the basement, too.

As Nellie June and I finished, the young man came in, Harry, who had followed me up the big hill last night before dark and tried to give me his shirt. He looked startled by the morning, startled by me, and Mrs. Grant laughed at him as she handed him a big mug full of steaming coffee. "Here you go Harry," she'd said. "Get your wits about you! I'm going to need you to help me pull the rest of the potatoes and cabbages from the garden; we'll get a good frost any day now, mark my words. It's on its way down from the hills; I can feel it." As Harry lifted the mug to his lips, I lifted my eyes and met his. He began to smile and I looked away. I cannot be friends with anyone. I am not even who I am.

Nellie June said we should watch the train leave and she wanted to show me as well the new houses for the chickens and the hogs, which appeared to fill her with excitement, and we left the kitchen, climbed the stairs, and stepped outside as the golden light of morning shimmered across the hills.

Yesterday Nellie June had rattled on as she showed me how to do the work—so many sheets and towels! She told me about the hotel, about the village to the south where she was from and about her plans to someday leave Alaska and go see the "real USA" where there are beaches to sunbathe on and where in some places winter never even comes. I had smiled as I listened, even though the talk reminded me of Jackson and myself, how we used to be, so full of dreams. Now Jackson was the problem I had, how because of him I would not be able to stay. I would have to leave whenever it was I would get paid, and until then I would have to make sure he did not see me again.

So when we heard the yelling, and heard Jackson say my name—

"What is her name? Is it Sophia?"

"No, it's not Sophia, Jackson! It's Sonja somebody! For God's sake let me go!"

—I knew what I must do. Nellie June ran toward the yelling and

I ran as fast as I could away from it. Jackson would look for me in and around the hotel. The train was readying for departure; it was rumbling as it sat on the steel tracks, like an animal resting before the run. Young men in matching clothing were carrying bags and suitcases out to the platform, and people were streaming in and out of the hotel. I ran away from it, invisible as the wind; people like me, I had learned on my journey here, were nothing to the larger world.

I ran to the foot bridge and hurried across, scrambled up the trail and disappeared from view. I found a spot out of the wind and sat there, my back against a rock, wondering if I could slip unnoticed onto a train, hide, and let it take me away. There were advantages with being easily unseen. Perhaps that is how it has been all my life. I had always thought that Jackson had seen me, had known me. Would always believe me. When I rose from the water of the bay and stowed away on two different boats, first to leave the island then to leave Juneau for Seward, I learned how unseen I was. When I enquired at the railroad office about a job in Findlay, I had to stand in the middle of the room and say, "Excuse me, sir," three times before the man behind the desk knew I was there. No one noticed when I rummaged through garbage cans and found the sweater and the old bag that became my possessions; no one noticed when I took the notebook and the pen that someone had left behind in the railroad bunk house where they let me stay until the next train north. No one asked for proof of the name I gave or questioned me about anything. Are the ties we have with others the things that make us real? I feel like I have become a ghost, as if I failed to survive the waters of the bay.

When I stepped off the train, before seeing Jackson, I had thought I had found the most beautiful place. I had thought, maybe someday I could bring Peter here, and we could have a different life.

I worry for Peter. However, I know Father Mikhail. All he will see is what he wants to see in Peter, and he will take good care of him. Peter will be safe from hurt and harm, as long as I and my evil tongue are among the dead.

The wind was cold this morning as I sat against the rock, and I did not have my sweater. I knew that soon I would need to start my work, and I worried that Jackson would spot me when I tried to return to the hotel. I heard something coming along the trail; I knew it could be a bear, but suspected it was more likely the young man Harry, looking for me, and so it was, and I tried to smile when he found me and act as if all was normal.

"Sonja!" he said. "We were looking for you. I thought you might be here."

I smiled at him and did not move. I feared what questions he would ask.

He sat down beside me and tipped his face back as if the sun could win its fight against the cold wind. "Does Jackson frighten you?" he asked.

Of course they must wonder why I ran away. "I don't know him," was all I could think of to say.

"Nothing to be afraid of."

"Did he hurt you?" The glimpse I had seen showed Jackson pressing Harry against the wall.

"No! No, not at all. He's a pretty strong guy though, I'll tell you that."

I could feel without looking at him how his brow furrowed as he thought, his eyes focused on the distant hills.

"He seems to think you're someone else."

I shrugged in response. I felt Harry's eyes, now, on the side of my face.

"Well, he got a good talking to, from the hotel manager," Harry said. "Told him to stay away for a while, so he'll probably hide out in the hills with that dog of his for a week or two. There's no reason, though, to be afraid of Jackson. He's been around here a few years now and never hurt anybody. This was the first trouble he ever caused."

"All right," I said. A reprieve. I have never been this lucky before. Except I also know Jackson. Once an idea is in his head, it is hard for him to let it go.

CHAPTER THREE

EMILY WELLS
FALL 1974

Sometimes, to take our mind off things, Thomas and I went down to the old hotel site and rooted around for artifacts. After the hotel burned, the railroad decided to bulldoze into the ground the little assembly of cottages that had once housed staff along with the various other outbuildings connected to the running of both the hotel and the trains. We'd learned these things from the old conductor on the train, the first day of our arrival. We'd boarded the train in Anchorage, after two turbulence-filled plane rides and a sketchy night in a cheap hotel with some frantic shopping in between. The train ride was long and slow and there was plenty of time for talk. The farther north we got, the younger and scruffier the passengers became; we saw our future selves in these young woods people in their patched jeans and tie-dyed long john shirts and backpacks full of supplies to be carried into the woods to wherever their cabins were. At that point Thomas and I did not blend in, newly showered and Thomas scruff-free, our clothes California cool and not yet embedded with dirt. We chatted briefly with another couple, Monique and Raoul, who boarded the train in the small village that was the closest to where we were heading and who got off at a stop about halfway between the village and Findlay. They lived by a lake, they said, two miles off the railroad and where a number of their friends lived, too, in a circle of cabins that ringed the water.

"That sounds nice," I had said, and Monique noted, as the train slowed in the approach to their stop, "There's no one living at Findlay these days," and Thomas squeezed my hand. Out the window of the train Thomas and I saw a small group of people who were there, it looked like, to meet Monique and Raoul. As the train had traveled through miles of trees, broken only by the occasional stretch by the river or by a swamp on the non-river side, it had grown emptier, and now with Monique and Raoul's departure the only ones left besides me and Thomas were the people traveling to Fairbanks: a mother with a pack of children of varying ages, and a variety of older people who, it seemed, were not happy to see people like me and Thomas.

THE DAY AFTER WE FOUND THE bone, and the morning after I saw the wolf, we drank some bad coffee around the campfire, cooked some equally bad oatmeal, put on our daypacks, and hiked the mile down to where the land flattened and where the hotel and the community of Findlay had once been on a small sliver of land along the river. We did not talk about the bone; I had told Thomas about the wolf, and all he said was, "You should have woken me up." As a precaution, Thomas brought along the shotgun which he didn't know how to use and which he carried awkwardly, alternating between a one-handed approach and a two-handed one. When we got there, bursting out of the undergrowth that was finally thinning as we plunged deeper into the brief Alaskan fall, he set the shotgun down on the gravel beside the rails of the main track, glad to be rid of it. We went about tromping through the brush between the river and the rails, where the hotel and many of the assorted other buildings had been, to see what buried objects the earth might have spit back up.

The ground held traces of what once was; the faint outline of where the hotel had stood remained, like a shadow without substance or source. As I parted bushes and kicked at patches of earth I thought how, if one did not have knowledge of the hotel and its little community's former existence, the average person would never guess that anything had ever been there other than the meadow-like grasses and dense bushes and scattered trees. If you knew to look, there were clues everywhere and in everything—bits and pieces, fragments of a reality that had once been. In prior excursions we'd found an old bottle, miraculously intact, a spoon, and a doorknob. On this day Thomas found a hinge, a pull for a drawer, and a badly burnt tea kettle. I found another doorknob, a big round metal button, and a small broken bottle, one that possibly had once held perfume. We took our treasures to the riverbank and sat for a while, watching the wide gray water and enjoying the breeze that traveled with it. I could feel the presence of the hotel behind me as if it were a living thing wanting resurrection. It had seventy-five rooms by the time it burned down. A laundry, a kitchen, a basement bar. Fireplaces. Toilets. The swimming pool, and along with the golf course, there was a tennis court and, in the winter, a ski area in the hills. All had been here, in this nowhere land, a spot that fell halfway between where the railroad started in Seward and ended in Fairbanks. Now, all was gone; vanished. "It was the most beautiful place you could imagine," said the old conductor, who we had seen again when we'd returned to Anchorage to file our staking at the land office. His name was Harry, and he'd been a younger man once and had worked at the hotel in the late 1920s. "A different world," he'd said.

THOMAS WAS SULLEN AND QUIET AS we sat by the river. He stood, picked up a rock and tossed it into the water. I could tell he was thinking about something, and I waited. Finally, he said, "We could throw it into the river."

"Throw what?" I asked, though of course I knew what he meant.

"The bone. Throw it in and get on with building our home."

"We can't do that, Thomas."

Thomas threw some more rocks and wouldn't look at me. I gave him his time, his room, and finally he said, "Can you believe they actually had a foot bridge across this thing? How did they do that?" He sat back down next to me, and together we gazed across the wide expanse of river. On the other side was Findlay Ridge, large and looming. The ridge was the reason, apparently, for the suspension bridge that had stretched between two tall towers. A trail from the bridge wound its way to the top of the ridge and continued on to where our friend Harry the conductor said a gazebo stood to this day, a shelter that was built for the hotel hikers to rest in and view the massive Alaska Range in the distance.

"It's like living inside a movie," Thomas said. "Crazy, huh?"

I smiled, happy he was diverted, though I wondered what kind of movie were we in. We didn't know yet, and I felt the weight of that unknowing pressed like a wall in front of us.

"It makes you think, though, doesn't it," Thomas went on. "Right behind us there was once a friggin' seventy-five room hotel. With a bar! Out here in the middle of god-damn nowhere. I almost wish it was still there."

"We wouldn't be here if it was," I said. Was I correcting again, or simply reminding?

Thomas looked down at the silty shore, shadows on his face. "Maybe we could have had both," he said, drawing circles in the gray silt with his finger. "Does it have to be one thing or the other, Em?" His eyes looked sideways toward mine. So blue, like an evening sky. Why was he asking me when it was all up to him?

"Maybe someday," I said, "when we're ready." Before he could say something I added, quickly, "This is not a prison, Thomas, right? This was wanted. We wanted this. We want this. That's why we're both upset right now, over the bone. We have a dream. A new dream, yes, but still a dream."

He kissed me then, his hands around my face, and I felt the spark of him shooting through me. We pulled at our clothes and lost ourselves in each other for a time, in front of the river and the railroad tracks and the shadow of the forgotten hotel, this world that was now ours and no one else's. Or so we thought.

WHEN WE RETURNED TO CAMP, WE RESTARTED the campfire and cooked Spam and potatoes in a frying pan which we ate directly from when the food was done. Thomas played guitar and sang for a while, stretching his long legs out in front of him, his back leaning against a rock, the sparks from the fire meeting the sound of his voice and spinning together through the quiet Alaska night. Later we crawled into the tent and I read *Trinity* out loud until Thomas fell asleep, then once again I went outside to pee in the last of the light. I looked up at the hill, just to prove to myself nothing was there.

But something was there.

It was a man, looking down at me.

"Thomas!" I hissed, not moving and trying not to breathe. "There's someone on the hill!" By the time Thomas thrashed his way out of the tent the figure was gone, vanished, and I had to convince even myself that it had been real. Maybe it had been a shadow, a whisper, my own demon following me to this new, northern place.

HARRY HARBOUR
FALL 1974

I THOUGHT MORE THAN ONCE I SHOULD tell them, the young couple on the train. Not everything. Maybe something like, *Not the best place for building around here.* Or, more truthfully: *The place has a curse on it.* When they'd said they were getting off at Findlay, I'd felt a shattering thud inside, like a sledgehammer slamming against ancient ice. "Findlay?" I'd said. "Well, that's nothing more than a ghost town now. No one goes there, and there's nobody around for miles."

"Exactly," the young fellow said. He stuck out his hand. "I'm Thomas Findlay, and this is my love, Emily Wells."

What's in a name, I'd thought, remembering the Shakespeare of my youth. I knew at that moment Findlay was more than a random milepost on the railroad for them and they would likely stay awhile. I knew exactly how I felt about that, and the cold hand of the past pressed itself against my heart.

FALL 1927

IT WAS A WEEK AND A day after Sonja Antonov arrived that Cora was on the southbound, sooner than I'd expected, though she was a swift and deadly hunter and her plans were known to change in a flash so you never could be too sure. There she was, hanging out of the baggage car as the train pulled up to the platform.

"Harry!" she called, and with big arching arm gestures summoned me over to her. "You've got to see this!" Herman pulled the sliding door the rest of the way open and the smell of dead meat hit my nostrils. "What do you think, Harry?" Cora asked. "Meet Marty!"

On the floor of the baggage car was the head of a massive moose, small wooden crates propped on either side of it, over the tops of which the antlers were sprawled like sideways growing trees. My eyes landed on those of the dead animal's, and I felt for a moment it was saying something to me, something about how he had been big and powerful and strong and had roamed the wild lands like a king. Then in a second he was brought down. Like if it could happen to him, it could happen to anyone or anything. If I could, I would have told him it was Cora that did it, she's a killer and a wily one at that, and it was his bad luck that he crossed her path. Or her good luck, which was probably the case.

"That's a good one, Cora," I said, and I wanted to apologize for those words, wanted to say to the dead moose, "Sorry she got you." I looked away instead and started helping Cora, who had jumped from the baggage car onto the platform and was unloading her gear.

"I'm sending Marty here and what's left of him on down to Anchorage tomorrow," she said. "Your dad will hang on to him for me until I catch up. Here—" she lifted a bloody game bag and plopped it in my arms— "here's a little something for the kitchen. And the staff. Have a few steaks on me!" She laughed and pulled her rifles off the train. "Next year you're coming with me, Harry— no excuses. Hang on to that ticket."

I smiled and was damn glad next year was a good three hundred and sixty or so days away. The upcoming caribou hunt would be more than enough for the near future.

I had intended to help Cora bring in her gear; however, the bloody bag in my arms posed a bit of a problem—it wasn't something you could set down anywhere and I could also already feel the blood soaking into my shirt. "Be right back, Cora," I said and started to walk off the platform, wondering how I could make my way into the kitchen unseen. Cora yelled after me not to worry, and did she look at all like a woman who couldn't carry her own bags? I slipped inside the hotel, skirted the edge of the dining room, in which the train outside the windows thankfully provided a distraction to the diners, and made it into the main level kitchen. A few of the girls wrinkled their noses at me. Mrs. Grant met me in the middle of the room and relieved me of my bloody burden. "Cora Allen," was all she said and took it over to the counter for cleaning and cutting. "Better get that shirt soaking in some cold water, Harry."

I nodded, finding myself unusually thankful for Cora and her bag of meat. I slipped down the stairs in the corner of the kitchen to the basement, went down the long hallway to the laundry, holding my arms over my chest to hide as much of the blood as I could. I didn't know a lot about what went on in the laundry, though I assumed, of course, a lot of washing. Since Sonja's arrival I'd been trying to sort it all out. Mrs. Johnson was the boss down there, her round face always flushed from the heat, her sleeves rolled up her pudgy arms. The laundry was a place of big business, and like the rest of the basement it whispered the secrets of an underground world. Everybody knew the laundry brought in a lot of money, washing and starching the laundry from the hospitals in Anchorage and Nenana and all the other railroad related laundry along the line in addition to everything at the hotel.

Mrs. Johnson was there in the laundry that day when I went in with my moose blood-soaked shirt, her face red and sweaty, and she said, "What is it now, Harry?"

I had been going down to the laundry a lot of late, delivering such things as a gentleman's fish-slimed trousers or the sweater Mrs. Arlington spilled coffee on. I uncrossed my arms and spread them wide so Mrs. Johnson could see the extent of the damage on my shirt. "Cora Allen I suppose," she said. "Sonja! Come help young Harry here. He's a bloody mess!"

From the corner of the laundry I saw her turn, and she smiled shyly as she crossed the room toward me. "Harry, what has happened?" she said.

I almost swore I would never dread the arrival of Cora Allen again; however, even in that bright, innocent moment I knew that would be an impossible pledge.

"It's only moose blood," I managed, grateful now for the awful feel of my clothes stuck to my skin.

"Let us put it into some water to soak," she said.

Next thing I knew she was unbuttoning my shirt, top to bottom, briskly and efficiently as if she were Mrs. Johnson, and the nearness of her was almost more than I could stand. I could smell the clean pretty smell of her hair, could feel her breath whisper across the skin on my throat.

She pulled the shirt down off my arms, held it gingerly by the collar, looked me over and said, "Oh dear, Harry."

"What?" I asked, the color rising in my cheeks. Could she see that my blood was swimming faster, my chest moving more rapidly?

"Your undershirt. It looks like you were stabbed in the chest, Harry. Take it off and give it to me."

I hesitated. I thought about Jackson Keats, how I saw him once, on a hot day last July, down at the river fishing with his shirt off and his pants rolled up to his knees. There were some female guests from the hotel with me, and they gawked at him shamelessly. I tied flies onto fishing poles for them and showed them how to cast and reel. But all they wanted to do was look at Jackson, and finally I gave up, picked up my pole and landed a ten-inch rainbow on the first cast.

I pulled the shirt up over my head. Sonja took it and stared at my bare chest, her eyes wide. I felt my heart beating, and hoped she couldn't see it there, thumping against my breastbone like someone trapped behind a locked door.

She said, "I think I'd better get you a washcloth, Harry," and whipped around. I looked down at my chest, at the big circle of blood painted there.

JACKSON KEATS
FALL 1927

"GO AHEAD AND RUN, SOPHIA; I will not chase after you, though your furry friend might do differently." He paused, eyes locked on hers, and added, "Or shall I call you Sonja? Is that who you are now?"

Jackson did not stay away from the hotel, as he had been told to do. Instead he watched from a distance and waited. Days passed. On this evening, as the light was beginning to fade, his opportunity came.

He saw her emerge alone from the hotel and begin to walk along the trail to the suspension bridge. No one was about—no fishermen, no Harry, all driven inside by the gloomy chill of a sky that would either rain soon or snow. The river was murky and dark, and a silence hung heavy in the air until it kissed the ever steady, always present drumbeat of the river.

He let Sophia cross the bridge and begin to climb the steep trail up the ridge before he followed her. He and Snowy Day were over halfway across the wide river when she reappeared, scrambling down the trail and not stopping until she reached the bridge and looked up and saw him there. A big grizzly appeared on the trail she had just walked on, and Snowy Day tipped his nose up into the air. Jackson's gaze flipped between Sophia—whose round little mouth hung open as she struggled to catch her breath and, he imagined, assess her current situation—and the bear that lingered above her. Jackson knew not to meet its eyes and he carefully lifted his hand to silently tell Sophia—for it was her—it was her!—to be still, and for a moment they were joined—he, Sophia, and Snowy Day—as they waited for the bear to decide. At last the bear turned and disappeared from sight, and everything that was broken between him and Sophia fell like shattered glass all around as the moment of unity collapsed.

Sophia did not answer after he spoke, and her eyes shifted away. She did not move as if she hoped to fade into the growing dark. Jackson knew he had her trapped on the bridge. She could not return to the safety of the hotel and her new friends without going straight through him; she could turn and flee up the ridge trail, though the bear could be there, hidden around some dark bend.

She could jump. He saw the trajectory of her gaze fall to the river below.

"Sophia no!" he said, a sense of panic sweeping through him. Perhaps he did not know Sophia anymore. Perhaps he never did. "No. That is not necessary. I will leave; I will leave."

He lifted his hands and took several backward steps. "Only please, please—let me know it is you. Everyone thinks you are dead and I think I am going mad!"

As he spoke he felt incredible joy cutting through his anger and his pain. No matter how much of a mystery she was to him now, he knew this was her, and knew it was no ghost that stood before him. "Please talk to me, Sophia. Remember who I am. Remember who we were to each other, before the trouble."

She continued to stare at the rushing water below. The wind made a lonely sound as it rattled through the cables of the footbridge.

At last, her lips moved, and in a flat, trembling voice she said, "There was no time before the trouble, Jackson. There was only our ignorance of it."

He felt again this terrible feeling that there was something he had not seen. What more could there have possibly been than what Sophia had already told him? That in itself was beyond belief.

"How could that be, Sophia?" he'd asked her. "You know how it is here. You do anything and everyone somehow magically knows. How could a secret like that live in a village like this?"

The secret was of her mother and Father Mikhail. An impossible thing. Sophia herself did not know until her mother lay on her deathbed. Even if it was true, Sophia's mother should never have burdened her daughter with such information. They could have been married, he and Sophia, and Peter would have had a home with them.

"Why did you come here?" he asked her now.

"Why did you?" She lifted her eyes and let them meet his. He flinched at the hardness in her stare.

"How can you let Peter think you are dead?"

Her eyes flashed brightly with sudden tears. "Because I would be, if I had stayed."

"No, Sophia," he said quickly and without fully processing the thought. She looked away from him. Slowly she removed the bandana from around her throat—his, he recognized—and pulled off the tattered wool sweater she wore.

"Sophia, no," he said. *Please stop*.

She lifted her blouse. The skin on her stomach was blotched

with a strange yellow color which echoed itself around her throat. She turned around. There again was the same painful yellow color, this in the shape of a boot.

"Ilian Nicholai?" he asked, trying to keep his voice steady. Even Ilian's oldest brother, Dmitri, who was Jackson's good friend, thought it was possible that Ilian could do such a thing.

She shook her head. "It was never Ilian. And now Ilian has been gone from the village, the same as you."

"It can't be Father Mikhail. It can't."

She pulled the blouse back down and replaced the bandana and the old sweater. "Will you let me pass?" she asked.

"Yes." He moved aside and held the collar on Snowy Day.

She silently slid by without looking at him, then stopped and said, without turning around, "If you tell them, they will come for me."

Before he could reply she started walking again and crossed the bridge without a backward glance. He watched her, in the disappearing light, on the trail to the lighted, happy hotel until she folded into the shadow of the building. Snowy Day tugged against his hold on the dog's collar, catching the scent of the bear on the wind.

"Come Snow," he said. "Let us go home."

They made their way across the bridge and set off toward the hills. He felt heavy as he walked, as if his boots were made of stone. Sophia could not have done that to herself, he knew, yet he could not believe Father Mikhail would do such a thing. If he did not believe that, how could he ever be with Sophia again, how could it ever be between them as it once was? It could not, and he felt the heaviness in his boots wrap itself around his heart.

SOPHIA PETERSEN
FALL 1927

HE FOUND ME THERE, ON THE bridge, and I saw my Jackson at long last. Did he mock me when he said, "Or shall I call you Sonja? Is that who you are now?"

I think so. How easy it must be to be him, and he is not capable of even seeing that. It is always easier to be a man in this world. A woman without a man is a woman unprotected, and you could say a woman with a bad man is unprotected as well. Thank God Peter was born a man; I am always thankful for that.

Jackson does not believe me even at the sight of these other bruises, ones that refuse to heal. Nothing has changed. But I am not telling him the truth, am I? There would be no point. Surely he would not believe me, and if he did it would crush him beyond repair. That and the other secret I carry. To believe any of those he must believe this one thing first: that Father Mikhail is not a good man.

I let Jackson know, as plain as I could, that I must not be found. I can only hope he has love left for me somewhere inside of him.

What if he does? I feel an ember of hope in the depths of my heart, though there is so much to stomp it back down. Our love has failed already, before it had time to really be. And besides, who would want me now?

But if he did. And if I could. Here we are, both of us, in the place we had heard about and dreamed about. Here we are.

I am so tired of thinking.

HARRY WAS THERE WHEN I RETURNED to the hotel. I walked to the front, drawn to the friendly light on the platform, and there was Harry, leaning against the wall beside the door. He straightened when he saw me.

"You all right, Sonja?"

"Yes." I was breathless and I shook. I added quickly, "There was a bear, on the trail to the ridge. He followed me back to the bridge."

"Grizzly?"

"Yes."

He nodded. "They're still out there. I wish the snow would come and tell them it's time to skedaddle."

"Skedaddle?"

"Yeah—get out of here, get going, go back to their dens."

"Oh." Had he seen me and Jackson on the bridge? I waited for him to say something; he didn't.

"I suppose they'll get going soon enough," he said. "I'm happy to walk with you next time you go. We could take Nellie June with us and she'd tell that bear where to go."

I smiled. "Yes, perhaps she would."

"And Cora's here of course. I think I'll save the bear's life and not mention it to her."

I smiled a second time. I had heard, in the past few days, the talk of Harry's aunt and had seen her restlessly roaming the grounds. "How long will your aunt be visiting?" I asked.

Harry said with a bit of a smile, "She's not my aunt. I mean, not in the literal meaning of the word. You know how it is in Alaska— people adopt each other all the time to make up for the family they left behind in the states."

I smiled and knew what he meant, though on the island, people had left family back in Russia. Like Mr. Wassily, with the ancient father and sisters and brothers he said he would never see again. No one in the village other than Mr. Wassily adopted my mother and Peter and me; it was the opposite of that.

Harry's brow furrowed. "You cold?"

"A little bit, yes."

"Come in by the fire," he said, tipping his head toward the door.

I thought for a moment, how lovely that would be: those soft-looking leather chairs, the big fireplace and the beautiful rugs, the laughter of the guests.

It wasn't my place. "I am tired," I said. "Thank you, Harry." I made to move, yet remained there in the light. I could feel Harry's eyes on me.

"Things going okay in the laundry?" he asked.

"Yes. I like it very much." He was taken aback a bit by my words, I could sense. I imagine that is not often the response.

"I could probably get you up in the dining room if you'd like that better," he said.

I shook my head. "The laundry is fine." I feel safe there, with Mrs. Johnson and Nellie June, in that world where all bad things are washed away and made clean.

"Okay," Harry said. I smiled at him in thanks for his kindness, and our eyes met. I looked away quickly and felt his eyes lingering.

"Oh," I said. "We have your shirts. They are clean; we removed all of the blood."

"Really? That's wonderful, Sonja! I figured they were goners."

"No, they are clean."

Why did I not want to leave his presence? Jackson loomed like a stormy black cloud. Jackson, who had once shone like a star in the night.

"I could get them for you," I said.

"Oh—that's all right Sonja. No need to trouble yourself."

Then we heard voices of people coming up from the dark river—men's voices, and a robust woman's laugh.

"Dang that's Cora," Harry said. "Look, why don't I go down to the basement with you and get those shirts?"

I smiled, and for the first time in a very long time I wanted to laugh. "We had better hurry, Harry, if you want to escape your aunt."

Together we slipped out of the pool of light, left the platform, and went around the corner to the basement door. He walked behind me down the stairs, then beside me through the recreation room and past the storage rooms to the hall that led to the laundry.

It was unusually quiet there; the hotel was between busy seasons, and many of the railroad workers were sent north to remove a slide of large rocks from the tracks. We could hear Nellie June, though, from the trainman's reading room, laughing and playing a game of cards with some of the men left behind. Soon Harry and I were in soft light and shadows in the dimly lit approach to the laundry door.

"Wait here," I said. "I will go get them." I left him by the door and slipped inside the dark clean warmth of the laundry, the machines all quiet for the night, the smells of bleach and starch and steam hanging in the air. I forgot where the light was. I knew where to find the shirts and made my way through the darkness to them. When I came back across the floor, I bumped into something living and gave a small cry.

"Oh—sorry! It's me, Sonja. Harry. I didn't mean to scare you."

I did actually laugh a little. "Oh! I am glad—glad it is you. I should not be so easily frightened!"

"Nah—I should've let you know I was in here," he said.

"It's all right. I could not find the light."

"I think I know where it is. Follow me," he said, and I let him take my hand and lead me across the room. Even though I do not know him, I felt strangely safe with Harry holding my hand, the two of us cloaked in the protection of the dark in the warm, quiet, room.

"Wait," I said, as I heard his free hand searching the wall. "Do not turn it on. Wait for a moment." What was I thinking? Surely he must have thought something of that, of the soft intimacy that swirled around us. Perhaps he thought that he should kiss me; I felt his warm breath on the top of my head, and his hand seemed nothing more than an extension of my own—familiar and comforting.

"Are you all right, Sonja?" he asked again.

I took a breath and said, "Yes. Thank you. It is so peaceful, in the dark. Here—I have your shirts." I carefully slipped my hand out of his and handed him his freshly cleaned clothes. We crossed the room through the darkness and found the door.

"Sonja," he said, when we emerged into the light of the hall, "would you like to—go for a walk sometime?"

I had a feeling for a moment, of being young and free. A normal young woman standing in a hallway with a normal young man who had just held her hand. "I like to walk," I said. It wasn't yes, and it wasn't no. It satisfied him enough for a smile.

"Maybe we'll do that sometime," he said. He started to turn, then stopped. "Have you got everything you need around here?"

"Yes," I said. "Thank you, Harry."

"Nothing I could get you?"

I shook my head then said, "Is there a place to borrow books?"

A smile spread over his face. "Not officially. I'm a collector of books, you might say, and I'm always happy to share. I'll bring some by. What kind do you like?"

"Anything. Stories. I like books that tell stories."

"Do you like Shakespeare?"

"I do not know that."

He tipped his head and smiled gently. "I'll be sure to bring you some."

"Thank you, Harry."

"All right. Well, goodnight, Sonja."

"Goodnight, Harry."

That feeling again. Yet as I watched him walk down the long hallway, I could see how much distance there was between who I am and who he thinks I am, someone I never was and will never be. Had I given him hope? In my hindsight for this day, I see that it was cruel. My future is nothing near normal and is filled with its own relentless cruelty.

CHAPTER FOUR

EMILY WELLS
FALL 1974

WE DIDN'T SLEEP EASY THAT NIGHT, the night I saw the figure on the hill or thought I did, flinching at every sound and keeping the shotgun within quick reach. "Maybe we should get a dog," I whispered.

"Maybe we should get a cabin," Thomas replied. When light began to seep through the thin walls of the tent, I finally drifted off. When I woke, Thomas was not in the tent. I pulled a sweater on, shoved my feet into my canvas tennis shoes, and crawled outside. In the quiet I could hear him up by the cabin site, doing something. Shoveling? That's what it sounded like. The campfire smoldered, and the coffee in the pot was warm. I needed a few minutes and filled a tin mug with coffee, splashed in what was left of the can of milk, and sat down on the rock Thomas had leaned against the night before. Thomas, I determined, was either digging the rest of the post holes or looking for more bones. Or both.

My back was to the hill as I sat and drank, staring at the sputters of smoke gasping out from the gray ashes of the nearly dead fire. I should stir it up, I knew, get it going again before it was too late. That was always easier than starting all over. I didn't even have the energy for that, my mind consumed. Did I or did I not see a figure on the hill? Hadn't I seen many figures this past year, shadows in the dark, in the corners of quiet rooms, down side streets, in hallways, behind drapes, in the yard of the small green house in Sacramento where Thomas and I tried to start over? In the light of morning, in this peaceful wilderness sanctuary where I had felt safe despite bears and wolves and all the wild things around me, it seemed impossible that what I saw on the hill last night had been anything more than an illusion.

I had to focus on those thoughts for a while before shifting to Thomas. What was he doing, how was he feeling, how would he feel at the end of the day? Was it even possible to build a cabin before winter? We had a pile of logs, peeled and ready, the result of weeks of work, waiting under a brown canvas tarp. They were closer to the camp site than the cabin site. I thought again that we should build here, and leave the hill alone, though I knew Thomas would have none of it. Even if I could bend him to the idea, he would resent it. I finished the coffee, slipped Thomas' down vest on over my sweater, and walked toward the hill.

Golden, Thomas was golden, I reminded myself as I climbed. Even when he lived in Sacramento, people would come from as far as LA to see Findlay perform. The other fellows—all very good—faded into the background behind Thomas, and all Thomas had to do was stay vertical and stand in front of the mike and sing. People saw something in Thomas they could relate to, sensed something in the way he looked at them as if he knew them, and that they in return knew him, knew how his policeman father had thrown him around when he was a kid; knew how his mother lived off cigarettes and coffee and beer in a small airless house with three other women who did the same, all of them as thin and pale as if they were made of paper. Thomas adored his mother, and when the money started rolling in he took fistfuls of it to her, but she waved it away and said, "It would kill me, Thomas." His father had a new wife, a nice house and an over-indulged daughter. When he saw Thomas, he would slap him on the back as if nothing untoward had ever transpired between them, and for the rest of the visit he would tell stories about his arrests and chide Thomas over and over about how he'd better not ever come across him at a hippie party or in a drug house, wouldn't that be a laugh—and wouldn't the other fellows just crack up if he had to arrest his own son. "If you see me coming, you'd better run," he'd say. Thomas already knew to do that.

My own family was the opposite: steady, reliable, a mother who cooked meals and monitored activities, a father who worked as a pharmacist and whose favorite time of every day was the time when he came home each evening. I had two sisters, both on track to finish their degrees, unlike me. I was loved all the same, and as Thomas' reputation grew like branches sprouting at lightning speed from a swiftly growing tree, my family watched in awe. I had hitched my wagon to a star.

That was before they realized the lifestyle choices Thomas and I were making, before the photographs of us drunk or stoned or both. Before they knew about the trips to the hospital and before it started coming apart like cotton candy in the wind.

I didn't want to think about all that, the same as I didn't want to think about the shape of the strange man in the dark on the hill, or about the bone that occupied my shawl. I moved toward Thomas like the moon chasing the sun and soon crested the hill. Thomas would shine again, in one sort of way or another, and I would be there with him when he did.

HE WAS FLUSHED AND SWEATY, AND he smiled when he saw me as he threw another shovelful of dirt over his shoulder. He had dug the post holes, all of them, his X of twine trembling as it linked the corners of the space. Something was different, though—something was off. "Thomas," I said, "what did you do?"

"Do you like it?" he said, his chest heaving. He finally stopped and leaned forward on the handle of the shovel.

"You moved the cabin," I said, stating the obvious. He had taken the front right hole that he had dug the day before yesterday, the one that was kitty-corner from the one which I had dug, the bone hole, and made that the front left corner, as if the cabin had simply turned over.

"No bones! No bones, Em."

"What time did you get up?" I asked. There was a knot growing in my stomach.

"I don't know." He hadn't quite caught his breath. "Around five?"

"Are you all right?"

"All right? Of course I am. I've got this figured out, Emily. You see, it doesn't have to be one thing or the other. They can have that spot—whoever. We'll just build here. Let them dig their holes! When they're done, we can plant a garden there. Or let it go wild. Whatever we want."

"Are you okay with the cabin being here?" I asked cautiously. Thomas had been very certain of the original spot.

"It's fine. Really. We can get those posts in any time now, then start hauling up the logs."

My mind filled with what-ifs as I nodded. I knew we should talk about the man from last night, but every good moment Thomas had was a good moment. He surprised me and brought it up himself.

"No tracks," he said with a sweep of his arm. "I looked everywhere. There are no tracks up here except ours."

How could he tell. The ground was rocky and grassy, at once open and dense and complex, like a large rustic meadow. In all our ramblings across the hills the only tracks we were able to discern were the pointed hoof marks of moose and caribou. I said, "I think I imagined it, Thomas."

He looked at me for a moment, trying to read my face. "Really?"

I nodded. "It's the only thing that makes sense. We haven't seen any sign of anybody living around here, and we checked at the land office, too. It must have been—just me doing my thing again." I hadn't been able to hide it all from Thomas, my jumps and starts and sudden little cries.

"Oh Em," he said and came across the invisible cabin space to me, wrapping me in his arms. "I thought all that had stopped."

"It has," I said, then added quietly, "for the most part." Thomas thought it was connected to my own past drug use, that I'd had a "bad trip" at some point, and the jumpiness and imagining things were a lingering side effect. I sometimes pretended that it was. "Breakfast?" I asked.

He smiled and nodded.

"Let's make pancakes," I said. One day, one moment, at a time.

Harry Harbour
Fall 1974

THOMAS FINDLAY AND EMILY WELLS WERE part of what I guess you would call a movement of sorts—some spill over from the 60s where young people were "going back to the land" and "finding Mother Earth," brought to these unsettled stretches of land along the Alaska Railroad by a state sponsored "Open to Entry" program. They'd get off at their stops with their backpacks and their hippie clothes and disappear into the woods, probably thinking people like me didn't know a thing about "connecting with nature," though they were nice enough, all of them, and I would laugh inside at their youthful naivety. I imagine someone like Cora, and all those tough old sourdoughs like her, would either impress the hell out of them or scare them to death or a little of both. The things they did, the things they survived. I suppose I had some of that youthful naivety myself, back before things went bad when all I had to worry about was that upcoming caribou hunt and how I was pretty sure I couldn't live up to whatever it was Cora expected of me. I wasn't excited in the least about the prospect of killing an animal and above all didn't want to lose sight of Sonja Antonov. I couldn't wait until it was over. Too soon I would wish to God I could just go back to the days when that hunt was all that loomed in front of me.

FALL 1927

"LIKE THIS, HARRY—HERE. UP ON YOUR SHOULDER a bit more. For God's sake you don't want to crack your skinny little chest when it backfires on you."

Cora shoved the butt of the rifle against the inside of my shoulder. We were a good mile or more from the hotel, up in the hills, target practicing, getting ready for the caribou hunt. This year she was going to hunt in "her old territory" of Deadhorse Hill—Findlay—for the first time since the hotel had been built. And, of course, I was going with her. "It's about time you shot something, Harry," she'd been saying for the last year or more. "We could set up a winter camp out in the hills. There's nothing like it—just the wind, the stars, and a good sleeping bag." I'd hoped she'd change her mind. So far she showed no signs of that.

For now it meant I had to follow her up hills and over nonexistent trails to where we were far enough from the hotel as not to be heard too keenly. We went a lot farther than I thought was necessary; I think Cora meant to give me a good workout in the process.

"Okay," she said. "Try it now. Take a minute and adjust your aim. Pretend that's your caribou there, aim for the head. There's really not as much meat on them as you'd think, and you don't want to ruin an inch of it." She stepped back and I looked down the sights of Cora's old 30.06 rifle. The target was a long tree trunk sticking out of the ground at an angle. The jagged top where the tree had broken—probably by some fierce wind that blew through—was the head; the rest of it was supposed to be various parts of the body. Cora admitted it took a bit of a stretch of the imagination to see it that way. I dutifully took my aim, squeezed my finger over the trigger and let the kick of the gun jolt me backwards.

"Damn it Harry! You've got a gut-shot animal there!"

"Sorry, Cora." My shoulder was getting sore, and I wanted to stop. Cora must have sensed that because she said quickly, "A few more rounds, Harry. You're gonna hit that head before we leave here. Didn't your father teach you how to shoot a gun? Holy mercy!"

I looked down at the frosty ground and tried to clear my head. We'd see caribou right here in these hills sometimes—even crossing the river—as they'd wander down from the tundra a few miles farther along. They always looked like peaceful creatures, just minding their own business as they grazed on the ground, the big bulls with their elaborate and majestic tangles of antlers sprouting from their heads. No, I had no interest whatsoever in bringing one down. For today, I was ready to head back to the hotel.

"What have I got to do, Cora? Shoot the head?"

"Yep. Shoot the head."

I lifted the butt of the rifle to my shoulder. Before I could shoot Cora said, "Where exactly does that Jackson fellow live?"

"What?"

"Jackson Keats. Where's his cabin?"

"I don't really know," I said. "Somewhere out this way, a few more miles probably. Right before the tundra, I think. Hey," I said, an idea popping into my head. "Maybe it's not a good idea to go hunting around here."

Cora laughed. "Nice try, Harry; however, we're going out a lot farther than he would be. He can't be that far, the way he shows up at the hotel."

There was something in the way she said that last sentence. She was circling around something. "Have you seen him?" I asked. "He's supposed to be staying clear of the place for a while."

"I suppose the suspension bridge isn't really the hotel," she said.

I lifted my face away from the rifle. "He was on the bridge? When?"

"Last night. Just before dark."

I looked at Cora. The question I wanted to ask hung in the chilly air between us. I wasn't going to give her the satisfaction of actually asking it. I put my face back down against the gun and tried to aim.

"He wasn't alone," Cora said.

"Cora, I am trying to aim this rifle."

"All right all right!" I could feel her eyes watching me. "That new laundry girl was up there with him."

I felt her words as sure as I felt the rifle kick my shoulder each time I pulled the trigger. Sonja was jittery— she would have been, after encountering a bear. Or had she seen Jackson instead? Or both? A strange feeling began to work its way through me, and I grit my teeth against it. However—I told myself—whatever happened, she didn't seem happy, not when she first came out of the dark and into the light at the front of the hotel. And the laundry room, the warm dark of the place and the two of us there, my hand holding hers. It had been all I'd been able to think about, from that moment to this, what I felt when part of me was connected to part of her. Now Cora had thrown kerosene all over my thoughts and I was waiting for the match.

I pressed the butt of the rifle deeper into the crook of my shoulder, checked my aim and shot. Bits of wood flew off the top of the trunk.

"Good job, Harry!" Cora said. "That's what happens when you quit thinking about what you're doing and just do it."

My shoulder hurt, and I stared at the top of the trunk. I put the rifle strap across my chest, and we headed back to the hotel.

JACKSON KEATS
FALL 1927

"IS IT ILIAN NICHOLAI, WHO STILL BEATS YOU?"

"Ilian Nicholai has never beaten me, Jackson."

Those words, so recently spoken, rode the current of his thoughts as Jackson stood in the cold river, washing the salmon stench off Snowy Day. He should not have come again to the hotel, but he had written a second letter to his father. Something had been bothering him since his encounter with Sophia on the bridge. What had Jackson said in that first letter, the one he wrote the night he sat at his table until the light began to creep again into the sky?

I thought I saw her today—

He'd realized those words may have been a mistake. He was beginning to think that everything may have been a mistake.

There she had been, on the bridge, lifting her clothes so he could see her injuries. The yellow color of her stomach, the darker circles near her ribs. The yellow footprint on her back, tinged with gray. He was a fool. Someone in the village was harming Sophia. It was so when he was there; it was so after he had left. He'd believed the story that it was one time, that Ilian Nicholai had gotten into some vodka, despite the Prohibition, and lost his mind. Jackson did not question it. Why would he have? The man confessed, was punished and repentant. No one in Ilian's family—his two brothers and his mother, Mrs. Nicholai—had said Ilian would not have done that. But had Jackson's belief in the story been a mistake after all? How many mistakes had he made? Until Sophia would talk to him, he could not calculate the damage he may have caused. He must know, he must understand, he must not do more harm to either of their lives.

Papa—

Please inform me if there is any news about Sophia. Of course I did not see her here; it was my grief, creating ghosts. I need to know what happened to her. She would not willingly leave Peter behind. You know that. Was she afraid of someone, in the village? Had someone been hurting her?

Perhaps when she accused Father Mikhail of those things, she had meant someone else. Perhaps it was a cry for help that we did not hear. Perhaps we were wrong to judge her. Please tell me what you know.

Jackson

To mail the new letter, he'd had to go to the hotel. The train would not be arriving until tomorrow and not leaving until the day after; however, he did not want to allow himself the opportunity to change his mind. He had to mail the letter. He had to erase from his father's thoughts the idea that Sophia might be here.

Jackson had to be sure to be seen by as few hotel people as possible because he was supposed to stay away. He was certain, though, that Shirley would take his letter. She was always kind to him. He'd needed to catch the end of her shift, with the hope that the manager would be down in the basement in the trainman's reading room, and many of the guests would have wandered to the dining room.

When he had gotten there, it had been as he'd thought. He'd slipped through the doors as if he'd had every right to, and Shirley was behind the front desk.

She started to say hello and instead clamped her mouth shut, leaned forward, and whispered, "Hello Jackson," when he handed the letter to her with the coins for the postage. "I've no mail for you. I'm sorry."

He'd shook his head to say, *Do not worry*, and left as quickly as he came.

Outside, he found Snowy Day had disappeared from the platform. Jackson whistled quietly for his dog and hurried around to the back of the hotel where the river was. Snow was always after the dead rotting corpses of the spawned-out salmon that washed up on the edge of the receding water.

The dog was there, sniffing along the shore. Jackson was about to yell for him when there was Sophia, coming from around the other corner. They'd both stopped, a span of distance between them. Jackson was aware of the windows in the rows of rooms, staring at him.

"Sophia," he'd said quickly, moving closer. "Please talk to me. Please tell me what has happened."

"I told you once, Jackson. That is enough." She lifted her hand to say, *Don't come any closer.*

Jackson stopped. "Snow!" he pleaded, trying not to raise his voice. "Come!" The dog ignored him. He looked back at Sophia. "It is not Ilian Nicholai who beats you?"

"Ilian Nicholai has never beaten me, Jackson. He is not even there anymore! Didn't you hear me? Or perhaps you think that I am lying."

"Then who, Sophia, who?"

She turned and walked swiftly away.

"Sophia!" he'd called, louder than he should. He looked to the river. "Snow. Please come." The dog continued down the sliver of beach in a rare moment of rebellion.

Now the dog had the stench of the dead salmon in his fur, Jackson was wet past his knees, and he was sure someone somewhere must have seen him. None of that mattered. The past two years, he had found peace, in this river, in this magical land of hills and trees and tundra and snow, something like peace, with Snowy Day by his side. He did not mind leaving the village behind, though he missed his father despite the man's overzealous devotion to his adopted religion. Jackson had wanted to leave the place from the moment he was old enough to imagine a life beyond it. Except that life he dreamed of included Sophia, and it did not include leaving the village in disgrace.

He'd felt responsible. His initial belief in Sophia gave her the courage to confront Father Mikhail. Before that horrible day in the church, though, doubt had crept into his heart. She had been so angry, after all, that her mother was not allowed burial in the cemetery. She could not let that go. So when Ilian Nicholai confessed to the assault, it made sense to Jackson, that her anger and her grief and the horrors of the assault caused her to lose her senses.

Father Mikhail was friends to everyone. He kept them all going, through the bad times. He had always helped Sophia and her family.

"You'll need something more than water to get that smell out."

Jackson turned. It was that crazy women, the hotel boy's aunt. Though Jackson could always see that she was not the least bit crazy.

"I brought you some vinegar." She had a bottle with her and an old coffee can which she filled with water from the river. She poured half of the bottle into the can and handed it to Jackson. "Pour it over him and rub it in and let it sit for about five minutes before rinsing him. Then see if you have to do it again."

"Thank you," Jackson said, taking the can.

"Beautiful dog. I had one looked something like that back when I lived here. Best damned dog. Malamute—plenty of wolf in them. Knew when to bark and knew when to shut it."

Jackson smiled, rubbing the vinegar water into Snow's fur. "Snow does the same," he said. "That is good for a dog."

"It is at that," the woman said. "He did, however, have an inordinate love of dead salmon, that's for dammed sure."

Jackson nodded. "This one too. The river becomes the graveyard for these fish."

The woman looked up and down the length of the moving water appraisingly. "Isn't that so. Those salmon are a miracle of nature, aren't they, smelly as they are in this final state of theirs. Born in these distant northern waters, finding their way to the ocean, eventually coming back after traveling God only knows how far, spawning and dying, like clockwork, like they've got a little clock ticking away in their scaly bodies, telling them what to do. And plenty of them feeding the world along the way." The woman looked at the water as she spoke, then out at the hills on the other side.

"You had the roadhouse here. Before the train came," Jackson said.

"That I did. Most beautiful place on God's green earth. Wouldn't know it by the name. Deadhorse Hill."

"Where were the dead horses?"

"Well, that was before my time, in the early days of surveying this area. I'd always thought it happened on that big hill about a mile back. It was somewhere along the canyon, not too far out." She pointed past the hotel to the hills that faced it. "Poor things. I suppose I'd jump off a cliff, too, rather than let a bear tear me to shreds." She looked at Jackson and caught his eye. "Speaking of which, I hear you've been roughing up my Harry."

Jackson looked down at Snow. "Oh. I did not mean to—to do that. I was upset. I am sorry."

"It's all right," she said. "Harry's a good sport and took it in stride. It was over that new girl, right?"

"I thought I knew her. I was mistaken." Once he would not lie for Sophia. He would do that now. At least until he knew the truth.

"Sounds like you're from the same part of the country."

"She is probably also from a Russian Orthodox village. There is more than one, in the territory."

The woman nodded. Jackson felt her eyes on him.

"I'm Cora Allen, by the way."

"Jackson Keats."

"That, I already know. Give him a good rinse and he'll smell better than he did. I'll leave you the vinegar in case you need to do it again—just don't let Mrs. Grant see you with it and for God's sake don't tell her I was the one who stole it from her pantry."

"Thank you," Jackson said, and the woman walked back toward the hotel. Jackson wished that he could follow, wondering where in that building of many rooms and windows Sophia had gone.

Sophia Petersen
Fall 1927

I do not think Jackson will tell. He keeps pressing me for the truth; I keep telling him the truth. He does not notice this—or something. Does not want to hear it. When my mother told me her truth, I was more ready for it because I already knew Father Mikhail was not always who he appeared to be.

The first time I learned that I was seven years old. Jackson was chasing some boys on the way to school. One of them ran into me and I fell into the mud, and I dropped the precious library books I had been carrying. How could I return them now? How would I ever be allowed any more? The library at the school was very small, and now that I am grown I see how the contents of the shelves were tightly controlled, though in my world a book was a book and I read for the words as much as the story, for the sound of them and the shape of them on the page. Jackson was sorry and took me to Father Mikhail's. Father Mikhail ordered Mrs. Nicholai to clean me up; as she did, she made a point of telling me I came from a filthy house and I do not think she was talking about actual dirt.

"I don't why the Father bothers with people like you," she had said.

When she was finished, Jackson was gone and Father Mikhail insisted I have some tea. I am sure Mrs. Nicholai did not approve. She served us in the small sitting room with log walls and a smokey fire where Father Mikhail watched me carefully and smiled at me the whole time.

"Mrs. Nicholai will tidy the books, and I will make sure they are returned to the library," he said.

I looked at the floor and murmured a thank you.

"What did you say, Sophia? I could not hear."

"Thank you, Father."

"Perhaps you should look at my face when you say that."

I looked toward him. "Thank you."

"My eyes, Sophia, look me in the eyes when you thank me. You can do that, yes?"

I nodded and tried again. "Thank you, Father Mikhail." I struggled to keep my eyes on his. I felt how they wanted to pull away, to look elsewhere.

"That's a good girl. You are a good girl, aren't you, Sophia?"

I nodded.

"It is important you be good, better than most. And obedient, as well—to God, the Church, to me. Is this correct?"

"Yes, Father."

"The eyes, Sophia, look me in the eyes, little one."

Again, I forced my eyes on his. It was not that he was terrible to look at; on the contrary, Father Mikhail had a small, clever face with a straight, pointed nose and fine arching brows, fine straight teeth and dimples in his smooth cheeks above his short beard when he smiled. His eyes were a blue-grey, the color of ice on the water. It was like a burning feeling when my eyes met his, like sticking a tongue on frozen metal.

"You and your mother mean very much to me, Sophia. I will always look after you, do you understand?"

I nodded.

"Say it, Sophia. Use your words."

"Yes, Father."

"That is better. Now come here."

My tea sat untouched on the table between us. I had longed for it—tea, with sugar! —and he must have seen my eyes on it as he said, "You will have your tea, after you first come to me."

Uneasily I moved around the little table between us and stood near him.

"A little closer, Sophia."

I stepped closer. His hand touched my cheek.

"You are so beautiful, Sophia, so like your mother."

I said nothing and felt my face flush and burn.

"Say thank you, Sophia."

"Thank you, Fa—"

"Ah—the eyes. Look at my eyes."

The nearness of him. My face was level with his while he sat. I clenched my teeth and looked at him. "Thank you, Father."

"Now kiss me, here." He touched his long fingers to his bearded cheek. How was I to do that? I was not far from the door. I wanted to be back outside, running to the school. Why oh why did Jackson Keats leave me there?

"It is all right, my child. Say thank you, and kiss my cheek, then you may have your tea."

I closed my eyes.

"No—look at me, Sophia."

I opened my eyes. I felt suddenly as if I were in a dream. "Thank you, Father," I heard myself say. My eyes grew closer to his, were swallowed by his, as I leaned forward and pressed my lips against his cheek. He smelled of clean soap. The lashes on one of my eyes fluttered against his own. I pulled my face away, slowly and carefully. He smiled.

"Bless you my child," he said. "You are a good girl, Sophia; you must always be so. Now drink your tea, and I will have Mrs. Nicholai walk you back to the school."

I have no voice for what I felt that day. Now so much later I know why, for the rest of that day, I struggled not to cry in the school. At the time I did not know. I only knew that something was not right.

Here, tonight, in our little room as we readied for bed, Nellie June said, "You know about the horses, don't you?"

We could hear voices from the reading room, where not much reading appeared to be done. Nellie June had very kindly found me a few things in the hotel's lost and found box—a flannel nightgown, some boy's socks, and a few underthings I washed first in the bleach. I told her my luggage had been lost from off a boat. She seemed to believe that, and said how that happens in the river sometimes, things are lost from out of boats.

"What horses?" I asked.

"The ones that died," she said. "This place used to be called Deadhorse, you know. Deadhorse Hill."

"I did not know that," I said.

"Well it's true. Ask Crazy Cora about it."

"Why does everyone call her Crazy?" I asked. "She does not seem so crazy to me."

"Well, I don't think she's crazy, either," Nellie June said. "As a matter of fact, I wouldn't mind being like her a little—she certainly seems to do what she wants! Anyway, she used to run a roadhouse here, before the hotel, called the Deadhorse Roadhouse.

They used horses for everything back in those days. Horses and dogs. Before the train, you see. In the summer they could use the river, to go back and forth and send and receive deliveries and all that, but in the winter, they used dog teams and in both the summer and the winter they used horses for whatever the boats or the dog teams couldn't do."

We lay on our cots. Nellie June left a light on as she knew I liked to write before sleeping. "Anyway," she said, "there was a team of horses on one of those hills in front of the hotel here, and along comes this great big grizzly bear ready to kill them all and the horses go crazy with fear and jump off the edge of the hill—it was kind of like a cliff you see, it was so steep—to try to get away from the bear and they died anyway, from the fall. Think about that. They saved themselves from the bear, though what they did to save themselves killed them all!"

"That is all true?" My voice floated in the space between our cots.

"Yeah. I mean, the fact there were horses and a hill and a bear and the horses died trying to get away from the bear by jumping off the hill, that's all true. Now, the stories vary about which hill it was, how many horses there were, how big the bear was and all that, but the story always ends the same. The horses died."

"That's a terrible story," I said. "I wish someone had saved them."

In the quiet of the room I could hear Nellie June nodding her head as it rested against her pillow. "Yeah. Me too. The right person at the right time coming along and boom! Shoot that damned bear."

"Perhaps the gun would scare them as well and they would have run off the hill anyway," I said. I could see it in my mind, how that could have been.

Nellie June thought for a moment. "Hmm. Well, could be they were too stupid to save."

"Perhaps," I said, and we said goodnight. I continue to think of those horses and wish the story had ended some other way.

CHAPTER FIVE

EMILY WELLS
FALL 1974

THE NEXT MORNING, I WOKE TO FIND MYSELF ALONE in the tent once more. I listened and didn't hear Thomas outside. I didn't hear anything. I pulled myself from the bed. I had slept in, I realized. Thomas must have started work on the hill without me.

Outside the tent, the campfire was dead, the ashes cold. No fire this morning. I rinsed and filled the enamel coffee pot, using the last of the water, and was about to put it on the camp stove when my eyes wandered up to the hill. The coffee could wait. I left the coffeepot on the unlit stove and began to climb, the tiny black flies swarming around me as the wind remained absent.

The hill was empty. This was so unexpected I felt for a moment I had no air, as if I'd been hit in the stomach. Where would he go? I scanned the vast, rolling terrain, then walked to the canyon edge of our hill and looked at the trees and rocks below, at Deadhorse Creek, winding its way down from some distant nowhere. I wondered why I did that. Of course Thomas wouldn't be down there.

We got water from the stream farther down, where the sides of the canyon were diminished and manageable. Maybe that's where he was. That made sense: we failed to get water yesterday. I hurried back down to the camp, only to find that all the water jugs were there. I crawled inside the tent and reached past Thomas' side of the bed to the space between the camp mattress and the wall of the tent. The shotgun was there.

I pulled myself up to my knees. I forced myself to take several long, deep breaths, like Thomas and I would do during that stretch of time when we were meditating. Clear my head. Where would he go?

Fishing. He could have gone fishing. I hurried out of the tent and looked to the side of it, where we kept the fishing poles under the shelter of the rain flap. They, too, were there. If he had taken the shotgun with him, I might have thought he'd gone hunting, though we didn't know how to hunt, didn't know if we wanted to. We had no way to refrigerate meat, and larger animals would spoil before we could eat them. The spruce hens were tempting, though, as were the ptarmigan we would sometimes see up on the hills closer to the tundra. At this point the shotgun was purely for protection. If he went somewhere, he had left the shotgun here for me, even though like him I didn't really know how to use it.

A thought gripped my heart. The man. Had Thomas seen the man, and gone after him? That felt like the most logical explanation, even though I knew he wouldn't do that and leave me here unknowing in the tent. I hurried back up the hill and spun in circles as I searched from one direction to the next. "Thomas!" I yelled into the nothing. "Thomas!" If he had disappeared into those hills, there was nothing I could do. No way I could follow. No way I could find him.

Maybe, I thought with renewed hope, he went back to the old hotel site in the hope of finding some old something we could use, or maybe he thought he'd left something the last time we were there. I returned to camp, looked longingly at the waiting coffee pot, sprayed myself down with bug dope, and headed out.

We had, by this point, developed a sort of trail that grew easier to find and follow with every excursion. It was pretty simple; if you kept going down you would end up at the tracks. I did lose the trail several times before I finally made it, feeling a flood of relief at the sight of the rails. They were empty and silent but connected. I could walk in either direction and eventually would be somewhere; I could touch them and be connected to Anchorage and Fairbanks and everything in between. Or I could simply stand there, for hours or for days, and sooner or later a train would come. Without the tracks Thomas and I would be floating in a sea of wilderness, unable to tell when we had found the shore.

"Thomas!" I yelled, into the graveyard of the old hotel. "Thomas!" Again nothing answered; all I could hear was the low murmur of the river, the occasional rustle of the leaves when the gasp of a weak wind puffed past. I sat down on the rails, my hands gripping the metal on either side of me. Why would he do this? Of course I imagined him hurt—maybe he'd heard something, went to the edge of the hill to look, and fell. That story again. The horses. The bear. The hill. But I had looked. Even with the tangle of bushes and alders, I would have seen him there, below.

Wouldn't I?

Bugs swarmed around me, oblivious of the chemicals I'd sprayed all over myself. I was hungry. I was thirsty. I was hounded by black flies and a few late-season mosquitoes. I closed my eyes and did some more deep breathing. Eventually the silence didn't sound so silent, as if the volume on all the sounds I'd been vaguely aware of had been turned up. The river roared; the trees whispered with the voices of a thousand branches—some barren, some holding on to what was left of their fading, dying leaves. There were gulls somewhere along the river, reluctant to leave the dead salmon that had washed up on the shore and fly south; I was surrounded by an army of birds hidden in the trees. *It's okay*, I told myself. *It's okay, it's okay, it's okay.* My mantra for more than the last year. The day Thomas fell off the stage, and I thought it was the end of him. We survived that. We survived when he fell into the swimming pool and was barely found in time, his body asleep and drowning, then that other which came later, which propelled us all this way.

I opened my eyes and stood. Wherever he was, he had to be okay. After all we'd been through, it couldn't be otherwise. I looked up the tracks, north, nothing; I looked down the tracks to the south, no—wait. Something moved, roughly a mile away where the tracks gently curved as they followed the river. Tiny. Tiny and tall. It was hard to see what it was; it could have been a moose, maybe, straight on, but as my heart beat against my chest I knew it was a person. As I began walking toward it, I knew it was *my* person. Relief flooded through me even as I saw the tiny, tall figure stumble and fall and stay on the tracks unmoving and I knew I had to get there, before a train, before a bear, before any person that might wish him harm. I started to run. I had to get there, and I knew I would, because I always did. It could never be any other way.

HARRY HARBOUR
FALL 1974

THERE WAS SO MUCH I DIDN'T know. I guess in some ways that's the blessing of youth (and beyond, really): you think you've got it figured out. You've still got all those brain cells, you see, you've got your strong bodies and your freshly minted looks. What you don't have is hindsight. I wouldn't go so far as to call it wisdom, because hindsight is granted after the fact, after you were dumb enough in the first place to mess things up. Wisdom is seeing it right to begin with. Everything else is hindsight, pure hindsight. It's easy for me now to see where things were headed, like a winding river with only one way to go.

FALL 1927

CORA HAD ANOTHER DAY TO TERRORIZE the hotel staff before
heading south to Anchorage to pick up her moose head and
whatever meat she didn't gift to my parents. A little voice was
telling me to go with her, take some time off, spend the winter
with my folks in Anchorage. There was no way I would do that
though. Besides the fact that I was in the middle of some drama
about a mysterious beautiful girl who appeared out of nowhere,
an equally mysterious mountain man who seemed to know her
from somewhere, and I myself uncertain and waiting to see if
there was any room for me in that story, the Findlay Hotel in
itself was an addiction. Every arriving train held the excitement
of new possibilities as new guests and guests who were like old
friends came spilling out onto the platform, bringing fresh faces
and news from the world beyond.

The setting was full of the little dramas of woods life: bear tracks
around the hotel in the slush of the first snow, a herd of caribou
moving through the distant hills, the sound of a wolf, howling up
into the night, or an owl somewhere, hooting away in the trees on
the far side of the river. September in Alaska brought the return
of the dark, starry nights and on those rare and lucky nights, the
Northern Lights would dance around above us. Fall and winter
brought a slight dip in the visitors, but the fishermen were still
coming and there were plenty of people still making that long trip
from Seward or Anchorage up to Fairbanks or going the opposite
way. With limited roads throughout the state, the train was the
connection from one part of Alaska to another.

After Cora left I felt, as I always did, relief. There was also a
feeling of deflation; say what you would about her, she was always
interesting and could fill a room all by herself, like that spirit of
Christmas Present in Dickens' *A Christmas Carol*. Everything
felt a little less after she left. Those last few days, though, I had
felt how she was watching me, and I knew she was searching

for and sorting out my secrets. It was hard to have any privacy, around Cora.

The morning she left she caught me with a pile of books in my arms, heading toward the kitchen and the basement stairs.

"What are you doing, Harry, starting a library?" she asked from where she sat in the dining room, woofing down a stack of sourdough pancakes.

I stopped and cursed myself; I should not have let her see me. "Just making a loan," I said and hoped that would be enough.

"Where'd you get all that reading material?" she asked.

"The books are mine, Cora," I said and they were; I had previously lent them to the hotel as a whole, making a stack in the lobby by the big chairs near the fireplace. A place like that needed books. However, right now I needed the books back.

I could see by the look on Cora's face that she knew what I was doing with them, and I could see she didn't approve. I knew she'd followed Jackson down to the river the other night (I got an earful from Mrs. Grant about some pilfered vinegar, too). She wouldn't say what they'd talked about besides dogs and dead horses. I knew better. Cora was sticking her nose in my business.

"Train will be leaving soon," Cora said, her face softening a bit. "Go deliver your books then come say goodbye."

"I will," I said, and went to the basement. Sonja and Nellie June were already busy in the laundry, and I left the books stacked neatly by the door to their room. She would be surprised, when they came back, and I hoped Nellie June wouldn't think they were meant for her, though about the only things I'd ever seen her read were left-behind newspapers and magazines all about life somewhere else. I guess books were about somewhere else, too, though I didn't see how reading a magazine article about life in the Bahamas was on the same scale as *Great Expectations* or anything that came out of Shakespeare's pen. When Sonja said she liked to read books, I felt an excitement flutter through me. There was a connection, like one set of train tracks attaching to another where the siding ended.

I returned to the dining room in short order. On the platform the passengers were starting to gather for the long ride into
Anchorage.

"Harry," Cora said, and I could tell by her tone this was going
to be annoying in the least. "What does the hotel know about your
friend Sonja?"

I said, "I don't really know. Why?"

"Where's she from?"

"Some village in the Southeast. Near Juneau, I think."

"Family?"

I shrugged. "Most people have family, don't they, Cora?"

"Not everyone, Harry. So here's a question for you: Hasn't anyone noticed the poor girl wears the same clothes day after day?
How she keeps them clean I don't know—maybe she rinses them
out in the laundry at night?"

"She didn't arrive with much, Cora—is that a crime?" I had the
answer to this mystery and wanted to see how far Cora would take
it. She didn't bite at all, just looked at me.

"Actually," I said, "apparently her bags were lost at sea in some
mishap on her way here. That's what she told Nellie June."

I had indeed noticed her lack of warm clothing, what with
winter breathing down our necks. Nellie June said she'd look for
some proper clothes for her, and I planned on giving my mom a
call and see if she had any old things handy that she could send
up on the train.

"Harry," Cora said, stopping herself for a moment. "It takes a
while to get to know someone. Remember that, hmm?"

I didn't respond. Somewhere inside I knew she was right,
though I was determined to ignore everything Cora wasn't saying,
like the name Jackson Keats.

"Just treat her the way you treat ice on a lake in the fall, Harry,"
Cora went on. "One step at a time, and don't be afraid of turning
around. Always remember you might not know what the situation
is out there in the middle, okay?"

I tried to bite my tongue. It didn't work. "She's a sweet young woman, Cora. It's not her fault she doesn't have much."

"You're missing the point, Harry."

My arms were crossed in front of me, and I looked out at the platform. "Train will be leaving soon," I said.

"I know that. Walk out there with me and don't be sour. Come along."

She stood and I followed her out. Her remaining gear had already been loaded into the baggage car. She walked up to the car and told Herman to fetch out the smaller of her rifles, the .22.

"Take this and practice shooting, Harry," she said, handing it to me. "Go spruce hen hunting or something. I'll be back once it's caribou time. We'll be hunting before you know it."

"Okay, Cora."

"Oh come on, Harry, don't be so glum about it," she said as she boarded. "We're going to have a great time, and I'm gonna see you get your first animal if it's the last thing I do. You'll like it once you get the hang of it."

That first hunt would be my last . . . another thing I didn't yet know.

JACKSON KEATS
FALL 1927

"SOPHIA PETERSEN, WHERE ARE YOU GOING?"

"Home. We are trying to get home, Jackson."

Jackson remembered the night. He and Sophia were teenagers, him a few years older, and he looked at her differently now. Jackson often found himself, after checking on his father's boat, crossing the point of land that reached like a gnarly finger into the sea and separated the village from the bay where Sophia Petersen lived. A few others lived in the area as well, people looking for distance or privacy, Jackson did not know.

"Why are you out in this weather?" Jackson asked her. "You'll be blown into the sea." A storm was moving in, and even in the little bay the wind was fierce and the ocean rolled.

"Our mother is not feeling good and needed medicine."

Jackson knew what the medicine was. Homemade and prohibited vodka, probably given to them from old Wassily farther down the shore.

"Your mother should not drink the vodka."

"My mother is frightened by the wind."

"Why bring the boy?" How Sophia's mother had another child was a mystery; she had no suitors and few visitors. No man in the village would touch her, and Anna Petersen tended to only leave the bay to come to church, at the order of Father Mikhail.

Sophia's mother was a whore, after all. Jackson's father said whores find a way.

"He wanted to come," Sophia said. "We're not afraid of the rain, Jackson."

"Maybe tonight you should be."

"Peter come," she said, pulling on the boy's hand. "Let us keep moving."

Peter ignored her and looked at Jackson and smiled.

"Peter, come!"

"I'll walk with you," Jackson said, returning Peter's smile.

"There's no need."

"It's not safe out tonight, Sophia."

"Then why are you out and not at home?"

"I needed to pull up our skiff."

Sophia made a face, something between a smirk and a smile. "Jackson your skiff is on the other side of the point."

"I wanted to walk."

"Maybe Peter and I wanted to walk, too, yet you admonish us for being out in the wind and the rain."

Jackson was uncertain of the meaning of the word "admonish." He refused to let that show on his face. Looked down upon as she was, everyone knew Sophia Petersen did better than most of them in the school.

"I am bigger than you," he said.

Sophia scoffed. "Not by so much!"

Was it sinful, what he was doing? Was he being dishonest, by not telling the truth of why he came this way? Was he being sinful by wanting nothing more than to be in the company of this child of sin?

"I wanted to see . . . if everything was all right," he said.

"All right?" she questioned. "You mean, with the beaches? The waves? The wind in the trees? Or is it the rain itself you worry about, Jackson?"

He felt color rise into his cheeks. "The beaches, and the waves. And people whose houses are built too close." Even though it was built upon a little knoll, Sophia Petersen's house was very close to the sea. The wind pounded it relentlessly; on days such as this, Jackson feared it would blow away.

Sophia looked at him. Strands of her hair had blown loose from her braids, and the cold clip of the wind had turned her cheeks and her delicate little nose the color of wild roses. Her eyes held onto his, and Jackson felt a tremor shiver through him. Eyes the color of a blue sky they so rarely saw; her braids like the sun, circling above.

She turned her face and looked at the sea. "You do not need to check on us, Jackson."

"I wasn't, I—"

"Father Mikhail protects us."

There was something in her tone, a bitterness. Did Sophia's family need protection, from something more than the weather?

"From who?" he asked. No one in the village would harm them, he was certain. With thoughts and words and stares, perhaps, but no one wished them actual harm.

"From the people like you," she said and returned her gaze to him.

Jackson did not know what to say. He turned sharply and walked away, leaving Sophia and Peter to their wind beaten beach. He would never hurt her. Never.

Somehow, even in that time, she knew that he would. There was more to it, though—Jackson knew now there was something important he did not know.

"SHE MUST TALK TO ME, SNOW, SHE MUST TELL me what has happened," Jackson said to his dog.

He sat at his table, looking out the window at the rolling hills. Winter would come soon, bringing the cold and the falling snow. He did not want to chase Sophia away. He would not soon forget the awful feeling of imagining her dead. As long as she was here, he could look out for her. As long as she was here, he could hope. He worried she would disappear as quickly as she had appeared.

He did not like to think about their last days together. How he begged and pleaded with her to confess the lie; how she refused, how she asked him how he could not believe her, how he went back to Ilian Nicholai's confession—why would he confess to something he did not do? It made no sense, and neither did her accusation of Father Mikhail. Father Mikhail had been in the village his entire career and had never hurt a single soul.

"This has to stop, Jackson," his father had said. "Sophia must confess, and you both must pray for forgiveness. Father Mikhail will grant it; first you must clear your souls."

Jackson went to the Father. He'd said, "Please forgive me, Father Mikhail. I did not know what I was doing; I did not think Sophia capable of telling such a lie."

"Yet you thought me capable of inflicting harm on her?"

Jackson shook his head. "I did not know what I was doing." Wasn't that written somewhere, hadn't Jesus Christ once said, "Father, forgive them, for they know not what they do"?

"Have you and Sophia sinned, Jackson?"

His heart nearly stopped. The kisses above the cemetery—yes, more than once—and what happened on the beach. How did the Father know? Jackson knew he could not lie. "Yes," he said quietly.

"Then you are as guilty of this as she is. Sin will drive a person mad. You must tell me. You must tell me everything."

Then he did. Father Mikhail pressed his hand on the top of Jackson's head, and so firmly did his fingers grip Jackson's scalp that Jackson's eyes watered in pain.

"I forgive you, Jackson. Now you must ask God's forgiveness and you must stay away from Sophia," Father Mikhail said. "Her soul is lost, and you will only cause her further pain and sorrow. What you have taken from her she can never get back; you have doomed her to a life like her mother's, one of sadness and sorrow and sin."

"I will marry her, Father! We have always wanted to marry."

"It is too late for that, my son. Because of the sins you have both committed, Sophia is lost, and only God can find her and bring her back. You, Jackson, must leave her alone, for the sake of her soul and for yours."

What a fool he had been, to think that God would hate him and Sophia for loving each other! Here in this quiet wilderness Jackson had found God in the stillness of a winter day, in the majestic beauty of the bright sun on the mountain range, in the soft sound of the rain on the sod roof of his cabin. He no longer needed a church to feel close to his maker; God was here, everywhere—God was in him and in Sophia, too.

He must find out what had happened to Sophia, even if it led him to a truth he did not want to know. He saw how that was, now, as if in all his existence he had been looking at life through an unclean window, and now the glass was rinsed clean.

SOPHIA PETERSEN
FALL 1927

I GREW UP IN A HOUSE BUILT ON A BARREN windswept rise above

the water. My mother's father had built it for her, after she became pregnant and was banished from the village.

She had told me she loved someone once. Always when I asked, she did not say who. There was the young man, who had been taken by the sea. Could he be the one who fathered me, I had always wondered, the young man she loved, who drowned during a fishing trip out to sea in a boat that proved too small for the waves that grew that day? Was she banished because they had done something out of wedlock that created me? Or was the story of the transient fisherman who forced himself upon her the true one? All my life I had wondered, and this knowledge was not among the secrets my mother told me when she died.

Why I did not insist she tell me, in that final time, I do not know. Perhaps because I was too distracted—no, consumed—by what she did reveal.

Jackson and I had our mishap, if I must call it that, one day when the wind whipped rain drove us from the shorefront where we'd met, halfway between my house and his. It was like the wind would lift us off the ground and twirl us into the air. Just off the beach was an enormous tree that had been tossed up over the edge of the sand by whatever storm carried it here from some other island. We hurried to it and lay down beside it, hoping the breath of its girth would protect us. Yes, we were safe from the wind but now not from each other; as we lay there while the world raged around us Jackson's hand found mine and I turned my face to his. He was not the bearded wild man he is now; he was not much more than a boy then, with cheeks soft and smooth and eyes that caught the light and danced within it. We stared at each other for a long time before I placed my hand on the soft warmth of his face, and he twisted slightly to kiss it so gently. Then he kissed it some more and his lips found mine and we kissed in a way that we could not stop. We moved in a way I had never imagined, as if there was a language inside of us we had always known and only then remembered.

"It is all right, Sophia," Jackson said afterwards, when we were tangled and sweaty and my legs were smeared with my own blood, "we will be married soon." He pressed his forehead into that place between my shoulder and my neck, and I let my fingers wander through his dark curls and felt that for the first time I was smiling at the world...and the world was smiling back.

MAYBE I SHOULD NOT WRITE SO MUCH ABOUT the past. It is all like a twisting sword into my heart. The pain of the bad things that happened. The pain of the loss of the good.

I had an adventure today. I will write about that now instead.

This afternoon a pipe in the laundry was hissing steam and needed fixing; Mrs. Johnson told us we could be free for the rest of the day. Of course that meant we had to work this evening to get caught up, but to be "free" in the middle of the day felt like a blessing, though there was a promise of such things to come as hotel business entered a between time—the big summer season had ended, and extra winter business waited on the snow.

"Let's make some sandwiches and go wander," Nellie June said.

"Wander? Wander where?"

"Let's ask Harry if he would take us up that hill."

"What hill?" I asked, though I was quite sure I knew what she meant. Yes, that was something I wanted to do, I told her.

Harry was by the river talking to an old man who was fishing. The day was gray and very chilly. I felt the wind cutting through the loops in the knitting of my found sweater. I pulled the sleeves down over my fingers. The sky reminded me of Jackson, of the name he called his dog. Snowy Day. The day felt like snow.

"Harry!" Nellie June said.

Harry turned, and I could see the surprise on his face to see us there. The chilly air had reddened both his cheeks and his nose, and his brown eyes were bright with the sting of the temperature. The wind moved through his brown hair, and I could see that he was not un-handsome. Different than Jackson, who was all strength and fierceness and like the wild swirl of a stormy day. Harry had a calmness and steadiness to both his looks and his mannerisms, like the bay in front of my old house when the wind was quiet. Once his surprise passed, he smiled.

"What brings you ladies down this way?" he asked.

"We want to see the hill," Nellie June said.

"The hill?" Harry asked.

"You know, where the horses died."

"Oh—that hill. Well, no one's quite exactly sure which hill that is."

"There must be some possibilities," Nellie June said. "Some likely suspects. You must have some ideas, Harry."

He smiled again. "Well, sure I do."

"Want to show us?" Nellie June told Harry about the broken pipe.

Harry looked at his gentleman. "Are you all set for a while, Mr. O'Malley?"

The man—who had thick glasses and a matching red plaid jacket and hat—nodded and said, "I think I can manage, Harry. Thanks for your company and expertise."

"Anytime, sir," Harry said. He glanced at me and I could see hesitation in his eyes. "Will you be warm enough, Sonja?" he asked.

I nodded, but I did not think so.

"All right," he said. "We'll be in the trees part of the way, that'll help."

So we left the hotel, crossed the train tracks, and walked toward the hills that rimmed the creek, pushing our way through the brittle brush. There was no trail for us and Nellie June asked Harry why we couldn't follow the streambed; Harry said we would not be able to climb out of the canyon once we found the hill. She also asked about what she called the "tundra trail," that was a fiant footpath I had noticed leading away from the front of the hotel.

"Too far east," Harry said.

"Well, I'm glad I brought those sandwiches," Nellie June said as the land began to rise. "This is going to wear me out!"

All three of us laughed at that, and for a moment I was swept away with a feeling I did not know much of in my life, a feeling of being young and free and with friends. Of course none of it was true except, yes, I am young. I am a prisoner of my past and of my future, and I do not think you can have real friends if people don't even know who you really are.

As it is on the other side of the river, the higher we climbed the fewer the trees and the stronger the wind. At least the sweater was thick, and the rigors of the walk made my blood flow warmly. I decided to let myself enjoy the day and forget for a time everything except the moment I was in; however, Jackson kept creeping into my thoughts and I could feel him there, in those hills. Where did he live, I wondered—was it far? For the first time I let myself think about his life since the island and was struck by an image of him alone in these hills, day after day, night after night with only his dog and the wind for company. I felt something begin to move inside of me, and I thought again of his face so close to mine, the feel of his hand entwined with my own. I could feel for a moment who I once was and all that he had meant to me. Oh Jackson, Jackson, you have paid such a price, too.

Soon I could see where Harry was taking us. We came up the gentler side of a steep hill and the view opened before us. Down below we could see the hotel, the shape of a giant T, and the river and the little bridge, then that master of a hill that rose up on the other side and the little thread-like trail that zigged and zagged its way to the top. There were no mountains today as there were at times in a not-so-distant distance; they were shrouded in an angry gray.

"Over here," Harry said, walking toward one side of the hill. "I'd always thought this might be the place. A wagon wheel was found once, down near the bottom."

"What would anyone be doing with a team of horses way up

here?" Nellie June asked. She stretched her neck forward to peer at the edge from a safe distance.

"Surveyors," Harry said. "They had to go all over the place, to get their mapping done."

The hill went steeply down. I stepped close to the edge and saw the trees and rocks and a winding stream below. I felt the full force of the wind, closed my eyes for a moment and wondered what it would be like, to fall into the wind, to feel the nothingness all around, to know there was not anything ever again to worry about, ever.

Free. That's what it would feel like, to be free.

Someone touched my arm, gently, and I could feel the hand holding on tightly to my sweater. "Maybe don't stand so close, Sonja," Harry said. I opened my eyes and looked at him. Something passed between us as we stood there, close together with him gripping the loose excess of the sweater, something that felt like I knew him, and he knew me, and our paths were woven together like the strands of knitted yarn on my sleeve.

"Yes, of course," I said, and he did not let go of me until we were safely away.

NOW I SEE MY YELLOW BELLY, and I think of pain. What if I had taken that moment, before Harry came to my side, and fallen into the wind? Yet I didn't. It would have been all over, and now it is not. What will become of me? Father Mikhail made it clear what would happen, had I not fled. I would be beaten until the baby inside of me or I or both of us were dead.

CHAPTER SIX

EMILY WELLS
FALL 1974

IT TOOK ME A LONG TIME TO GET THOMAS back to camp. When I first reached him, I quickly ascertained that somehow, somewhere, he had gotten drunk. In his shirt pocket there was a baggie of pot. I looked down the tracks. Somewhere there was someone who had these things, and Thomas had found him or her. Of course he would. It must have been someone we'd met on the train. Raymie, perhaps? As far as we knew, he was closest, about four miles south down the tracks and off in the woods somewhere.

I was too grateful that he was more or less okay to be angry. I knew he needed these things—beer and pot and sometimes peppermint schnapps. We never thought we would give up everything. I sat on the rail beside him, swatting at the bugs and listening for trains, and let him sleep, his face peaceful and calm. This was okay; we could manage this. A little beer and pot or schnapps in the woods would be fine.

After a time, he began to stir, opened his eyes, and looked up at me and smiled. "Hello beautiful," he said.

"Hello yourself."

"What are you doing out here?"

"Looking for you."

"Oh—well, I guess you found me."

I nodded. "Don't do this again, Thomas. Please. It's scary out here."

He reached his hand toward mine. "Sorry," he said. "I went to see that Raymie guy. He'd said to come by anytime, remember? He's pretty nice, Em. You'd like him! I told him you thought you saw someone, and he said it was probably just the old trapper."

I felt a physical jolt inside. "The old trapper?"

"Yeah—he's got a big scar across one side of his face. He's back in the hills somewhere and not many people actually see him. Don't worry, Emily, he's totally fine—totally. Raymie said."

What Raymie said or didn't say about a stranger in the woods would make no difference to that shadow-self that now lived inside of me; I would imagine the trapper everywhere.

"What else did Raymie say?" I asked, unable to stop the edge of uneasiness that danced along the outline of my words.

"What? Oh—well, Raymie said that he could help us get the logs up the hill. He's really nice, Em. Do you want to go see him?"

"Raymie? Not today, Thomas, we need to get you home." Had I really seen someone on the hill, and had it been the trapper?

"He's really a great guy, Em. He says we don't have to worry about the trapper guy. Really. So it's good I went see him, right?"

"We have to get back to camp, Thomas," I said, avoiding his last question. "We need to get you into bed."

"I'm fine. It's really comfortable here."

"I'm tired, I'm hungry. Let's please go back to camp."

His eyes turned to the sky, and he lay there unspeaking for a time before saying, "House of bones."

"What?"

"Of all the places out here—look at all this fucking land, Em, we could have had any of it and what do we do? We pick the place of bones."

"Bone. A bone."

"Don't correct me, Em, you're always correcting me, did you know that? Why would there be one bone? Just one bone. There's got to be more up there. How many bones do we have?"

Too many. Too many to fathom. Recently I had begun to doubt my own self. How did I know for sure it was a human bone? What made me think I knew what all the bones of all the animals looked like? Nursing school felt like a long time ago, and it was something I failed to finish. Couldn't it be a wolf bone or a dog bone, a small bear even? This was a place where people once lived and many others came to stay. Who is to say no one buried a beloved pet on top of our gorgeous hill?

"Thomas," I said quietly. "Maybe I made a mistake." Out of the corner of my eye I saw the look of panic and pain sweep over his face.

"Oh no, Em, no. I'm a fuck-up, I know. I fuck everything up, just like my old man always said. But we're all right, Emily, aren't we? Aren't we?"

"Thomas—Thomas, shh. Of course we're all right! That's not what I meant. You're not a mistake, Thomas; you're my family. My *family*. Always and forever. I was talking about the bone. Maybe I was wrong about it. Maybe it is a dog bone or something like that. Wolf or coyote. It could be anything."

I watched his face clear and light, his lips opening like the blooms on a rose. "Do you think?"

"Yes. Maybe."

"So maybe we should just forget about it."

"Yes. Maybe," I repeated. The "maybe" kept creeping in there, and I couldn't seem to stop it.

"We'd better get busy building that cabin. Raymie says we've got the rest of September before we're going to start getting pretty cold in the tent."

"I know," I said. At this point there was only half of September left; it had barely been August when we'd arrived, the leaves on the birch trees green and the air full of mosquitoes. Somehow, we had squandered away our time.

Thomas pushed himself up on his elbows. "We'd better go get to work!"

"Yes," I said, though of course no work would get done today. Anything to get him moving. Anything to get him back to camp.

He stood, wobbled, and I grabbed him and held on. He leaned on me like a wounded soldier as we slowly shuffled along. Once when we were finally on the trail to camp he decided he had to lie down and I waited, the little black flies relentless, until at last I could get him going again. Camp never looked so good, and when at last I got him inside the tent and onto the bed I allowed myself to cry silently outside while I drank the water I had poured into the coffee pot. I probably would have made a lousy nurse. Other people's pain absorbed right into me, though I always managed to hold back the tears until the crisis was over. I grabbed two of the smaller water jugs and made the trip through the brush and everything else to where the sides of the canyon eased and I could get to the stream. As I filled them with cold clear water, I wondered why I wasn't afraid of the animals here. We'd seen bears, both black and brown, and we'd seen moose, all from a distance, though when the undergrowth was high and thick as it was in August, we'd always known we could walk right into a bear. Now there was the trapper, and I felt exposed in the openness of the streambed. I would be glad, I realized, when our neighbor Raymie came to help. Maybe.

Thomas slept most of the day. When he emerged from the tent in the evening, I had the two water jugs filled, the campfire burning and a pan of potatoes and canned ham sizzling on the camp stove. His apology came the way it always did; he wrapped his arms around me from behind, his head hung and his forehead pressed against the top of my shoulder.

"You are too good for me, Emily Wells," he whispered. "I'm such a piece of shit."

"You're not a piece of shit, Thomas. You must stop saying that, okay?"

"Forgive me?"

"Of course, Thomas! The only thing I'm upset about was that I didn't know where you were." That wasn't entirely true. The idea that he was capable of falling asleep on the railroad tracks haunted me. It was a new thing to worry about, and now when I heard those nighttime trains—freight trains, barreling through—I knew I would reach for Thomas, to make sure that he was there.

AFTER DINNER, AFTER SINGING, AFTER SEX, Thomas slept softly beside me in the tent. I lay there thinking about the bone from the hill. If it was a human bone, there should be more right there, just beyond the edges of the hole. However, if a wild animal had carried the bone to where we'd found it, the rest of it could be scattered who knows where. It was still light, and I decided to walk up the hill and take a quick look into the hole.

The evening was peaceful and quiet, and I felt calm and secure. I knew what Thomas meant about the hill, the sense of safety it provided as the views unfolded while I climbed and I could see there were no bears, or no people, in sight. Just me and Thomas, and all of this. Everything would be okay.

Thomas' new layout for the cabin awaited me, and I spent some time standing where the front door would be, gazing at the view it would afford. Years ago, did the people from the hotel walk up here to pick berries in the late summer or to ski in the winter, or come here when they wanted an excursion different than the massive ridge across the river? I tried to imagine what kinds of people they were: enigmas, reflections of the state they lived in, blends of extremes like the hotel itself, a luxury hotel in the middle of a vast, rugged, and wild land. What kind of people would me and Thomas be, after years here? The almost rock star and the almost nurse, living in a handmade 16-by-20-foot cabin on a hill in nowhere, Alaska.

I was so absorbed in my thoughts I nearly forgot why I had climbed the hill in the first place. I looked toward the spot where the now abandoned corner was supposed to be. I didn't see it right away, so I walked over and looked more closely, finding an impression in the ground filled with fresh dirt where the hole had been. So Thomas filled it. I felt a pang of resentment as we hadn't decided yet what we were going to do about the bone, and Thomas and I made decisions together. I wondered if seeing the hole there every time he came up to work was too much for him, and he was too ashamed to tell me he couldn't take it. Despite those thoughts, I felt a small crack caused by his secret decision, and it hurt. There were not to be anymore secrets between us. Wasn't his going off to visit Raymie whatever-his-name-was also a secret? No, I reasoned, he had not intended to keep that from me, though there was a shadowy feeling whispering at me in the far corners of my mind. It would have been easy to leave me a note.

It would have been easy to wake me and say, "Hey, want to come?" Now I had to decide if I should raise the issue of the hole or leave it for now…or wait to see if he would tell me himself.

I went back to the tent and crawled into bed. My backpack was directly across from me, and I stared at it in the dim light. It kept saying, come look, just look, beckoning me forward. I tried closing my eyes against it, but it didn't work. Finally, I slipped over to it, quietly unzipped the bottom compartment, reached in and felt my shawl. It was empty. The shawl was neatly folded, no longer wrapped around the bone. I felt beneath it and emptied the entire compartment. It wasn't there. I pulled everything from the pack—top, bottom, side pockets until it was completely empty. No bone. For good measure I searched through Thomas' pack, both of our duffels, and every box or bag in the entire tent. Oh, Thomas. He hadn't just filled the hole—he had reburied the bone. I looked over my shoulder at his sleeping face, peaceful and beautiful in the quiet light. Okay, I told myself; maybe that is where the bone was supposed to be. After putting things away as best as I could I slipped back in beside him. Sleep was long in coming.

What I did not know was that Thomas thought it was me who had reburied the bone.

HARRY HARBOUR
FALL 1974

WHAT WOULD I DO DIFFERENTLY? GOD WHERE do I begin. The problem is I was operating in the dark. I didn't know jack-shit, pardon the phrase—and I didn't have any hindsight on anything because nothing much had happened yet in my then-short life. That moment on the hill should have taught me something; I saw it there, in her face. She had thought about jumping. Why?

If I could go back now, what could I do to change the outcome of this story? Oh, more than a few things. If I could be the big fat hand of an all-knowing God who saw everything and knew everything, I would change things you can be damned sure of that. Unfortunately I'm only that all-knowing person now, after everything happened. I guess if there was one thing I could send backwards through time to myself it would be this message: Harry, keep your eyes open. Things are happening all around you, and some things are not as they seem. And for heaven's sake stay away from guns. I guess I'm not too sure about that last tip. Because, if—. One thing I have learned, is a lot about that. The old if-this-then-that. If-not-this, then not that.

Best to just tell the damned story. My failures will speak for themselves.

FALL 1927

PICNICS ON THE HILL ON AFTERNOONS when the girls had breaks from the laundry became something we did, Nellie June and Sonja and me, the two of them obsessed about the idea of the poor dead horses. Now that the brush had dissipated, the hike was a lot easier than the trail across the suspension bridge, and the view was nearly as good. Plus we were on the same side of the river as the hotel in the event of bears and things like that. They were still prowling about, even though we were heading into winter full speed with dustings of snow on the mountains creeping lower and lower. I made whatever excuses I needed to get away with the two of them—to spend time with Sonja for obvious reasons and realizing that Nellie June was a lot nicer of a gal than I had previously thought. Also, there was something about the impending onset of winter that made us feel we had to get out into the country as much as we could before snowshoes became necessary, and I guess we were naturally drawn together as we were all of a certain age.

I had called my mom on the hotel phone and asked her to rustle up some warm clothes for Sonja, and I also asked that maybe she should send up the wool skirt I wore when I had to play Viola/ Cesario in a production of *Twelfth Night* in my old school. My mom had made the skirt, and I guessed it would fit Sonja and be of her style, and I was right in that.

"Thank you, Harry," Sonja said when I gave her the little bundle that came up on the train. There was a tan wool coat with a good lining, some wool mittens and a knitted hat. We'd found some boots that one of the smaller-footed railroad fellows had abandoned the last winter, and I had snuck one of my flannel shirts into the bundle so I could secretly give her something of mine. None of it was perfect; later on when she had some money, she could order things of her own choosing. For now, it would have to do. It was getting cold fast.

She thanked me for the books, too; she looked forward to reading them when she got the chance. I wanted her to say more, like what kinds of books she read growing up, but she didn't; in general I couldn't get much out of her, about anything, try as I might—just bits and pieces, like broken glass she was afraid to touch.

"Do you have any siblings?" I asked her one day on the hill.

"A brother," she said quietly, looking out at the view and not at me.

"What's his name?"

There was a pause before she said, "Peter."

I was about to ask another question about Peter, when she said quickly, "Do you have brothers and sisters, Harry?"

"I'm an only child. Is Peter—"

"What about you, Nellie June?" she interrupted.

From the look on Nellie June's face I could tell she'd already told Sonja about her family—three boys and two girls, Nellie June the oldest; their dad worked for the railroad same as my own. Nellie June missed her siblings and now that things were slowing down and Sonja was all trained up in the laundry, Nellie June would probably start making the occasional trip "down the tracks," as we'd say, to the village for visits, like for her upcoming birthday.

Nellie June wrinkled her nose and looked at Sonja and said, "Oh, you know about them already. And Harry certainly does."

By that point I'd gotten the message that was hidden in the exchange: Sonja didn't want to talk about her family, at least not about Peter. Despite the fact I knew nothing about Peter, including how old he was, my mind began to think of all kinds of things: he was crippled like Tiny Tim, he was actually dead and she couldn't face it, or he was being held hostage by an evil uncle or someone of the sort. That's what too much time in a place like Findlay would do to you—the sweeping hills, the wild animals, the soaring views and all the different people coming and going and beneath everything the silence and stillness of the wilderness—it fed the imagination, and there was also plenty of time for reading and I read nearly everything I could get my hands on.

Nellie June and I exchanged a look, and Nellie June gave a little shrug.

Sonja said, "What is that?"

"Where?' I asked, and rose from the cold frosty ground, happy to have an excuse to stand beside her.

"There," she said, and pointed to a distant hill. I leaned in closer to follow the trajectory of her finger, my eyes squinting as my face hovered next to hers. She had a clean, soapy scent, and her warm breath smelled like the apple she had eaten from our picnic lunch. Every cell in my body burned with the longing to turn my face and kiss those soft pink lips. I swallowed hard against it and struggled to find my voice.

"On that hill? That one over there?" I asked.

"No—to the left a bit, Harry. It is on the top of the hill, near the center of it. Oh! Now I see two."

My eyes caught the moving forms, stick figure animals crossing over the top. "Caribou," I whispered, sensing with dread the approaching hunting trip with Cora.

"Caribou," Sonja whispered back. We were locked in a moment together, full of awe and wonder. There was a startling bang on my shoulder and Nellie June was there, shoving the binoculars we'd borrowed from the hotel at me.

"You'll see them better with these," she said.

I sighed, took them and handed them to Sonja.

She lifted them to her eyes, focused, and said, "They are amazing! So beautiful! There are three now that I see."

I stopped her when she started to hand me the binoculars. "Go on—keep looking for a bit," I said. "Nellie June and I have seen our share of caribou." Sonja smiled and put the glasses back over her eyes. Her head swept to the east and she let out a tiny gasp. Nellie June and I followed her gaze and saw a distant flash of grayish white.

"That'd be Jackson," I said. "At least his dog at any rate." The little speck of gray/white was soon followed by a larger, darker form that came over the rise of a hill and suddenly stopped.

"He sees us," said Nellie June.

"He does," I agreed.

Sonja tore the binoculars from her eyes and handed them back to Nellie June. "Shall we go now?" she said.

"If you're ready," I said.

"Might as well," Nellie June said. "Getting cold up here."

We packed up our things and headed down the hill. I carried with me that feeling again, the one I always felt when there was a collision of Sonja and Jackson—that there was something important I did not know.

JACKSON KEATS
FALL 1927

THE DAY JACKSON LEFT THE ISLAND AND SAID goodbye to his father was stormy and gray, as of course it would be.

They'd already had the talk of where Jackson was going; "Nowhere," Jackson had said, and his father said, "Somewhere."

Jackson did indeed know where he was going, to the place he and Sophia had talked about, that mythical land of mountains and caribou and days filled with blue skies and sun. He would not share this with his father, not yet. He had with him the money he had been saving for when he married Sophia.

Jackson had already said goodbye to Dmitri Nicholai, who warmly gripped his hand and said, "You will be all right, Jackson. I am sure you will be home soon. And I am very sorry about Ilian, and what he did."

Now Jackson stood before his father, who said, "The boat will get you to Juneau. You could stay there, you know, until everything turns right again."

Right again? Jackson could not imagine anything ever being right again. It was irrelevant if his father was right, if Father Mikhail was right, and if God was on their side: it was ruined here for Jackson. Every day that he woke was a day he wished wasn't. The only days he wanted were the days before Sophia's mother fell sick; the days where he and Sophia wandered the beach or sat on the hill above the cemetery, talking of their dreams and being happy only to be near one another. Days when the villagers admired Jackson and waved and called his name when they saw him about. What had happened? These two years later, it remained unclear to Jackson, and it certainly wasn't clear on the day he left his father and the island behind.

"If you stayed in Juneau, I could visit you as well," his father had said. Jackson worried his father would cry. But his father was the one who had told Jackson he had to go.

"It has all been too upsetting, for the church and for the community," his father had said, repeating his words from days before. "Father Mikhail has told me you and Sophia must be separated and I could not agree more, given what has happened. It is for your own good, Jackson. Sophia is not right in the head. Because of that, Father Mikhail says Sophia cannot be the one to leave. And there is Peter to think about. You *will* be able to come home one day, I know it, Jackson. I believe you are an innocent, and it was only the goodness of your heart that led you astray."

Jackson said, "Did you not love my mother?"

His father stilled, surprised by the question. "Your mother was not like Sophia, Jackson. She was of the church, her parents were good and godly, and she would not let me touch her until we were properly married. That is what a godly woman would do."

Jackson froze. So his father knew what he and Sophia had done. Father Mikhail should *not* have told him—or anyone. It was Jackson's confession, words that were between him, the priest, and God. Jackson had always been proud of his father's friendship with Father Mikhail. It elevated them in the community and gave his father someone to talk to who also had no wife. On that day Jackson was able to see how their friendship was now working against him.

"Anything that happened between me and Sophia was my doing," Jackson had said.

"And so now you must leave."

That was it, those were his father's parting words. He'd tried to embrace Jackson after Jackson lifted his bag; Jackson shrugged him off and walked out of the door. He had been to Juneau before, once with his father and once with some fishermen he was working for, and the thought of going there did not frighten him. He had a sleeping bag and a tarp in his backpack, money in his pocket, and he would be all right, though the thought of being there filled him with emptiness. The wind would whisper of Sophia, and the water would always call him home. If he had to go, he would go, and he would find that great river and those big hills and the mountains that rested like gods on the horizon. He clung to that vision as the fishing boat where he bought passage pulled away from the island and he stood on the deck and watched the place where he had always lived slip away into the water and the fog, the rain pouring down onto him and a great emptiness opening inside of him.

He spent three miserable days in Juneau, staying close to the docks where he slept under his tarp as the rain beat down. At night drunk men came and went from the boats, and when he went into the town in the mornings for food, he would see the unluckier ones who had no boats slumped against the walls of buildings along the side streets, the Prohibition's cracks and failings in the territory on display. After eating, Jackson would walk away from the town, down the small stretches of road, and one day he walked over ten miles down a wide trail to the glacier, and there he stopped and stared at it, longing for the ancient, pristine wisdom held frozen in the massive chunks of strange blue ice.

At last he was able to find a boat headed for Seward, and from there he could ride the train into the wild depths of Alaska. It wasn't until, days later, when he was sitting on a train moving north, that Jackson felt something stirring inside, some sort of hope, a feeling that maybe he could find someone new inside himself, a new way to live.

It was the country that was bringing him back to life. As he sat on the train watching the miles slide slowly by, he savored every change in the landscape: hills and rocks and cliff faces, mountain passes and tunnels even, rivers and lakes and later the ocean again as the train neared the town of Anchorage. He felt the new land ahead of him calling him, as if he knew he was going to the place where he would live the remainder of his days. As the train left Anchorage behind, it moved through endless forests full of tall white birches crowned with gold leaves and the straight and pointed spruce trees, cloaked in their coats of green needles. There was a village, near the end of the day, and a bridge that spanned a great gray river while another such river ran beside the railroad tracks, flitting in and out of the trees. The sky was blue. In the distance there were white mountains, bigger and brighter than anything Jackson had ever seen.

Later there was a long slow bend that followed the big gray river. Soon he saw the famed hotel up ahead, so startling in that landscape of hills and river and distant mountains. There was a handful of other buildings, too, like little homes lining up obediently beside the hotel. A thread of a bridge spanned the great river, and hills rose on either side.

As Jackson stepped down off the train the conductor said, "Here to work?" and Jackson said, "No," and nothing more, though the words he felt hovered unspoken on his tongue: *I am here to live.* As he moved away from the train and into a world that was clear and sharp and vibrant, he knew that was what he could do. Live.

It was then his life here began, with the train ride followed by one camp after another as he worked his way into the hills that overlooked the face of the hotel. When he found his spot, within the tree line but high enough where the trees were scattered and scarce and the hills were clear and clean and the world felt open and wide, he planted what was left of his life into the ground like a seed and felt it start to grow.

Now it had come to him, the biggest miracle of his journey, bigger than the pup he'd found one day abandoned several miles from the hotel, and that was Sophia, tossed out of the sea and off a train. In this clear mountain-fed air the island and the church and all the troubles there were like a different life he had lived, or a dream he once had that did not end very well. Here, now, perhaps he would at last learn the truth. What he knew most about Sophia, as much as he knew anything about himself, was that she would not willingly abandon Peter. Something had happened to make her do that, and Jackson—and his father, and the village—had gotten something terribly wrong. Father Mikhail. That something had to be Father Mikhail. Jackson had thought about the priest many times in his solitude. He remembered the day he took Sophia to him, the day when she and the books she carried tumbled into the muddy street. He had known that day when Sophia came to school looking tearful and afraid. He had known that Father Mikhail had done something to her, that either hurt her or frightened her. Jackson had buried the feeling beneath what was safe and familiar despite his child's empathy and instinct telling him that something was not right. Could she forgive him?

"Come Snow," Jackson said and put on his wool coat. He needed to walk the hills, and he would let his feet take him where they always took him now that Sophia was here: to the view of the hotel, where maybe he could catch a glimpse of her, a distant figure in an old thin skirt.

The day was gray, and the wind blew cold from the north. It felt like snow, and Jackson said, to his beloved pet, "A day for you, Snow. Snowy Day." The snow, when it came, always made things more difficult, but the world it created was white and magical and bright.

As he walked, he saw first two then three caribou on a distant hill. He should be hunting—a moose, a caribou, something—but today he was glad he did not bring his gun. Let the caribou have their day. He had plenty of dried fish to eat and all the harvest from his gardens. He looked to the land in front of him, sensing something, and saw three figures on one of the many hills that loomed above the hotel. His heart leapt. One was Sophia. He knew her anywhere, and from any distance. Now.

SOPHIA PETERSEN
FALL 1927

I CANNOT ESCAPE JACKSON. EVERYWHERE I GO he seems to appear, as if he can smell me in the wind and knows always where I am. My time here runs short. Doesn't it? Even if he could swear to me he would not tell anyone I had survived, how could we possibly live anywhere near each other, we two who once wanted only to vanquish the very air least a breath of it come between us?

Today Jackson had stood before me on the hill and said, "Sophia, forgive me," and I'd said, "For what, Jackson? For which betrayal? Where do we begin?"

I had come up the side of the hill of the dead horses and there he was, his big white dog beside him. He had seen us, me and Harry and Nellie June, the day before yesterday when we stood on the hill and saw him off across the land—toward the tundra, Nellie June had told me—and today he had somehow known I was coming that way again. He is watching me, perhaps? For what purpose—to report back to the village?

"My friends are coming," I said when I saw him there, on the hill of the dead horses, though I knew today they were not. Harry had taken a man fishing, and Nellie June was suffering from her monthly. I had wanted to see the view, and I wanted to feel the wind.

There was something else. I had wanted to see the place that went steeply down again, that tentative edge that had taunted me, and I wanted to see, if on a different day I might feel a different way.

"Sophia, please."

"Go away, Jackson," I said. I no longer wanted to be there; I turned around and began the walk back the way I came. He did not follow. I felt the piercing loss of who we each had once been.

I feel, at this moment and at times that hit me like a hammer in the face, that all I have left is my story. If I am to tell this story I must tell it, but for whom do I write these words? It is a story that should never be shared. Perhaps I write it only for myself, and perhaps that is enough.

ONE DAY AFTER MY MOTHER'S BURIAL, Peter was in school and there was a knock on the door. I opened it to Father Mikhail, who asked if he could come in.

"No!" I said and made to slam the door in his face. He was quick and held the door while I pushed.

"Sophia, there are things we must discuss."

"Discuss with me? Were there things you 'discussed' with my mother as well?"

"I do not know of what you speak, Sophia."

"You know. You know! She told me—she told me what you did to her!" I had meant to talk without stopping, but the look on Father Mikhail's face took my very breath away. Fear, anger, and shock. So my mother had surprised him, after all those years.

I found my voice and went on: "And if you do not allow her to be reburied in the village cemetery like a proper, worthy person I will tell! I will tell everyone!" His grip on the door had eased, and I was able to get it closed. I pulled the latch as he walked briskly away.

Later that day, when I went to pick up Peter from the school, he had been invited by Mrs. Nicholai to spend the night and play with a little boy who she was watching at the time. Peter's little face showed how he would like to do that, the same as when he asked to return to school, even though our mother was not long in the grave. The funeral—if one could even call it that— had been rushed; there was no service, with only me and Peter, Father Mikhail, Jackson, and old Mr. Wassily in attendance on the lonely spot outside of the village beside those few others found unworthy of proper burial. I had been too wracked with my own grief to try to stop it, too concerned for Peter, and my anger had not yet found its feet deep inside me.

So I let Peter go to Mrs. Nicholai's home, and before I left the village I went looking for Jackson and found him down at the dock with his father.

"Sophia!" he said while his father glared at me sullenly. Of course he wanted a better match for Jackson. Jackson said his father would come around, and that he spent too much time with Father Mikhail and the church people. Jackson believed his father would remember how he himself had to once seek the acceptance of those same people and that same church, and he would eventually accept me.

Jackson was certain of it. "My father is a good man," he'd said. "He would want me to be happy."

"Sophia, what is wrong?" Jackson asked that day at the dock then quickly checked himself. "I'm sorry. Of course I know what is wrong. Father, please excuse me. Sophia, let us walk." I turned and he followed, and we walked without speaking up to our spot above the cemetery, where I let my rage at my mother's burial fly out into the wind and ran away down the hill, Jackson calling after me.

That night I found my mother's vodka, a half a bottle she must have forgotten, otherwise it would have been long gone, and I drank a glass of it. It did not help; it only made me want to rage against the walls of the house like a storm-driven wind.

"I will stop you!" I shouted, into the quiet emptiness that death brings to a home. "I will make you pay!" How big I felt in that moment, and brave and justified. When the knocking came on the door I was glad—I would throw Father Mikhail out into the wind and kick him as he left. I pulled open the door. It was not who I expected.

I do not like to think about it, that first beating, the surprise of it coming from those hands. I knew what it meant. Father Mikhail was telling me how it was to be.

I was tossed onto the floor, thrown against the wall, kicked in my stomach, my back, my legs, my arms—everywhere that would not be seen—and left in a crumpled heap. It took a long time for me to be able to move, to make it to the door and pull the latch closed. The following day I limped as I walked to the school to bring Peter home. No one asked me what was wrong. I wanted to scream for their help, though I knew I would not be believed. I knew, too, that I had to make some move and did not know what. I would have to plan something, and I believed I would have Jackson on my side.

What would the people here, at the hotel, think if they knew of this? Jackson—I know what he would think and feel, if he believed it. Most people, I do think, could not imagine that this could be true. I should have known better, than to try to tell the village. And I did not tell the entire truth, about the beating, but the fact that it was Father Mikhail's will that it happened was the truth. Father Mikhail and only he was responsible for what was done to me.

What if I had told Jackson the entire truth? Then his disbelief in me would be twice what it was. I feel, though, that there must be some purpose in our both arriving here. That God has willed it; *why* I do not know.

Nellie June and Harry have found some warm clothes for me. I realize I have never had friends—only Jackson, and Mama, and Peter and Mr. Wassily; my grandfather while he lived. There are also books from Harry which I am trying to read, but my own story keeps distracting me, along with my constant worry for Peter and how sad he must be, believing that I have died.

He doesn't even have Jackson anymore. In those days after Jackson went away it was hard to see how Peter would stand outside and look at the ocean, wishing it would bring Jackson back to the island. Little would he dream that Jackson and I are both in the same place now. If only I had brought Peter with me! Why didn't I? Because I thought that night that I would die. Because I was fleeing for my life. And as before, Peter was not at home when I was attacked.

Now that I have not died, could I go back somehow and get Peter, and take him away from there? I do not see how I could do that, on my own. Do I walk bravely down the street, for all to see? Or do I sneak around in the night and kidnap my own brother as he sleeps. Could I get Nellie June or Harry, these new friends I have now, to get Peter for me?

Or Jackson. Peter would be so very happy to see him. Do I dare to ask him? Do I dare to imagine that saving Peter might be God's reason for sending both me and Jackson to the very same place?

No. Perhaps I can at least ask Jackson to find out how Peter is doing. Can I trust him that much?

CHAPTER SEVEN

EMILY WELLS

FALL 1974

I HAD TO GO TO TOWN TO GET SOMETHING called a come-a-long, which we would need to get the logs up the hill after Raymie arrived. Thomas said we wouldn't have to pay him; he said Raymie volunteered and didn't want compensation. I thought we should pay him, and we could, though when our money ran out I didn't know when we could get some more, or how. I also didn't know what might happen, leaving Thomas there on his own, and I didn't know what might happen to me, in Anchorage on my own. I didn't know if I really saw a figure on the hill, and I didn't know why Thomas reburied the bone, or why he didn't tell me that he did. I didn't know why I felt such dread.

Times like that, I would force myself to remember things, so I could compare the "then" to the now. After San Francisco and the breakup of the band—wait, not a breakup. After San Francisco and after Thomas was fired by the band that was his own creation, we moved back to Sacramento and rented a little green house with a garden in back and an arched pathway to the front door. It felt tucked away from the street and the sidewalk, a world all its own. I loved it—except for the big plate glass window in the front that stared back at me with bottomless eyes every black-dark night. I had heavy velvet curtains made and each night pulled them tightly closed; they couldn't change, however, what I knew was there on the other side: darkness and the unknown. Thomas, too, struggled in those days, in that sweet little house where we were going to start everything over, and I needed all my almost nursing skills to keep him level. Pot was a necessary medication, as was peppermint schnapps. With beer between. If he got drunk enough he would forget what his body really wanted: opioids. Heroin. The stuff that would take him so far away he would not even notice when he slept on the bottom of a pool. That was our battle, when we lived in the little green house, to keep him, to keep his cravings, caged and to keep him from walking out the door alone.

Each morning we sat across from one another, exhausted. Thomas from drinking; me, from staring at the velvet curtains and daring them to move. Always his hand or my hand would reach across the table, and we would sit like that, our hands entwined, drinking tea or coffee and watching the birds outside the kitchen window.

We didn't last long. Finally one evening Thomas came out of the bedroom and made for the door. It was locked and I had the key. He began screaming that he needed to leave, he needed to go out; he began pleading. "Please, just this once, I just need—"

Then he started yelling again and throwing the furniture. I had not closed the velvet curtains yet; I could still make out shapes in the yard in the fading light. Thomas looked at that window, that big sheet of glass, and before I could even begin to think of what he might do he ran straight through it and it shattered into hundreds of sharp, piercing shards.

Another trip to the hospital. Thomas was stitched up like a torn toy, and his scars—some big and some little—were scattered across the front of him.

Here we were, now, over twenty miles from the nearest any-thing that resembled a town. If he got drunk at the neighbor's once in a while that was fine. As long as there weren't needles there, and dangerous stuff to fill them with. *Here* was better, bones in the ground and possible strangers on the hill included. Yet I remained uneasy as I readied myself to get on the train. I pulled on clothes that had not been worn since our last trip to the city, things too fancy for woods life—flared colored cords and a silk paisley blouse and my fringed suede jacket—relics of that past life—and I scrubbed the dirt out from beneath my finger-nails. Because my hair was thick and full and layered you couldn't really tell how dirty it was, though I knew it smelled like campfire smoke. It would have to do until I reached the hotel and a shower, and when I got on the train Harry the conductor said, "Don't you look lovely this evening, Miss Wells."

"Thank you, Harry," I said, looking anxiously over my shoulder for a last glimpse of Thomas, waving to the train. I found a seat and settled in for the long quiet ride.

The train blew its whistle and started to stop shortly after I'd gotten on. It was a flag stop train, which meant that anyone on any stretch could flag it down and hop on. From the nearness of this stop to ours, I guessed it was likely Raymie. I waited apprehen-sively. What sort of fellow, besides Thomas, would get drunk first thing in the morning? I could have laughed at myself, thinking that; San Francisco was one big party, though I always tried to keep the mornings clean. Maybe a little coke; definitely no alcohol.

When Raymie strolled into the car I remembered him, from when Thomas had talked to him on that previous train ride. He gave me a brief glance, sat in an empty seat across the aisle and several seats in front of me. After about a minute he turned around and looked at me.

"Aren't you Emily?" he asked.

I said I was, and he switched seats to the one right across the aisle from me.

"I'm Raymie Weatherell," he said.

"Hi."

"Yeah—hi. Thomas make it home okay the other day?" His eyes were round and a calm green, like a still, quiet pond.

I hesitated. His face invited me to be honest, to say something like, "Sort of," or "More or less." I did not want to do that to Thomas, though—wouldn't do it. My dear wonderful, wounded Thomas. "Yes," I said, "of course."

He smiled and nodded. I could feel how he had seen my hesitation, or heard the unconvincing firmness of my "Yes, of course." He took in a breath as if to say something, stopped as if changing his mind, and said instead, "How are things going, up there?"

"Good!" I said, too cheerfully.

He tipped his head to one side as if studying me. "Thomas said you saw someone. On your hill?"

"Oh," I said, suddenly embarrassed. "Maybe. It was sort of dark, so I'm not totally sure."

"There is an old trapper, who lives somewhere back there."

"Thomas told me," I said. "I—I'm just not sure." Nor was I sure if that was a good thing or a bad thing, if the trapper had been there. It might be worse, I had been thinking, if I had imagined it, if I was actually really seeing things that had more substance than the flitting shadows that had been haunting me.

"He's supposed to be a good guy," Raymie said. "Some of the railroad guys know him. He doesn't come out much."

"Oh," I said.

"He's apparently got a big scar across one side of his face. That's how you'd know if it was him."

"Okay."

"I'd love to run into him," Raymie went on. "The stories he must have."

"Stories?" I asked, aware that I must seem like the most boring person he had ever spoken to. I knew I was considered to be pretty, but I was no Thomas. Thomas could engage people with laughter and smiles and stories of his own. He was a good listener, too, and he made those around him feel special. I was often at a loss for words.

"Yeah—well, like that scar on his face. Might be some kind of a story there." When I didn't respond he added, "Sorry—I'm a writer. That's just how I think."

"Oh," I said. "Well, what do you write?"

"Nothing I can make a living at," he said, and added: "Poetry. I write a few stories every so often, but I'm pretty stuck on poetry."

"How do you make your living?" I asked. Thomas and I really needed to figure out that part of our own plan.

"I'm a biologist. What that means for me is that I go to the western part of the state for a few months in the summer and count fish."

The whistle blew, and the train started the slow process of stopping again.

"Count fish? Really?" I asked.

"Yeah—crazy job," Raymie said and stood. "I'm actually getting off here—visiting the hippies. I'll come by in a few days." He paused, looking down at me. "That's all right with you? Thomas said you could use some help."

I nodded, though I wasn't sure. He seemed nice enough, but how does one really know? "Yes—thank you," I added quickly. "That would be great, actually."

"Okay." He smiled. I felt him taking me in—my jacket and my silver hoop earrings, my pointy leather boots sticking out from the belled bottoms of my purple cords. "Sounds great! I'll see you soon."

"Yeah—see you. Thanks," I said and watched him walk down the length of the train car to where Harry waited for him.

I crossed the aisle and looked out the window and saw Raymie hop down off the train, skipping over the little steps Harry had placed there for him and the two of them having a laugh about it. There were some people there to meet him; I recognized Monique and Raoul, happy to see him. I felt a flush of a strange jealousy as I imagined their evening: going back to a warm cabin, passing the pipe and maybe a bottle of something, laughing together and nothing going crazy, everybody staying in some sort of sphere of normalcy.

Hours later I was in a hotel room in downtown Anchorage. Nicer than we really could afford, but the well-lit halls and the nicely dressed people and the all-night desk clerk gave me a slight feeling of comfort and safety. Slight. I quickly searched the room and locked the door, pushed the room's two chairs up against it, and pulled the drapes across the black windows.

HARRY HARBOUR
FALL 1974

WHAT'S IN A NAME? IT'S STRANGE how that small little line echoes around for me, from the day I met Thomas Findlay back to the days when I was trying to figure out if Sonja was Sonja or really the Sophia that Jackson Keats seemed to think she was. At my small little Anchorage high school, I'd been part of the drama club. That's where my love of Shakespeare began, and I actually spent some time back in those youthful days taking the "all the world's a stage" thing a bit literally and trying to see the things going on around me as scenes in a play. Maybe I missed my calling, there. But when the final act came and things fell the way they fell, I knew the best life for a man with a dark secret was a quiet life, not a life in any spotlight at all.

Back then, though, before all that, I was determined to find out who Sonja Antonov was. If I could.

FALL 1927

THAT .22 CORA STUCK ME WITH lived in a corner of my room since she got on the train. I didn't have time for target practicing, I told myself. After all, I was lord of the bellhops, resident fishing guide supreme. Or so I liked to think. The truth of it was, I was always handy when Walter the pool guy needed someone else to clean that darned thing or when Mrs. Grant needed some help in the garden or some guest thought he needed someone to carry his golf bags for him, though in terms of size our course was probably a bit of a joke. I was always whatever somebody else needed me to be.

I guess I could have said, as I looked at that .22 in the corner of my room, now Cora needed me to become a hunter. There was a reason, though, why it would be a good thing for me to learn how to shoot. If Nellie June and Sonja and I continued our hiking expeditions next spring when the bears were active, we might want to carry a gun along. It also occurred to me that Jackson Keats was a hunter and probably a pretty good shot. I thought of those ladies I was teaching to fish, the ones that just watched Jackson instead. Maybe Sonja Antonov would be different. At any rate, if I wanted to protect her and Nellie June from the spring bears, I had to learn to shoot a little better. You didn't always have twenty shots to get one right. Before anyone could grab me that afternoon to tend to some undone or ill-done chore, I put on my wool jacket, tossed a wool cap onto my head, grabbed the gun and headed out the door. The day was gray and cold as I climbed to the "hill of the dead horses" as Sonja called it. I loved the way she said that, it made it seem so grand somehow. The ground was frosty and we had yet to see some snow. This day certainly felt like snow; the clouds were low and heavy and gray, as they had been for a week now, and we were a bit past due.

When I crested the hill, the wind held a sharp edge as it pressed against my face, and I felt a chill run through me, though I wondered at that, as overall I felt fairly warm. I took note of it and went directly about figuring out what I was going to shoot at and from how far. The best I could find was a multi-pronged and very dead branch that had fallen off one of the few birches on the hill, alone on the remains of the once-flourishing brush and grasses as if tossed there by the wind. Fall was a good time for walking, with all the undergrowth beaten down; all that would end with the snow, though that in itself wasn't too bad if you had some decent snowshoes or could manage yourself on a pair of skis. I'd have to find Sonja some snowshoes, I thought as I jammed one end of the branch down into the space between two rocks that were half buried in the ground so it would stand. It was an insubstantial target if there ever was one, and I'd be lucky to hit it at all. I started at a fairly close range, something like twenty feet, and took a few shots which vanished into the air. I was pleased, though, by how comfortable the small caliber rifle was; there was none of that kick-back and not much noise, either, comparatively. I had plenty of the little brass-colored bullets so I kept trying, and eventually some of the areas of that branch began to shiver and tremble, and I even broke a piece off at one point. I saw how I needed to be farther away, more like if I was actually shooting something, and an idea struck me. I took off my wool cap and secured it to part of the branch and walked to the back edge of the hill.

I had a strange feeling, aiming at the hat that had so recently come off my head. It felt sort of macabre to be shooting at it, or at the very least seemed like some kind of bad luck. I did it anyway. After three shots I hit the damned thing and gave a little yelp of victory.

It was like a spell was broken. I shot that hat until it was a tattered rag of surrender hanging from that long-dead branch, and I even managed to shoot up the branch itself. Damn. I almost wished Cora was there with me to see it, though maybe if she was there looking over my shoulder I wouldn't have been able to free myself up enough to get it right. It was like in my theatre days. If I couldn't get a scene right, I had to go off somewhere on my own and stand before a blank wall or a row of empty chairs and then I'd get it right, and it would stick with me, and I could carry whatever I had snagged back onto the stage.

I felt pretty pleased as I pulled the shreds of my cap off what was left of the branch. I remained unexcited about killing a caribou, but I at least didn't want to make a fool out of myself or worse, wound one. It likely wasn't too long now before Cora would be getting off the train again. After that was over, the winter season would be getting under way and I'd be free of any family obligations until Christmas, when my folks would be expecting me. That would give me a lot of time, in the warm and jolly hotel, to see if I could get Sonja Antonov to let me hold her hand again.

I was thinking that thought and had turned to begin my journey down the hill when I saw something moving in the viewshed a little farther down closer to the hotel. My first thought was that it was a deer, not that we had deer here or anywhere in Alaska except on Kodiak Island and some places in the Southeast part of the state. I didn't need the hotel's binoculars that hung around my neck to soon see that it was Sonja, with her gold cap of braids circling her head and wearing the tan wool coat my mother had sent up from Anchorage. She held up her skirt as she hurried along, and I saw that she was on the trail that led up into the tundra, heading toward the general area where we had seen Jackson appear the day we'd seen the caribou.

I knew where she was going. I watched her for a few moments before I strapped the .22 across my chest and resolved to follow her.

JACKSON KEATS
FALL 1927

"ARE YOU LOST, SOPHIA?"

Jackson saw how Sophia jumped at the sound of his voice. She looked wildly about on the long slope of an open hill before she spotted him, sitting among the faded grasses, his back against a large rock, Snowy Day curled by his side.

She frowned. "Were you lying in wait for me, Jackson?"

"I was just sitting here, enjoying the view. Then you happened to come into it."

"And you sat there, waiting."

It was how they used to go at each other when they were

children. "What would you have me do? Get up and walk away? Or try to say hello to you, you who seems to hate me so much."

She did not reply at first. She looked at him as if thinking, as if weighing something, then said, "Can I sit here, oh stoic one?" She gestured at the empty place along the rock face.

He felt a smile wanting to burst across his face. "If the dog approves, yes."

She reached out her hand to Snowy Day, who sniffed it and delicately licked the top, as if kissing the hand of a queen. Jackson saw how red and raw Sophia's delicate little hand was, from laboring in the hotel laundry.

"I think he is all right with it," Jackson said, struggling to restrain the surge of happiness rushing through his heart when Sophia sat down on the other side of Snowy Day. "Why are you out here?" he asked.

"If you want me to say I am lost, I will say it. I am lost."

"Where are you wanting to be? Where were you going?"

"I was going to find where you live, to find you."

That big, expansive feeling again, in his chest. "Then you are not lost, because here I am."

"I only found you by accident. I did not find your home."

"You were going in the right direction, Sophia. My cabin is not far, though it is true you might not have found it." He didn't want her to get truly lost, if she ever tried again to find him. It was becoming very cold at night.

"Oh. Well, that is good for me to know."

"You do not want to get lost in these hills," he added.

"I'm sure there are worse things, Jackson." She had been looking out at the view since she sat, and now she turned her eyes at him and he flinched inside. "This is not about whether or not I forgive you," she said.

"All right."

"I need a favor from you, about Peter."

Jackson turned from her gaze and nodded. The light joy he had felt was flying away from him, and he hoped it would return. "I have thought about the boy, since hearing of your death."

"Do not be snide, Jackson."

"I am not."

"It is plain that I am not dead."

"Yes, but am I right that Peter does not know this?"

He heard a soft breath flutter out of her, like the beating wings of a dying bird. "That is correct."

"What is it you think I can do, to help the boy?"

She hesitated and looked away from him, staring down at the ground, cold and frosty. "It is not to help Peter. It is to help me," she said softly. "I thought . . . perhaps you could find out how he is doing, and what has happened to him since I left."

Jackson waited a moment, choosing his words carefully. "Sophia, you have told me how important it is that no one in the village finds out that you are here. You would wish them all—even Peter—to believe you dead. What is the danger, Sophia—can you tell me, and then I can gauge how best to help you?"

Her lips thinned and tightened. "I cannot tell you."

Jackson suppressed a sigh. "All right. This is what I think. If I start writing someone in the village, asking after Peter, do you not think some may think that odd?"

"I have only recently died. Someone in the village obviously told you. Everyone knows how fond you are of Peter. They would expect you to ask after him."

"Is it Father Mikhail, Sophia, like you said that day in the church?"

She did not respond.

"I could write my father," Jackson said, "but you know how close he is to Father Mikhail. He would tell him straight away." Of course there were the two letters he had already sent to his father. He could not tell Sophia about those. He could only hope that the second eclipsed the first and that his father did not say anything to Father Mikhail.

I thought I saw her today—

"Surely, there is someone besides your father you could write to?" Sophia asked. "You had friends, Jackson, the other boys who fished with their fathers, such as Stepan and Sasha. You could write to them."

He noticed she did not mention Dmitri, once his closest friend. "I don't even know if they are still there, Sophia," he said. He had been in this new place for nearly a year before he let his father know where he was. The letter from his father about Sophia was the first he had received from the village.

"Where else would they be? They were there this past summer. I saw them with my own eyes."

"I have not written even to Dmitri, or to any of my friends. I was banished, remember?"

Her face turned quickly and sharply to his, and her eyes narrowed. "You were banished, Jackson, because you told Father Mikhail what we did on the beach! You were banished, but you were allowed to be free! I was left to collect the rest of our punishment, Jackson, while you came here to—to—paradise!"

Her words fell into him like heavy stones. He knew what he had told Father Mikhail in his confession. "No one was to know—it was a confession, Sophia! He was bound by God not to tell!"

Her face twisted cruel, and she turned her head and spat onto the rocky ground. "Father Mikhail is not bound by any God worth worshipping, Jackson. How could you have ever chosen him over me? How?" She stood sharply and looked down at him. "Forget I asked. Forget everything, Jackson! Everything!"

"Sophia no!" he said as she turned, and he leapt to his feet and hurried after her, Snowy Day doing the same. "Sophia, please! It is not forgivable, I know! I was a fool, but I never ceased to love you, Sophia, though I tried to deny it. Never!" He caught her by the arm and she pulled hard against him. "Do not leave. Do not leave, please. Hit me, curse me, only stay and talk to me! I made a mistake, Sophia, and I am paying for it."

She stopped pulling and shook her arm free.

"I will get Peter for you," he said, realizing what Sophia would really want, and what he could do to try to make things right between them. "And bring him here so you could see for yourself how he is." If Sophia had truly died, he would have gone back to the village, banished or not, to help the boy. Why shouldn't he go back to retrieve him?

"I did not ask for that!"

"I will go back to the village and get him and bring him here. I will help you raise him, Sophia, and I will never ask you for a thing. Look at this place!" He swept his arm at the endless wild beauty around them. "It can be yours! It can be Peter's! And if anyone from the village came here to harm you, they would have to kill me first! Father Mikhail is nothing here—nothing! He does not matter to these people, or to these hills or that river there, down below. He is nothing here, and no one."

She watched him, and listened to him, and Jackson saw the anger leave her face. He felt hope once again. "You don't have to forgive me, Sophia. Hate me for eternity if you must. I will get Peter and bring him to you and help you both to live." He felt a tightness in his throat, and the push of tears against the back of his eyes. "I am so sorry, Sophia, for ever leaving you and Peter behind. Let me help you both, now."

She did not say anything as she stepped toward him, put her arms around him, and held him as he wept.

SOPHIA PETERSEN
FALL 1927

"DID YOU NOT EVER WONDER WHERE THE FOOD on your table came from, Sophia?"

"I did not think it was you."

"Well, it was the church, and I am the church."

"I thought—the sewing. All the sewing my mother did!"

All the sewing my mother did. Those words I spoke had echoed through my head that night. Father Mikhail had arrived again at the door, and this time I dared not send him away. He had brought with him a bundle of clothing and household items that needed mending. The same type of bundle he would bring my mother: the quilts and trousers and blouses and coats from the people of the village, along with items belonging to the church and to Father Mikhail himself. When he put them on the table he had said, "Here." That was it. I looked at the table, the tidy bundle. My mother had been gone three months. She had managed, somehow, to stow a little money away for me and Peter, so I was not worried about starvation yet, and I had my own little jobs that were continuing. I helped Mrs. Kozlov, a young woman in the village, do her growing family's laundry and beat the dirt from her rugs, and I cleaned the house of Mr. Wassily, who paid me even though when my mother lived we had owed him, always, for the vodka he would not let us pay for.

Mr. Wassily was very teary the first several times since her passing when I showed up at his door. "Brave Sophia!" he had said. "Brave Sophia." And his red-rimmed eyes looked redder than usual. When he paid me, he gave me 50 cents, much more than the normal, and I said to him, "You don't have to give me extra, Mr. Wassily."

"Oh, I do," he said. "The loss of a mother is a terrible thing. I was only six—young Peter's age—when I lost mine, and I never forgot how it feels. I will help you, Sophia. And when Peter is old enough, he can help me with the firewood."

"Thank you," I said, and felt my own eyes turning wet. Mr. Wassily was more newly removed from the Old Country than most of the people in the village. One Christmas he gave me a set of painted wooden dolls that nested inside each other, and it was among my very favorite things. I had seen one in Jackson's house, in one of the few times I had gone inside; it had been his mother's, and it sat on a wooden windowsill above the kitchen sink.

"It's a good kitchen," Jackson had said, as if that was what I was looking at. I was about to tell him it was the little set of Russian dolls that intrigued me and not the kitchen, lovely as it was, when we saw that his father was coming down the road and we slipped out the side door and ran down the beach, laughing the whole way.

By the time Father Mikhail brought the bundle of mending, Jackson had left the island. The mending, I knew, was Father Mikhail's way of saying, "All will go on as before, despite your insolence." More than half the village would not look at my face. Nothing was the same.

"I believe in forgiveness, Sophia," Mrs. Kozlov had said to me when she came round herself to ask me to keep coming to her house one day a week. "It should not all be about so much judgement."

Jackson was gone; Peter and Mr. Wassily and Mrs. Kozlov remained, as did Father Mikhail, despite my words, despite my hate for the very sight of him.

"I am here for you, Sophia," he said. "And for Peter of course. I will care for you like my family, and you are protected by the church."

"I do not want the sewing." It wasn't the work of it. It wasn't the thought of my mother's cracked and bleeding fingers, how she strained to see in the dull light of the kerosene lamp. It was that the sewing was always delivered by Father Mikhail, dropped off on one Thursday and picked up by him on the next. Every Thursday Peter and I were ushered from the house, to go fishing in the leaky boat or fetch the vodka from Mr. Wassily, and we were not to return until we saw the Father walking away down the dirty, rutted road.

"Father Mikhail must preach to me," my mother would say, "and grant me his blessings so I will be able to continue with the sewing work."

I did not know of things that went on between a man and a woman, and when I did, I did not know that a priest was very much a man.

"You will, Sophia, because you will need the sewing to survive," Father Mikhail told me that day.

"I will manage."

"Your mother," he said, as he walked out of the door, "left you too much to run wild."

As I watched him walk away, I saw that the sewing was still there, on the table where he had left it. I shoved it out into the entry.

A WEEK LATER HE REAPPEARED, DURING THE time of the day when Peter was at school. "I have come for the sewing, Sophia," he said when he entered. "I see it is there in the entry. So you have finished?"

"I did not do it," I said. I was making pea soup for myself and Peter, with carrots from our garden, my back to the priest.

"I guess I will have to wait," he said, "right here, until you do the sewing."

I turned into the room, a new feeling of panic fluttering through my insides. I looked at Father Mikhail. "You cannot do this," I said.

"Yes, yes I can, Sophia. I would like some tea while I wait, and you must begin on the sewing."

"I have my own jobs."

"You will not have those jobs anymore. Your first duty is to the church."

"Why?" I asked. "The church's duty has never been to me. All I want is for you and the church to leave me alone, and I will leave you alone."

"It is not so easy, Sophia."

"Please leave my house."

"And there is an example of why it is not so easy."

There was something in his voice that filled me with dread. Was there something my mother forgot to say?

"This is not your house; this house belongs to the church."

"You lie!"

"No, Sophia. Of the two of us, you are the liar. Never mind. Your mother sold the house to the church—to me—a very long time ago."

"Get out!"

"I will stay, here in my house, and you will sew."

"You are the spawn of the devil!" I hissed and spat on the floor. Quickly he was up and pushed me against the wall. I struggled. He was strong. I screamed and he shoved my face hard into the rough boards. With one hand he ripped off my skirt and then there was something hard and hot between my legs and into the place where only Jackson had been.

"No!" I cried and he slammed my face again. His movements ripped through me. He moaned and trembled then threw me to the floor.

"You are not a virgin so do not cry," he said. "Sin begets sin, Sophia, and there is no damage that can be done to someone already so broken. Now to the sewing, and to the tea, and Peter will know nothing of this."

I pulled myself up. I knew where a knife was, and I thought about killing him, but I knew, too, how that would doom Peter to an unbearable life. I tied up my ripped skirt, and I put on the kettle, and I found my mother's sewing kit. Hot tears pierced my eyes. Not from what the priest had done—those would come later. These were for Jackson, and the knowledge that he had betrayed the secret of that most sacred thing that had happened between us and doomed me to my mother's life.

Today I went to find Jackson. Today I held him as he wept. Today I asked him to help me find out how Peter was and he knew what I really wanted, he knew, and he said without me having to ask that he would get Peter from the village. Can I believe him? He said to me that Father Mikhail is nothing here. Nothing and no one. He said I did not have to ever forgive him, and suddenly I did.

CHAPTER EIGHT

EMILY WELLS
FALL 1974

"DID YOU HAVE A GOOD TIME?" Harry asked when I boarded the northbound train on the Tuesday after the Sunday when the southbound train had brought me down.

I nodded yes, though I felt more like I had survived something. Strangers in the street. Strangers in the hotel lobby. I had to keep reminding myself that whoever did what was done to me might not have been a stranger at all. It was someone who had to have known Thomas was not there. Thomas was in the hospital, after the pool incident, recovering from his near fatal overdose and drowning, and languishing in the beginning phases of opioid withdrawal.

I had missed so much. Like an idiot I'd had no idea. There was so much going on, people coming and going and endless parties and concerts and gigs. The record deal. The money. We were high on all kinds of excitement. The drugs felt like little more than a sideshow.

We knew, though, the same as everybody knew. Janis Joplin. Jimmy Hendrix. Jim Morrison. We knew. Somehow I didn't think that was us.

One night I came home from the hospital to our San Francisco apartment. It was dark inside, and I left the lights off as I walked over to the big picture window to take in the view and try to put everything that had happened into some kind of perspective. Then I felt something, and I'll always remember that feeling, like hundreds of tiny spiders crawling up my back. Before I could turn around a gloved hand clasped over my mouth and I was slammed up against a wall.

"Shh . . . hush little lamb. Hush." That was all he said. It was over before I could really absorb what was happening, and I was thrown violently onto the floor, and the man dressed all in black disappeared out the door and out of my life—but not really. He left his shadow behind, and it was always there, in the dark.

I never told Thomas. I never told anyone. For a long time that night all I could do was move enough to lock the door. This couldn't have happened, I kept thinking. I had locked the door. The apartment was on the tenth floor. No one else had a key, had they? This was a nice building. This was a good neighborhood. How did this happen, here?

Thomas would believe me, and all that would do was cause him pain. The same with my parents and my sisters. I had a bruise on my elbow from falling onto the floor; I knew that would not be enough to prove that what happened was unwanted. There would be those questions. Hadn't I waited too long to call the police? Hadn't I not struggled enough? Weren't Thomas and I known for extravagant parties with people coming and going at all hours? The newspapers might hear of it: *Emily Wells, girlfriend of Thomas Findlay, singer of the popular rock band Findlay. . .*

Nothing in the apartment was missing. The only sign that someone had been there was a pile of Thomas' papers—songs he was working on—that I had straightened on his desk, that were now disorganized in a sloppy pile. Was it a fan? Someone who wanted to get close to Thomas by getting close to me? Whoever it was, I thought I could leave him behind in San Francisco. I was wrong.

On the train that day I said to Harry, "I ate some ice cream, and I took one bath and two showers."

"Sounds like a holiday," Harry said with a smile.

We had chatted, of course, on my ride down on Sunday, about the weather, the bugs, the shift in the seasons. I had not asked Harry about what Raymie had said, about the trapper with the scar on his face, but I had not forgotten it. Now, after the train got on its way, Harry took a seat across from me, in order to say a proper hello, he said. I knew I had to ask, and ask now, or else feel the shadow of the unknown hanging on to me until another such chance appeared.

"Harry," I began, after answering his questions about our building progress (or lack of) and agreeing with his suggestion about how much easier it would be, to not build on the hill. "I heard something about a trapper who might live somewhere near Findlay. Someone with a scar on his face. Do you know anything about him?"

He had been looking out the window. His face didn't move, and for an uncomfortable moment his eyes met mine in the ghostly reflections of our faces in the glass. I saw something there.

The moment passed and he smiled. "Ahh—yes," he said. "He's not a cause for concern. More legend than anything."

"So he's out there somewhere?"

Harry raised his brows and shrugged. "I suppose he is," he said. "As far as I know at any rate."

"Oh. Okay," I said, not sure what he meant.

I expected more, something along the line of his usual favorites like the horses who fell or how three people died when the hotel burned down, or how his aunt felt there was a curse on the place. He smiled again, patted my shoulder and added, "People like to talk, especially about that area, you know, because of the hotel," and went back about his duties.

When the train neared Findlay, I noticed Harry was extra alert, and he continuously looked out the windows. Didn't he always, though, at least every one of the few times I'd ridden the train? Not for the first time I wondered what he felt when the train went past the old site, all overgrown like an untended grave. Did he see the hotel there every time, like an apparition, or did the site simply remind him of what it was like to be young, to have his life in front of him?

I wondered what Thomas and I would think, when we were older, what memories, triggered by this or that would flash through our thoughts, like the one that came to me then: Me and Thomas, in San Francisco, before everything. A scene, after a show, Thomas' arm around me as we pushed through the crowd, Thomas laughing, my hand hooked in the belt that circled his narrow hips, my face pressed against that space beneath his shoulder. A bouncer coming to help us get through to the car. People screaming and cheering, loving him. That was the best of it, that night. The top of the mountain, in the glorious light.

"Findlay!" Harry announced, as if there were more souls besides me getting off. He stood by the door as I stayed behind him with my arms full of bags that wouldn't fit in the boxes that went into the baggage car; the door hissed open and Harry leaned out to put down the step. He took several of my bags and guided me down, and I stopped midway and stared at the gravel and the woods. No Thomas. My heart lurched in my chest. I turned toward Harry and saw that he was looking elsewhere. I followed his gaze up toward our hill. Then, with a sudden burst, Thomas came flying out of a patch of alders and ran up to the baggage car just in time to grab the boxes. I began breathing again.

"There you go!" Harry said, delivering me to the gravel that bordered the rails. "Until next time!"

"Yes," I said, my eyes watching Thomas as he laughed and talked with the baggage man. "Thank you, Harry!"

I walked over to Thomas and the pile of my purchases, and together we waved at the baggage man and Harry, at the faces in the windows of the train as it passed. Suddenly Thomas grabbed me and lifted me up off the ground and twirled me around with the train moving beside us then kissed me long and hard after he set me down. I was flooded with happiness. For a moment everything else dissipated.

It was soon to pass. First, though, came the afternoon of hauling what we could up the long trail to the camp, leaving behind everything we thought would be of no interest to bears or other animals. Our packs were heavy and our arms were weighted. I could see how horses would work here, how they would be helpful on days like that. What I couldn't see was how a horse could be anything but a bear attractant and imagined they would always be hunted, always be vulnerable.

After we unpacked, Thomas grabbed my hand and led me up the hill. There, to my surprise, stood heavy log posts in the holes he had dug.

"Thomas!" I said and felt the sting of threatening tears as my heart swelled at the sight of the beginnings of the foundation of our new home. "Look what you did!"

Thomas glowed with pride in the golden light of the fading day. The chill in the wind that clipped across the hill was hard to miss, and there was a steely edge to the darkening sky. "Raymie is coming tomorrow. So it's happening, Em. Finally!"

He picked me up again and we laughed. Then we hurried back down the hill to our camp, as if the cold wind and the darkening sky were biting at our heels.

"SO SHOULD WE TELL RAYMIE ABOUT THE BONE?" Thomas asked that evening by a big bright fire. I brought back a case of peppermint schnapps—most of it left down by the tracks—and we celebrated the newly installed creosoted posts of the cabin. Thomas had the guitar out and he had just sung Jackson Browne's "Jamaica," one of our favorite songs. I'd sung with him, my harmony in pitch and though my voice was no match for his, he loved for me to sing with him, and I loved that he loved that.

"I don't know, Thomas," I said. In all the happiness of the afternoon I had momentarily forgotten about it, now there it was, that thing we hadn't dealt with.

"Maybe he'd have some ideas," he said, his fingers stopping their dance across the strings of the guitar. "Like, what he would do if he were us."

"Maybe," I said. It was a likely thing, that we would end up telling him about it. We would be up there every day, working right by the place where we'd found it, the place to which it had been returned, and every night we'd be here by the fire, drinking and talking.

"It would be great to just forget about it, wouldn't it?" Thomas said.

"Is that why you reburied it?"

He looked at me. "Why I what?"

"Reburied it. The bone."

He tipped his head, and his brow furrowed. "You mean you didn't?" he said.

"Didn't what?"

"Didn't rebury the bone?"

I felt the cold of the night against my back. "Thomas," I said slowly, "so you didn't take the bone from my pack and put it into the post hole and cover it back up?" My voice was rising, and I saw a sweep of concern brush across Thomas' face.

"No, Em, I didn't."

"Maybe when you were drunk?"

"I didn't move much, Em, from what I can remember. And you were here. You would have seen me."

"What made you think I had buried the bone?" I asked.

He shrugged. "I saw the hole was filled in, and when I felt your shawl, it was empty."

"Why didn't you say something?"

"Why didn't you?"

"Because I thought it was you," I said.

"No Em," he said. "Not me."

I knew that now.

HARRY HARBOUR
FALL 1927

THE WAY SHE HELD HIM, IT WAS DEEPER THAN most things. I could see that. It was more than youthful desire, more than friendship, more than simply love, even. It was tangled and complicated, and there was something in it like the river: strong and fierce and deep and eternal. He was crying, for God's sake, on her shoulder, this tough, dark fellow, and she was up on her tiptoes, holding him, saving him. That's what I thought as I watched. She was saving him, from whatever it was he had done to her, because I was quite certain, as I watched them, that somewhere along the line he had caused her great pain.

Somewhere along the line, they had loved each other. That was also pretty plain.

I should have turned back—I should have never started to follow her to begin with. I knew that. It made me look bad, it made me feel bad right on the spot as I watched them together through the hotel's binoculars like a proper spy, the two of them wrapped in a moment of something that was so very personal and painfully private. As I'd slunk along trying to keep out of sight, I'd convinced myself I was looking out for her. I would be there if she needed help, if she got lost, for example, and at one point it looked like she did: she spun around, looking, searching, though from my vantage point I could see Jackson there, sitting quietly, waiting for her to see him.

I had stumbled upon Jackson's trail a time to two, taking guests over to Deadhorse Creek to fish. There were traces of it in what I called "Last Chance Ravine" which was basically a little dip in the rising landscape where you could climb out of the emerging canyon before the sides got too steep. I also knew he used the tundra trail, too, and which one he used on what particular day probably depended on what else he was doing, like coming down to fish or looking to flush up some ptarmigan. Sonja must have guessed where she needed to go when we saw him from the hill. Or maybe she had figured it out some other way and some other time; as much as I tried to keep track of her, I had no idea what she did, when she was not in the laundry and not hiking with me and Nellie June. Cora was right that I didn't know her, I admitted bitterly; I did know, though, how I felt when I was in her company, like in a story I might have dreamed up once, or read in a book or felt in the words of a play I was in. If I waited long enough, if I had enough time. I was held fast in my feelings for her, and there was nothing I could do but wait.

When I finally, and much too late, turned away, I remembered something Cora once said, when I was a boy and she took me down to the mud flats that ringed Anchorage's Turnagain Arm, not too far from where my and my folks' house was, one day when the tide was out. She was warning me about the dangers of the flats, how they looked so calm and smooth and easy, like you could walk way out on them to where the water was now and be someplace you couldn't be when the tide was in. I had thought about that, lots of times; I'd wanted to ride my bike out there, as a matter of fact. It seemed mysterious, to stand where the water was deep and not have to get the least bit wet to do it except, well, I knew enough to know I'd probably get pretty muddy, especially if I rode my bike.

Cora said, "That long glossy beach isn't what it looks like, Harry. It's full of a danger you can't see and that's hard to imagine being real—like real to the point that it could take your life. There are places in those flats where your feet will sink and the mud will grab hold of you and you won't be able to move. People might see you out there and they'd come help you—like your mom and dad or maybe just some folks out walking on the shore—and try as they might, they wouldn't be able to get you out. Someone would fetch the fire brigade and they wouldn't be able to get you out. All the fellas from the whole town might even come and all together they would not be able to get you out. And you'd be stuck there, Harry, out on those flats."

I'd shrugged. It didn't sound too bad, though I wasn't sure how I'd be able to eat or go to the bathroom. Though for that first concern I was sure my mother would bring me out some dinner, and maybe some blankets if I was cold.

"Now that's a problem, Harry, being stuck out on those flats," Cora continued. "You might think it might not be too bad, and that eventually someone would be able to figure out how to get you out. However, there's another player in this, Harry, besides you and the hole you got stuck in, and that's the turning tide. When the water starts coming back to shore, there's nothing you or any living person or thing can do about it, and it will come sliding back, and it won't care that young Harry Harbour has his foot stuck there in the mud flats. It will keep coming, Harry, and it will go right over you, and it will still be over you long after you've gone and drowned and you're there like a strange tree growing on the ocean floor, only you won't grow anymore ever again."

By that point in the story my mouth was hanging open and my eyes were wide and fixed on some spot way out there on all that gray, that spot that would grab me and not let go.

I could almost feel again Cora's hand taking mine as I'd looked fixedly at my dirt-covered brown play shoes on that gray, soft ocean floor at the edge of the dry beach and the beginning of the wet flats.

"There's nothing you can do about a turning tide, Harry. Nothing. Remember that," she'd said. "Moral of that story, Harry: Don't be stuck when that tide turns."

As I walked back to the hotel, I finally knew the depth of what she meant.

JACKSON KEATS
FALL 1927

"WEREN'T YOU SCARED, JACKSON, COMING HERE all alone?" Sophia asked him, when they met on the hill of the dead horses, as Sophia called it, to discuss the rescue of Peter though they talked mostly of other things.

"Weren't you, Sophia?" he asked, and he looked into her blue eyes, the color of the waters of his old home on a rare fine day.

"I asked you first," she said. "It is only fair that you answer first."

He had placed his coat down for her to sit on, and he stretched out on the frosty ground beside her, Snowy Day lounging near his wool-clad legs.

"All right," he said, and began, looking out at the rolling country in front of him. "Yes, I was afraid, but I was also very—how would you say? Despondent. So much had happened, Sophia, as you remember, and things were not good between myself and my father. I had embarrassed him in the community, and he felt I had betrayed him, as if he were Father Mikhail himself. And I felt betrayed by him, that his love for me should surely be greater than his love of the church."

He caught himself there, noting how his words were so like Sophia's when she'd asked him how he could have chosen Father Mikhail over her.

"You and I," he said, continuing, "we were lost to each other, and I could not see a world where that might be corrected."

He looked at her, her gaze off across the hills, and she did not turn toward him. He swallowed the sigh he felt wanting to escape his lips and went on, if for no other reason than to keep her there beside him and prolong their conversation. "I became—angry, by the time my day of departure arrived. At my father, at everyone— even you, Sophia." He paused. This time he did not try to find her gaze. "I was afraid, as the island became smaller and smaller while I stood in the stern of the boat. What I was frightened of was the

way that my anger was leaving me, too, as the island vanished into
that sea of gray water, and I felt this empty hollow inside of me that
was waiting to swallow me whole. The only thing I had left was the
image my mind had formed that day you and I heard the stranger
speaking in the village store, of a grand hotel in the middle of a
wilderness filled with hills and animals and rivers full of fish. And
the closer I got to it, the bigger that image grew, like a seed inside
me, so that when I stepped off the train I was ready to welcome this
new land and find a new life."

He stopped there and waited. It was some long moments before
Sophia spoke, and Jackson savored the silence between them as it
was how they would be together sometimes, in the time before all
the trouble.

When she did speak Sophia only asked another question: "And
here, you are never afraid?"

He thought on the question, though the answer was not hard.
"There are times, yes, when I am afraid," Jackson said. "The winters
here can be cruel with cold, and there have been dark nights when
the freezing wind pounded against my cabin walls so fiercely that I
was afraid. Beyond those walls there was such cold darkness, such
bitter wind, so close to me where I was."

On those nights he would sit on the floor by Snowy Day, on
the rug made from the bear he had shot one spring. They would
stay close to the fire; even Snow knew that outside was nowhere he
wanted to be.

Sophia looked at him and placed her hand against his cheek.
Jackson dared not move. She dipped her head forward, like a swan to
the surface of the pond beneath it, and kissed him on the lips—lightly,
tentatively, and he knew how it was a test of some sort, how she was
seeing the way it would feel to her, to touch him again like that. Too
soon she lifted her face and took her lips away. Jackson wanted nothing more than to pull her toward him; instinct held him back.

"I was not afraid when I left," she said, "because though I wanted
to survive, I was no longer afraid to die."

Jackson felt those words stab their way deep inside him. "You must tell me what happened to you," he said softly. Very carefully he reached out and with a finger pushed the hair that had flown loose from her braids back off her face, letting his touch linger as long as he dared before dropping his hand.

"I cannot, Jackson."

"Why? There is no one here except for us and the wind."

"It will be painful for us both, when I do."

"So you will?"

"Yes. I will have to. But not today."

His mind filled with questions, like buried objects rising to the surface of the soil that held them. He knew he must stay silent. It was all he could do.

"Do you remember, Jackson," she said suddenly, "that day in the forest, when we found the waterfall?"

I could never forget, he wanted to say, but only nodded.

"It was like a dream, wasn't it?" she said, and he saw with delight that her face filled with joy.

It was four years ago. There had been sunshine that day, and it was warm and lovely. Peter was with them, and Jackson had to carry him as they hiked and climbed among the giant, ancient trees—the Sitka spruce, as wide as Jackson was tall. They were looking for it; Sophia knew the waterfall was there somewhere and held a memory of her grandfather taking her and her mother to it, many years before.

They heard the water before they saw it, and when they broke through the thick brush the waterfall was before them, shimmering in the sun. Peter, only four, gave a little cry of amazement and Sophia lifted him onto her hip. She stepped into the pool at the bottom of the waterfall and took herself and Peter beneath the glistening shower, the two of them laughing as the water rained down upon them. Jackson followed, and they went to the other side of the falling water, where there was a little spot where they could stand. The cold water made them shiver, and Jackson put his arms around the two of them as they looked out at the world through that shimmering curtain, into which Peter repeatedly placed his hand and laughed.

When they came back out, they found a little patch of dry ground where they could sit in the sun and get dry.

"Could we live here, Sophia, could we?" Peter had asked, and Sophia said, "When you are a little bit bigger, Peter, we will come here and build a house, okay?"

"Why do I have to be bigger?"

"So you can help with the building," Sophia said.

"Will we bring Mama with us?"

"Yes."

"And Jackson? Will Jackson come live at the waterfall, too?"

"I don't know; we have to ask," Sophia said and looked at him with a smile.

"Would you?" Peter asked, turning his little face to Jackson.

"Yes," he said. "I would."

"And would you help with the building?" Peter asked.

"Of course!"

"We don't have to wait, Sophia! Jackson can help us with the building! He is big already!"

"He probably could," Sophia said, and they laughed some more, and Jackson felt a cool salve wash over that wounded place inside of him that missed the mother he had lost too soon and the full happy home he had only briefly known.

Now Jackson expected Sophia to say something about that day; instead she only smiled and Jackson thought how that was enough, that was plenty, and he felt himself fill.

SOPHIA PETERSEN
FALL 1927

IT WAS JACKSON WHO TOLD ME Ilian Nicholai had confessed.

"Confessed?" I had said. "To what?"

"To beating you, Sophia! That is what he said. That it was him. Him!" Jackson stood before me in the open door of my mother's house. His face was white like frosted ice, and he was wild with distress.

"He is lying," I'd said. And Jackson threw his felt hat onto the ground.

"Why would he lie about a such a thing? He is going to be lashed, Sophia, lashed! And he has disgraced himself and his mother and his brothers. And now we are disgraced, and Peter and my father are, too, because you said it was Father Mikhail who beat you!"

"I did not say Father Mikhail was the one who beat me."

"You did! I heard it with my own ears, Sophia!"

"I said that he had done that to me. It is not in the way that you think. He knows, Jackson. He knows he is the cause."

"So now you say Father Mikhail did not beat you? And neither did Ilian Nicholai? Sophia, I feel I am losing my mind! Someone beat you, and you know who! You know!"

"Of course I know, Jackson!"

"Who, Sophia, who?"

"It was Father Mikhail who had that done to me! Father Mikhail!"

Jackson left, kicking sand down the beach.

I did not know what to think, or how it had come to pass that Ilian Nicholai was tangled up in my story. He was somebody I never noticed, only as the one of Mrs. Nicholai's three sons who was different from the other two. With a flush of shame I realized that, when it came to Ilian Nicholai, I was like all the others in the village, thinking I was somehow above him, though both his brothers treated me as if it was clear I was not above anyone even after Jackson had chosen me. Yet I always knew Ilian was not stupid, as some people said he was. He was simply odd; he did not like people and always looked very disheveled, even though his mother kept him in clean clothes—clothes which were mended frequently by my own mother. He had stringy straight hair that often fell into his eyes, and his face was narrow and pointed, giving him the look of a stray dog. His shoulders slumped forward as if he were trying to hide from the world. He and his mother—and his brothers before they grew and made homes of their own—were very dependent on Father Mikhail and the church. Their father had perished in the same boating accident that took my mother's young man. That is why, I am sure, he confessed to something he did not do.

Days after the "confession," I saw him wandering in the forest while I was picking mushrooms with Peter and I chased him down. He hid behind a massive tree. I knew he was there. I had left Peter with the mushrooms and could not waste time.

"You did not beat me, Ilian. You're not the one," I said to the tree. "You should not have said you did something you did not do. Now everyone thinks I'm a liar. Everyone! And that is because of you. You are the real liar. But I know that you were made to do it."

I waited. Nothing moved. I stepped closer to the tree, and he was off like a frightened rabbit.

"I did not want to!" he shouted as he ran. "You should not have accused Father Mikhail!"

Peter appeared, holding his little bucket of mushrooms, or I would have tried to catch him. I had to give up. Ilian was soon sent off to Juneau, and though I was careful to hide from him and anyone who might know me when I was there, waiting for a boat to Seward, once I covered my face and looked for him around the town. I did not see him, and I do not know what became of him. Perhaps now that I am dead to the village, he will be allowed to go home. I hope for that, even though he wronged me. Father Mikhail ruined his life, as well.

If he had told the truth, we both might have had a chance.

I think now, sometimes, of the church and wonder how it had come to be that our little, tiny village had its own priest. There were not so many priests in the territory, and they stayed with the bigger churches in the bigger communities, and the smaller places worshipped without and waited for their turn to have a priest come to visit. Perhaps the big church in Sitka was worried our little village was a village of Old Believers, who sought to avoid the changes the reforms of many years ago brought. For the Old Believers, however, being so close to a big church like the one in Sitka would have been too dangerous, and they would not have built a village there. Or perhaps Father Mikhail was being tucked away somewhere, or perhaps he was well connected in the church hierarchy and had decided, after some time in the village, that he wanted to stay and was allowed that luxury. I do not know. How different my mother's life would have been, had our little village not received the blessing of its very own priest.

I kissed Jackson today, when we met on the hill of the dead horses to plan our rescue of Peter, a subject we only lightly discussed, as if to keep the need for meeting ongoing. Though I had touched him only days before, when he cried and I held him, for a time on this day the curtain had drawn between us again, and I was as chilly as the wind that ripped across the hill, and I saw how that pained him. He was patient and answered my questions and told me a little of his life here. The curtain slowly thinned, and there was a moment when it lifted and I realized who it was who lay stretched out beside me in this place on this Earth, the wind wild in his dark hair. I felt for a moment how I used to feel, when we would sit in our spot on the hill above the cemetery, the air around us swirling with our longing for one another. I tipped my head down and I kissed him. I let myself have that, to feel the sweetness of memory flooding through me. I felt myself longing for a future we might yet have. A door was opening in my heart, and I quickly slammed it shut. I do think it is possible Jackson would have me in that future, even after he learns the whole of it, but in that moment of the kiss I saw that I could not face him, every day of my life after I tell him everything, and I felt my heart breaking all over again as I kissed him. I imagined those nights he described to me, of the wind pounding against the walls of his cabin in a way that was fearful, and I imagined myself outside of

his window, looking in, the wind and the snow blowing through
the hole that was my heart.

If I could have Peter, I could find a way to live, even though it
could not be here as Jackson dreams. Once he gets Peter, I will have
to say goodbye to him and to this beautiful country. I will have to
say goodbye to myself as well. The only future for Peter and me is
to go somewhere where no one knows us, and where—unlike my
sweet mother—I will take my secrets with me to my grave.

Except I will tell Jackson the truth before I leave. I will give him
that. It is the only thing that I can.

CHAPTER NINE

EMILY WELLS

FALL 1974

THE NIGHT BROUGHT LONG HOURS OF no sleep. Every rustle of bush or branch startled my heart; every whisper of wind opened my eyes. Thomas was awake, too, pretending he was sleeping in an attempt to help me settle. "I'm here," he'd said, and we'd switched places so that he and the gun were on the outside edge of the bed. His tone said, *I can't do much, but I can protect you.* Dear Thomas. Dear darling Thomas, and his heart of gold.

Someone had been in our tent, had taken the bone, and most likely put it back where we'd found it and covered it over. The thought of it left me raw inside, skinned of my skin. Was this some silent stalker watching us, waiting, slipping into the tent when we weren't looking, taking what was—his?

The figure on the hill. It had to be. Raymie's story of the scar-faced trapper hung heavily upon us. Harry did not deny the trapper's existence; he'd said so little, though, that I'd wondered if it really were just a legend. While we assumed the bone was reburied, we would not know until we dug it up again, which we would do in the morning. The question of what to do next remained, large and looming.

I did, at some point, fall asleep because suddenly I felt myself waking up, being pulled from a dream of trains and hills and Harry as a young man, not seeing me there, asking which way to go. With the flutter of my eyes the orange glow of the tent shot reality through me. Thomas was gone—yet again, and while I did not hear him nearby in the camp, I knew with absolute certainty he would not be far today. He'd left the shotgun in the tent beside me; this time I would take it with me. I was pretty sure I knew where he was.

I hurried out of the pile of sleeping bags and unzipped the door of the tent. There'd been no fire this morning, no coffee. I had no idea what time it was. I pulled on my boots and, carrying the shotgun, climbed the hill.

I heard him before I saw him. Sobbing? The idea of that sent my stomach down into my knees. No—it was breathing, hard breathing, and there was a clumping sound and the occasional clink of metal on rock. He was shoveling. I crested the hill and there he was, like a madman, shovel swinging, dirt flying, a hole long, wide, and deep. He was in the middle of it.

"It's here!" he said when he noticed me approaching.

"What?"

"The rest of it! Here! It's all here!"

I rushed over and looked. Panic pulsed through me, and I stifled a scream so as not to scare Thomas. I saw the round dull colored skull and a bony hand. "Thomas stop."

"What? Why?"

"Just stop!" My voice was too high. It screeched in my ears. Thomas froze. "Come out—come out of there," I said.

I reached for him. He took my hand, and I pulled him from the hole. We collapsed onto the ground, on our backs, chests heaving, tears on our cheeks, the sky flat and gray and vast above us.

Thomas grabbed my hand and our fingers wove together, and I imagined the world upside down, and Thomas and I falling into the gray void of sky that had been with us now, hovering and waiting, for the past year.

We fell asleep. I don't know how, and I don't know for how long, and some time later we both stirred when a light cold rain began to fall. We pulled ourselves into sitting positions and stared at the view. The rolling downward descent in front of us, the railroad tracks, and the flat of overgrown land between the rails and the river, and across the river the high steep rise of Findlay Ridge. Today something moved on top of the ridge and we both couldn't breathe until we sorted out what it was. A moose maybe? No—a caribou, its graceful antlers silhouetted against the gray. For a flash of a second I forgot our current situation and longed for my binoculars.

"Where's the herd?" I whispered.

"I don't know," Thomas whispered back. I don't know why we were whispering; we could have stood and screamed and our voices would never have reached across the river. "Maybe farther north?"

"Why is it separate from them?" I wondered.

There was a pause of silence, then Thomas said, "Why are we, Emily?"

My eyes slid to the side to look at him. "Don't," I said. "Don't talk like that."

"It's true. We're here because of me, cut off from the herd, here with our barely started cabin and our dead body in the ground. If that's not a bad omen, I don't know what is."

"It has nothing to do with us, Thomas."

He looked at me, laughed in a way that broke my heart, then looked back at the ridge across the river. "I don't know, Em. Out of thousands and thousands of acres of land, this spot right here was the one we chose. The one I chose. Me."

"We have ten acres, Thomas. Let's build down by camp."

"We should just leave, Emily. Let's go home."

"We can't."

"Of course we can."

"Thomas you'll die."

"I won't die, Emily."

I looked at the crook of his arm, covered now by his dirty flannel shirt. There was a river of scars there, there and between his toes, different from the places where he'd been stitched up after crashing through the window, little pale dots where the needle pushed in. I don't know how it had happened, how I didn't see it, how I was mistakenly glad he had cut down on his drinking and was finally sleeping. Every day was such a whirlwind blur: interviews, band practice, which show was next, spending money on velvet pants and fancy restaurants, the hours I had wasted in front of a mirror, wondering if I was good enough to be the girlfriend of someone as beautiful as Thomas. It didn't matter to me if he was almost famous. It didn't matter to me now that he was no longer on that trajectory. He was my person, my family, and all that mattered was keeping him safe, and with Thomas that meant keeping him safe from himself.

"I'd be afraid," I said. "I'd be afraid every minute of every day if we went back." And not just afraid for Thomas. I would not be able to breathe.

"And you're not afraid now?" Thomas said. "Someone came into our tent, Emily, and took the human bone that we'd found right over there!" He pointed with a stabbing motion to the now much larger hole. "Where there happens to be what looks like a complete, entire skeleton! If all this is not something to be afraid of, Emily, tell me what is, okay?"

For a flash of an instant I almost told him. The hand across my mouth, materializing from the darkness as if it was the darkness itself, suddenly with shape and form and strength.

"Hello!"

The voice rose up the hill from the trail from the camp. Thomas and I scrambled to our feet, hearts racing.

Thomas put his hand on my shoulder. "It's okay. It's Raymie."

"Hello on the hill!" we heard, the voice closer now.

We waited shakily as Raymie emerged from the side of the hill, wearing an olive-drab raincoat open at the front, a flannel shirt full of the colors of fall, leather boots and blue jeans with a wide leather belt from which hung a knife in a fringed leather sheath. *Confident and calm.* Those were the words that came to me, watching him ascend the hill. Someone who was easy with himself and with the world.

"Wow!" he said. "This is incredible." He spun around to see all the angles of the view, then tipped his face to the sky and felt the rain. "Come forth into the light of things, let nature be your teacher," he said, smiling, and wiped the rain from his forehead and pushed his thick light brown hair off his face.

Wordsworth. I remembered the poem from some long-ago English class. Then my mind started spinning with one thought: Keep him away from the hole.

Thomas said, "Hell yeah! Welcome to our kingdom, brother!" He stepped forward and shook Raymie's hand, turned him around, and we all went down to the camp.

I MADE COFFEE AND PUT SOME BACON in the frying pan while Thomas and Raymie put up another tarp and got the campfire going. Raymie had left his backpack leaning neatly against a birch tree.

"So you've got your corner posts in—great!" Raymie said, holding up a corner of a tarp for Thomas.

"Yeah," Thomas said, "except there's been a change of plan."

I looked over my shoulder and watched and listened. Raymie tipped his head to the side and studied Thomas.

"Um, Em and I—we just had a talk, and we decided it would best, for now—you know, with winter coming and all that—to put up a little place down here. Do something on the hill later on."

"Wow," Raymie said. "Starting from scratch, quicker though— it would definitely be quicker, with your stack of logs right here."

Thomas nodded.

"We'd better get busy," Raymie said.

I turned back to the stove and silently cried. After we ate, Thomas went back up the hill to get the shovel and the shotgun we had left there while Raymie and I, using the tape measure he'd brought with him, worked on marking out the new spot. Thomas took a while, and I knew it was because he was refilling the grave.

HARRY HARBOUR
FALL 1927

"HARRY, DO YOU HAVE TOOLS I COULD BORROW?"

"Tools, Sonja?"

"A hammer and a nail."

"Sure—I could find those for you. Come on."

Sonja followed me to one of the many outbuildings, where I grabbed a hammer and a nail of her choosing and we went back outside into the day.

When I asked her what she needed them for she said, "I will show you."

We went down to the riverbank, where Sonja had a little spot in the dead grasses. She had an old board on top of a flat rock which made a little table of sorts, and she had pieces of birch bark arranged in a little pile. These she spread out on the board, and I realized they had been cut into deliberate shapes.

"I'm making something," she said. "For Nellie June."

Nellie June's birthday was coming, and we were going to have a little party for her down in the rec room. It wouldn't really be her birthday yet; she was going south down the tracks to her village for a few weeks and so wouldn't be here on the actual day. Sonja took the hammer and the nail and made little holes in the bark along the edges of the pieces. She wore no gloves and her hands looked raw with the cold. I wanted badly to hold them and warm them for her.

I also thought how her arms had been wrapped around Jackson, how those hands had touched him and held him tight. I wanted to ask her—well, I wanted to ask her anything and everything. Then it came to me, as I sat there on the riverbank, that what mattered at that moment was the moment itself, watching her work as she wore the coat my mother had found for her, the comfortable silence between us, and the cold wind coming down the river that whispered of the winter days to come.

After she hammered for a while, she picked up some dried pieces of grass near where she sat, and she took two pieces of the bark and held them together as she worked the grass in and out of the holes she'd made. I saw what she was doing—making a little box of sorts and putting the pieces together with the grass.

"Where'd you learn to do that?" I asked. It was like something Alaska Native people made; my mother had some prized baskets made of birch bark like the one Sonja was making, and also some that were tightly woven from pale grasses, like the grass Sonja was using to stitch her box together. My father had gotten the baskets on a trip north to Fairbanks and my mother loved them even more than her collection of porcelain figures.

"Aren't they lovely," my mother would say. "And all made from nature. Imagine the skill and patience required!"

"I am teaching myself, right now," Sonja said, in answer to my question. "I am hoping it will be good enough to be a birthday present."

"For Nellie June? She'd like that. Alaska Native folks—they make baskets like that."

"People in Russia do this also," Sonja said. "My neighbor, Mr. Wassily, had some baskets like this that he had brought with him from the old country."

"The old country?" I asked.

"Russia, Harry. The 'old country' is what we sometimes call it." Sonja looked at me and smiled.

"Your whole family from there?"

"No," she said. "Not so much anymore."

I wasn't sure what she meant by that, and she must have seen my confusion because she said, "My mother was born here, in the territory, as were myself and Peter."

"And where do they live—your mother and Peter?"

"My mother has passed, Harry," she said softly.

I could have hit myself. "I am so sorry, Sonja."

"It is all right. Peter—." She stopped herself.

The name hung in the air, like a loose feather falling from the sky carrying so many questions with it. I watched her as she sewed, wanting badly for her to continue and fearing all was not well with her brother, either.

Eventually she gave me a quick glance and a little smile, and I said, "Sonja, can I ask you something?"

She looked at me.

"Why did you decide to come here?" The question wasn't what she'd thought it would be, I could see that on her face. I had managed to stop myself from asking about Peter.

"I heard about this beautiful place," she said. "The beautiful hotel in the wilderness."

I smiled at her words and looked out at the river, then back at the hotel with the hills rising on the other side of it, feeling the bite of cold in the air, the shifting into winter. I felt in that moment I had everything I could ever want—this place, this day, and this beautiful girl I was sitting beside. Of course, really, I had nothing except a job in a beautiful place and a tenuous friendship with a girl I had more than friendship feelings for. Nothing I wanted belonged to me, try as I might not to see it that way.

I looked up at the sky, just in time to see the first small flakes of snow swirling down.

"Here's the snow," I said, still looking up.

She stopped what she was doing and looked with me. "Oh!" she said. "It is so beautiful!" And we shared that, the coming of the first snow.

AT THE PARTY FOR NELLIE JUNE, down in the basement, I drank too much and spent most of the time waiting for Sonja to appear, looking for her through the in-and-out weaving of people coming and going. Nellie June herself came and went, leaving the rec room to wander into the trainman's reading room where the gents in there were all too happy to slip her a drink. Despite Prohibition, bootlegged or homemade alcohol found its way into the hotel fairly regularly, and that night there were plenty of little flasks being passed around. Nellie June had washed her hair for the party, and it hung loose and shiny around her shoulders, and under her over-sized flannel shirt she wore a dress, the shirt making the dress hard to see. It was a green flowery print and fell well past her knees. I knew Nellie June would have rather worn pants any day and likely felt she couldn't get away with it. Cora wore pants more times than not and never worried about getting away with anything.

At one point, as I looked, I saw Sonja there, standing shyly in a corner by the table. I made my way over to her and leaned against the wall.

"Hello, Harry," she said.

"Sonja," I said with a nod. "How'd your basket box come out?" As soon as the snow started, I'd had to leave and go back to my duties, which involved putting things back where they belonged in the sheds and under the eaves as we knew the snow was finally going to fall.

She had the gift folded in a white napkin. She pulled back the corners of the cloth and I saw the finished little basket. She'd carved a flower pattern into the sides; I imagined she'd taken the nail and kind of drew with it, going through one layer of the bark to the darker layer beneath.

"That's really nice, Sonja," I said.

And it was. I knew Nellie June would love it. My present for Nellie June was a book someone had left at the hotel last summer that I'd snatched up before anyone else could: *The Enchanted April* by a writer I'd never heard of called Elizabeth von Arnim. It was about women traveling to the Italian Riviera. I figured she'd like it if she took the time to read it.

Someone started the gramophone and music filled the room. People were finding partners and dancing.

I grabbed Sonja's free hand and said, "Come on—let's dance." I took the napkin wrapped basket from her and set it on the table.

"I do not know how to dance, Harry," she said, and I felt how I was holding her hand a little too tight.

"Oh, it's easy," I told her. "You just follow me," and I put my other hand on her waist and we began to move with the others.

The music swirled around us. I closed my eyes, breathing in the warm wonderful smell of her, like clothes dried on a line in the fresh air. A quick short time later I missed the end of the song, and I became aware of her voice saying, "Harry, the song is over. We must stop the dancing now."

I opened my eyes. The music had indeed ended, and my clammy hand remained on her waist, my other hand gripping hers. The realization of how I must have seemed in that moment hit me, and I quickly let her go and took a few steps back.

"Thank you, Harry," she said and walked away through the room into the clusters of people. I lost sight of her as other people talked to me and someone passed me a flask, and when I looked around for her again, she had disappeared.

JACKSON KEATS
FALL 1927

HER MOUTH WAS ON HIS, WARM and searching, her nose cold against his cheek, and he wondered at this change as both fear and joy spread through him. Sophia, Sophia. Somehow, they were back on the beach at home, and it was snowing in a way it never would, and Jackson asked himself, *What is happening?* Then he opened his eyes, realizing it was a dream.

He rose from his cot, stirred and fed the coals in the wood stove.

It was dark; Snowy Day looked up at him then closed his eyes as if to say, "Go back to sleep, Jackson."

Jackson knew that he could not. Sleep and contentment had both flown out the door the moment he saw Sophia on the train platform. Now he knew the simple life he had built for himself would never be enough. He needed Sophia with him in this world and in this life. Peter, too. If he could manage to bring Peter to Sophia, perhaps he would also bring her back to him.

Could it be so easy, to change a life? He had begun to realize, after he'd left the island, that there were some circumstances where you could choose to not let others have power over you. If he had known this two years ago, perhaps he might not have left. Or perhaps he may have anyway—though of his own choice. If he could bring Peter safely here, the three of them could be free to choose to live however they wanted, and maybe he and Sophia could find those old dreams again. If not, he would be good to his word to help her raise Peter.

The thought of returning to the island, though, made him nothing short of uneasy. There were so many unanswered questions. Before he dared go back, he would have to have some of those answers. Yes, he knew now it all had to come down to Father Mikhail; he also knew the priest would not have been the one to lay his fists onto Sophia. She had always insisted it was not Ilian Nicholai. There was no reason for her to lie about that, and if it was true Ilian no longer lived in the village, he could not be responsible for the bruises she had now, even if he was responsible for the first ones. Is she protecting someone—someone who beats her? Mr. Wassily perhaps? No—Jackson could not see that. The man had doted on Sophia and her mother, had been such good friends with Sophia's grandfather. Sophia had continued to visit him and work for him, even after the bruises appeared.

There were plenty of men in the village who were beholden to Father Mikhail, and there were others who worshipped him as a supreme leader. His own father. Dmitri and his other brother,

Alexsei. When they grew, they and their mother and Ilian were dependent on the help from the church, ever since they lost their father to the sea on the same boat that took Percy Petrovitch, who some continued to believe was Sophia's father. Dmitri and Alexsei had done well for themselves and have been dependent on no one for anything since they were old enough to captain their own boat, though their love for Father Mikhail remained. They did not defend Ilian, and they did not accuse him. Dmitri did, in his own way, make it plain that he did not believe Sophia's story. "I would believe my own brother did it, before I would believe that it was Father Mikhail," he had said. Why wouldn't Sophia tell him?

He wondered if he could simply walk into the village, locate Peter, and walk away with him. They could go overland, across the island, until they came to Sitka. Jackson knew the forests and his years here in this country had only increased his abilities to survive in the wild. From there he would have to find passage on a boat for them, to reach Seward where they could board the train. Jackson had no money—not enough for boat passage and train rides. He did have some furs, though, from the last winter's trapping season that he had not yet sold: several marten, and a wolf that had come to his cabin, his hungry eyes on Snowy Day. Mrs. Grant bought furs from him, as did some of the railroad men on occasion. Jackson remained leery of the hotel, since his scolding for pinning the hotel boy up against the wall. Perhaps enough time had passed, and he could speak with Mrs. Grant.

His dream. He thought of it as he put a kettle on the wood stove and looked out the window at the dark morning. The snow that had started yesterday afternoon was continuing, though lightly and delicately, and he wondered how deep it would get. Tomorrow he would try to meet Sophia again, on the hill of the dead horses. What would happen between them this time? Speaking with her was like trying to cross the river in the winter. It might be fine, or there might be an open channel beneath a bridge of snow. You had to be so very careful. Like in his dream Jackson felt both fear and joy. He sensed she had forgiven him, though he was unsure if that forgiveness was complete. He carried with him the last time he saw her before he left the island. He had waited, hidden in the trees on the point, for her to appear on the beach. He hurried over to her; the wind was blowing strong so she did not hear him come up behind her.

"Sophia!" he'd cried into the wind, and she whipped around. Her face was pale and pained. She wore the black dress she had worn since her mother died, a dress her mother had worn at the grandfather's funeral years before.

"What is it you want, Jackson?" she yelled back, the wind pulling strands of hair out from her crown of braids.

"I am to be leaving," he said, wishing she would come closer so he did not have to yell.

"And why do you have to be leaving, Jackson? Doesn't Father Mikhail still love you? Doesn't he?"

He could not tell her that he confessed their sin. He knew that she would believe he was leaving to be away from her and the trouble she had caused. He'd had no words to tell her it was not so.

Suddenly she had closed the distance between them and at once began to strike him on the chest with her hands clenched into tight little fists.

"No no no no no!" she screamed. "You leave then Jackson! You go! You go live a life that I can never have! You pig! I never want to see you again!" And she'd spun around and ran back to her house, where Jackson knew she would lock the door against him.

So many mistakes. He had made so many mistakes. He should have defied his father and Father Mikhail and stayed. He should not have left everything as it was.

He realized he had to temper his hopes. Both their hearts had been bent. How could anything ever be the same between them? He hoped Sophia would try; *he* would try, and he would start with getting Peter for her, somehow.

When the light finally crept into the sky, he opened the door and stepped out into the snow, holding his warm cup of tea in his hands. The snow lay across the land like a clean, soft blanket. He wondered what he would be doing and how he would be feeling on this day if Sophia had not reappeared into his life. He would be happy to see the snow; he would likely have a list of chores he would want to do—snowshoe out some of his trails, if the snow piled deep enough to warrant that, and start planning the winter trapline. Get out the sled and go find some more firewood. Busy, busy, busy. Life in the wild country was very busy, with all you needed to do to simply survive. When he'd first arrived, he saw how he could live here—live. Now he knew it would just be surviving, from one season to the next, if he could not bring Sophia back to him.

SOPHIA PETERSEN
FALL 1927

"SOPHIA, YOU MUST LISTEN, YOU MUST."

I held my mother's dry hand, day and night during her last time on this earth. She had given up the vodka when she started not feeling well; though it was too late for her to regain her health, she did regain her mind, and for a short time I had my mother back, the mother who ran in the wind on the beach with me, who told me stories of our family and from when she was a little girl. The mother who combed my hair and taught me how to braid. The mother who would sing me to sleep at night and would make me feel safe from the world.

"There is money, in the oatmeal tin in the kitchen," my mother said, in the last of her time. "Money I have saved. The seeds for the garden are on the shelf in the root cellar. Please stop going out in that old boat, Sophia. Please! I am so afraid you and Peter could drown. Please ask Jackson to fix it for you. Please."

On one of those days she said, "Sophia, take the money from the oatmeal tin and leave this place after I am gone. You and Peter. Go start another life in some better place. You will not be safe here!"

"I will be safe, Mama. Jackson will marry me, and he will take care of me and Peter."

"I am afraid," she said. "I am afraid." She did not say of what, and I had assumed she meant her death. I said, "Oh Mama! I love you so much! So much!" And she squeezed my hand as tears made their quiet way down the sides of her haggard face.

She was so beautiful once, a smiling girl with long blond braids. Even after I was born, and she had to live in disgrace outside the village, we were happy. My grandmother was frail and died when I was quite little; my grandfather provided for us and came often to our little house. My mother would cook for him while he fixed loose boards on the walls or shingles on the roof and always found the time to explore the beaches with me. He was a big man with broad shoulders, my grandfather Sergei. Mr. Wassily often had meals with us when my grandfather was visiting, and the two men would laugh and talk long past my bedtime. Too soon my grandfather left this world as well; it was a logging accident in the forest, and I remember the big, empty feeling that filled our little house. The church maintained my grandfather had debts, and my grandparents' small, simple house in the village was sold to cover these supposed debts, and Father Mikhail created the job of the sewing for my mother.

My mother was often sad, in the coming times.

I knew she was afraid; "Sophia," she would say, after several helpings of the "medicine," "we have no one to protect us now."

I began to learn that women on their own were vulnerable in this world, like animals in the wild without coats or claws.

I learned to fish, I learned to garden, I learned to collect driftwood for firewood to keep us warm, and I learned about the wild things we could harvest for food—mushrooms and berries and the Labrador tea. When Jackson became more than my friend, he would bring us ducks that he had killed, and big fish that he would catch on the boat with his father or when he was out with Dmitri Nicholai.

Peter was born amid all of this, when I was thirteen, and it was like having the sun itself living in our house; he was such a bright and happy little person. At the same time my mother sank further into the deep hole she often dwelt in, and I was so busy, taking care of Peter and going to school and helping to keep us fed, that I did not have much time to wonder where my happy mother went. I only knew she was gone. I began to realize the people of the village did not like us, though Father Mikhail said we must go to church on Sunday and would send one of the Nicholai boys out to fetch us if he thought we would not come. Always it was either Dmitri or Alexsei, never Ilian. Dmitri and Alexsei, who liked to act as if I did not exist.

"You need the church," I heard Father Mikhail tell my mother once. "You need God, Anna, as do your children."

"My children," she'd said and laughed in such a way that I knew the strange sound meant something different than what laughter usually means, yet even as I grew older I did not know what Father Mikhail was to her. I only knew that after my grandfather died, he came often to our house. At first my mother appeared pleased with his visits and would send me out to play; Peter was not even born yet before I saw the light fading within her. In my innocence I did not connect that with Father Mikhail, though I made sure never to be alone with him after the time I had fallen into the mud.

"I must tell you something, Sophia," my mother whispered on that last night after Father Mikhail left our house. "You must listen to me. You must!"

"I am here, Mama. I am listening."

"It is something very hard to hear. It is hard to say. But I must, I must tell you."

I pressed her hand up to my cheek. "You should rest, Mama. Rest."

A bitter smile. "There is no time to rest, my dear lovely Sophia." She took a ragged breath. "Are you certain he is gone?"

"Who? Father Mikhail? Yes, he has gone. He will come check on you in the morning."

"I will not be here in the morning."

"Mama do not say such a thing!"

"I must tell you."

I waited. It was hard for her to breathe; she was so tired and her body so wasted. Cancer, the doctor sent by the church had said; "It is God's will."

"I hate God!" I had shouted to the doctor. "I hate Him!" I ran out the door only soon to return, pulled back by an image of Peter's frightened little face.

Now Peter slept softly in his room as my mother lived her last in this world.

"Father Mikhail. You must be careful with him, Sophia."

I nodded. I had known this since the time of the mud.

"You must be very careful!"

"I will, Mama. I will! Do not worry."

"You don't understand, Sophia. I am his!"

I did not know what to say. I did not know what that meant. "His?" was all I managed.

"Listen, listen, Sophia. When he comes for the sewing. When you and Peter leave us together so we can pray. We are not praying, Sophia. He makes me do things, that I do not want you to have to do."

The color that had disappeared from my face came rushing back as I thought of what Jackson and I had done, on the beach in the wind. Father Mikhail was a priest! Surely, she couldn't mean that.

"He takes from me what he wants. He always has!"

"Mama—what do you mean? What has he done?" An idea was forming in my mind; one I did not want.

"I could not stop it, Sophia, I could not! I had to obey him. We have no one to protect us." She looked away from me and down at the bedclothes. "When I was younger—I did not mind. He was much kinder once, or perhaps I was more foolish."

"Peter—." Of course I had wondered, as I began to understand things, who Peter's father was.

She nodded. "No one must know that," she said. "No one must know of what I told you. No one! He will turn on you, Sophia, and I fear for Peter. It must be kept secret. I do not know what he would do to Peter if that truth came out. The secret keeps Peter safe, you see? You see that, Sophia? He is a priest. He cannot have children! Don't you see? It must be kept secret!"

I shook my head and pulled my hand away from hers. "No, Mama, no." It was impossible, to keep a secret such as that.

"Sophia you mustn't, you mustn't ever," she pleaded and grabbed back my hand. "I only tell you so someone knows, someone. For Peter's sake. As long as Father Mikhail lives, you must know nothing, Sophia, nothing! You must not tell a single living soul, Sophia, you mustn't, mustn't, mustn't."

That was when I thought about the lamp, and how easy it would be to set the house afire. I could never have done that, though, never, not with Peter sleeping under the same roof—even if I knew what would soon begin to happen to me.

"Then why did you tell me?" I said, struggling to keep the anger out of my voice. Not for my mother of course, but for the man who calls himself a priest.

"In case he comes for you," she said.

I THINK OF THIS TONIGHT. I THINK OF THIS ALWAYS. Tonight Nellie June had talked about her trip down to see her family, happy from her party, and it makes me feel very lonely. First there was the family of my mama, my grandpapa, and me; next there was the family of my mama, Peter, and me. Now I am here with no family; Peter is there with none.

What had I done to him, my Peter?

"You have to stand up to things, to the bad people of the world."
I had heard my grandpapa and Mr. Wassily talking one night, and
my grandpapa spoke those words. I grew up knowing what those
before me had done to be free. Here, in this new country, it was
supposed to be that way. Free. But we brought it with us, didn't
we—oppression. It lived quietly within our love for our church and
came silently with us, wherever we went.

CHAPTER TEN

EMILY WELLS
FALL 1974

PRODUCTIVE PEACE. THAT'S WHAT WE GOT with Raymie there: three weeks of productive peace. Raymie knew how to build a cabin, and we made progress each and every day. He and Thomas became fast friends, and I looked forward to his return to the campfire each morning. He'd been in Alaska for four years; he was from Southern Oregon, not far from Sacramento, and had family there he had not yet gone home to see.

"Don't you miss them—your family?" I asked him one morning while Thomas slept and he and I talked quietly by the fire.

"I'll get back there," he said, and I could tell there was something buried in those few simple words and the way he said them. I wondered how long it would be before Thomas and I would visit our own families. The things we think about when the future is unwritten in front of us.

During this time we didn't forget about the skeleton. It was the first thing I thought about each morning when I opened my eyes and the last thing Thomas and I would talk about each night, our faces close as we whispered inside the tent so Raymie wouldn't hear, though he had pitched his own tent away from ours. Within earshot, if we yelled, I had noted, and at the same time distant enough to leave me and Thomas to ourselves. Despite that, we whispered. And we worked hard to keep Raymie from going up the hill.

"The curse of the Findlays," Thomas whispered one morning in the tent. "My mom always said the Findlays were cursed—our branch, at least—and she always said I'm a Findlay through and through."

"I don't think you're cursed, Thomas."

"Gold slips through our hands and shit fills our shovels."

"I'm in your shovel, Thomas—don't you forget."

He kissed my temple and nuzzled his nose in my hair. "For better or for worse," he whispered.

"Not worse," I whispered back, smiling as his fingers stroked the side of my face. "It's always been for the better, Thomas."

"Oh come on," he said, "how many guys fall off stages, sleep on the bottom of a pool, run through a plate glass window, and pick a building site on top of a lonely mysterious grave?"

I kissed him, in part to keep myself from crying. The things we didn't talk about he just talked about—a good sign, I hoped, that he was seeing the reality of his situation with clear eyes.

"What if it's not a *lonely* grave?" I said, my lips half on his.

"What do you mean?"

"And not a mysterious one, either," I went on. "Think about it. Years ago there probably weren't many options around here for burying people. It could be the trapper—or whoever—is simply tending the grave—keeping an eye on it—not for a nefarious reason like murder, but because it's someone he cares about."

Maybe I was trying to justify the fact that all we had done about it was tamper with evidence, if there was any. I wondered, since we had reburied it, if it was too late for us to report it.

Thomas pulled me close. "Well that could be, lassie," he whispered with a smile. "However, I remain the fool who picked that spot of all the spots I could have picked."

"It's the most beautiful spot," I said. "You might not be the only one who thought that. Maybe that's all this is."

"Maybe," he said, kissing my forehead. "And we've been through worse, haven't we?"

"I love you Thomas Findlay," I whispered.

"I love you, Emily Wells."

We were coming to the end of things. But that morning felt like some kind of a beginning.

The following night was clear and cold. We had built up the fire, drank too much, and the three of us had lain down on a wool army surplus blanket and looked at the stars. Raymie was right; they were bigger and brighter than the stars I knew, though somehow they were the very same ones my sisters and I used to stare at when we'd do this very same thing—lay on a blanket in the yard—and I felt as if they were going to sprinkle themselves all over me as I floated up into the sky to meet them. Beside us the warmth from the fire reached out; I was closest to it, Raymie farthest, and while I kept offering to switch with him or Thomas so they could get warm, they both insisted I stay there. I let myself enjoy the feeling of being cared for and wanted the night to last and last as I listened to Raymie and Thomas go back and forth about bands they liked and bands they didn't, concerts they'd been to and what food they missed the most, living out here.

"French fries," Thomas said.

"Thai food," Raymie said.

I said, "Ice cream," and Raymie said he had an ice cream maker, and when the ice started to appear in the river, he'd bring it over and we'd make some.

The conversation shifted to what bands were big on the radio these days; Raymie had a battery-operated radio and on a clear day could get a signal all the way from Anchorage.

"Did you know there's a band named Findlay?" Raymie said. "Probably named for something else but hey—I heard this song they've got on the charts now and it's pretty good. Though I'm sure they never heard of Findlay, Alaska."

A blanket of cold fell over us. I reached for Thomas' hand. "What's the name of the song?" Thomas asked, words in the dark that carried so much weight with them.

"The Findlay song? Something like, 'Window.' Yeah. 'Window.' That's it."

I suppressed a cry of surprise and my mind screamed with messages: *Don't worry, Thomas, we'll get this figured out, of course they're assholes and they'll never get away with this they can't do this to you they—*

"Gotta take a leak," Thomas said, rising from the blanket. A few minutes later we heard him stumble off to bed. I could only hope he was drunk enough to go right to sleep, to forget about what he'd just heard. "Window" was a song Thomas had written for me. Thomas wrote nearly all the Findlay songs. For the album they had started recording before Thomas fell into the pool, "Window" was set to be the single.

"I should go, too," Raymie said. "Big day tomorrow." Tomorrow was roof day; the next, floor day, and then it would be time to set up the stove and cover the window holes with a plastic called Visqueen until we could get some glass. Then Raymie would be gone until I went to town and bought the real windows and he'd come back and help us put them in.

"We can't thank you enough for helping us, Raymie; you have to let us pay you something." I tried to sound normal as I felt an earthquake shifting around inside me.

"Nah," he said. "There's no need for that. I want to build a proper woodshed next fall; you can come help me with that if you want."

"I think we could do that," I said.

"You okay with the windows? That big one in front?" he asked.

"Yeah. Yeah, I guess."

His face turned toward mine, and he looked at me across the gap where Thomas had been. They'd left a much bigger hole for a window than I had wanted, in the front.

"We can change it," he said.

"No—you're right; I know it would be better, during the day, to have a nice window there."

He kept looking at me, as if my face were a page full of words he was trying to read. "Not at night though," he finally said.

"What?"

"A big window wouldn't be better at night. Not for you." He said it softly and without judgement.

I looked at the stars. I wanted to love the night again, and tonight I had been until the specter of the stolen song, here in the open under the stars with the fire and the woods and the big hill behind us where the skeleton lay. I loved this night, and I wasn't sure I would love the nights in the cabin; I feared reminders of the little green house, dark walls and black windows, and I feared those reminders would take me back to the fancy San Francisco apartment and the dark room and the window of night. I was raped. I was raped.

"I was raped," I whispered.

Raymie said nothing at first. Tears trickled out of my eyes and ran down my temples to my ears, little rivers of relief. Then Raymie said, whispering as well, "What happened?" and I told him, and when I finished, he reached across the empty space between us and grabbed my hand, and we lay like that for a while as the fire burned its way down to glowing coals and we went our separate ways to bed.

The next day at the cabin site Raymie said, "You know, it's going to be pretty hard getting a big window up from Anchorage and all the way back here without breaking it." He and I were handing long flattened poles for the roof up to Thomas, who was sitting on the ridge pole. I worried he would fall.

Thomas said, "I was wondering how we were going to do that." That morning in the tent, Thomas had whispered, "What was that about, Em? Why don't you want a nice window in the front? You don't think I would—do you?"

"No, of course not. That's not it."

"Then what is it?"

"Nothing. I just thought, you know, bears."

"Okay." There was a pause before he asked, "You sure?"

"Um hm."

"Okay."

The relief I had felt from finally telling someone what had happened to me was laced now with guilt and confusion. I had told Raymie, not Thomas, though I never knew how I could ever tell Thomas. He would blame himself for being in the hospital because he fell into a swimming pool and didn't wake up because he was overdosing on heroin. He didn't need the weight of that. Or so I told myself, to make myself feel better for my late-night confession to the wrong man.

"Thomas," I'd said, before we left the tent. There was a different window we should have been talking about. "The song."

He sighed and said, "Yeah, that sucks. They could at least have asked." When the band got rid of Thomas, Jimmy the manager tried to get Thomas to sign over permission to use his songs. Thomas refused. After that Thomas went to a lawyer and added my and his mother's names to the rights to his songs.

"I'll write the lawyer guy and let him straighten it out, Em," he'd said that morning in the tent. "We've got other things to think about. Like a roof!"

I did not believe it could be as easy as that. I let it go, hopeful that our new life was taking hold and Thomas really was okay with the whole thing.

Now Raymie said, "Well, you know—it might be just as good to have two smaller windows next to each other. It would have the effect of a bigger window, and smaller sheets of glass would be a lot easier to manage."

"Oh," Thomas said. "Kind of like what Emily was talking

about." I had suggested that when I was trying to change the window size.

"Yeah—basically."

"Sounds good to me," Thomas said. "How about you, Em?"

I nodded. Raymie had heard me, all the things I did not say.

SEVERAL DAYS LATER THOMAS AND I WERE building our first fire in the cabin. It was empty, sparse, and clean and gigantic compared to the tent. Raymie had left that morning, and his parting words were, "Best start packing up the camp. Snow's coming." Thomas and I had watched as he bounded down the trail, a man with a gun and a backpack, heading home.

As we lay there that first night, snuggled together in the bed we'd made on the floor by the stove, Thomas the happiest I'd seen in ages and falling asleep in my arms, I stared at the gray Visqueen-colored holes that were ghostly and luminous in the dark. I kept expecting to see shadows on the other side of those filmy gray eyes and I realized glass would be better; I realized that here, the outdoors—even at night—was a friendlier place than veiled, unclear space. I would have to get the windows, sooner rather than later.

HARRY HARBOUR
FALL 1974

I SEE NELLIE JUNE SOMETIMES; SHE GETS on the train now and again, I think just to stare at me malignantly. She knew something had happened. She knew her friend Sonja wouldn't leave just like that, vanished with never a word except a hasty note to Mrs. Johnson. Nellie June deserves to know the truth; I know that, and I've thought many times about leaving her a letter in my will, telling her what happened. There's already one letter with my will, and one from Cora as well. Cora had given me instructions that if ever I felt for certain that telling everything was the wrong thing to do,

I should burn the letters. If it wasn't for the grave, and the fact that there was someone more important than Nellie June who deserved to know the truth, I would have done that long ago.

FALL 1927

THE LAST TIME SONJA AND I spoke together—properly, the shadow of what was coming right in front of us unseen—she found me in the dining room having a cup of tea and did the unusual thing—for her—of taking the seat across the table from me. My heart thundered to life, and I stared at her unspeaking. It was the day after Nellie June's party, and I worried I had been too forceful, too clumsy, too much like someone who'd had too much to drink. Outside the windows the snow was falling, fast and furious. I was waiting for the train, for Cora.

"Harry," she said, and I watched her cheeks flush a delicate shade of pink. "I had never read William Shakespeare."

"You'd mentioned that," I stammered out, wondering if I should offer her some tea so she would stay longer while feeling like any move from me might send her scurrying back to the laundry like a frightened bird.

"Now I have," she said with a rare smile. "So wonderful! The people! All the problems. It is so hard to read, though—so difficult for me. I must keep stopping, to figure out the words. I was not schooled properly."

I shook my head. "Oh, no, Sonja, you're fine; I'm sure you were schooled fine. It takes a bit of reading him to get used to it; people talked differently in those days. I've had to read each play about four times before I could start to really understand it."

"Oh! That is such a relief. I have been feeling very—ignorant."

"Oh—no—you're not ignorant at all, Sonja." I knew how stupid I sounded.

"What is your favorite play?" she asked.

'Oh, well, that's a hard question," I said. "I kind of like them all. I guess I really like *Henry V*. I don't know. I was always fond of *Twelfth Night*, too; I played Viola in high school, when we did that play."

She laughed then quickly covered her mouth.

"I am sorry!" she said, smiling. "It is funny, Harry—Viola pretended to be man, and you were a man pretending to be a woman pretending to be a man?"

"Yep—that about sums it up. And really, in Shakespeare's day, that's how they did it. Women weren't allowed to do things like act in plays."

She nodded solemnly. "I could see how that would be so," she said.

"So you read that one?" I asked.

"Yes. I like it very much. Not so sad."

"What is *your* favorite?"

"Oh—I cannot say yet. I have not read many. But *A Midsummer Night's Dream*—so beautiful and mischievous."

"That's a good one," I said.

"You look sad, Harry," she said suddenly.

It caught me by surprise, and I looked at her, and she looked at me, and I felt a flood of all the things I longed to tell her, all the things I wanted to share with her, how I wanted to spend the rest of my life talking with her about Shakespeare and following her down trails through the woods.

"Oh—no—I'm—I'm not sad," I said. "My aunt's coming in on the train, and we're going to head out tomorrow morning to go caribou hunting."

"You don't want to go?"

"No—not really. I mean, I love the country—I know it's going to be beautiful—I just don't get excited at the thought of killing things the way Cora does."

What I really wanted to say was that I couldn't stand the thought of being away from her for a few days, having to wonder and worry what she and Jackson Keats might be up to, what it was between them, and what it was she wasn't telling us.

"She knows how to survive," Sonja said. "It is good for a woman to know those things."

"Oh yeah—Cora does indeed know how to do that."

She reached across the table and unexpectedly touched my hand. She was happy; that was obvious. My heart was cracking thinking I knew the reason for that.

"I hope you have a good time, Harry. Nellie June would be very excited, if you brought back a dead animal! I must get back to the laundry. Thank you again so much for the books. I will give them back to you soon."

"Oh—you can keep them for as long as you want," I said, watching her rise, feeling her hand slip away from mine. I tried to swallow but my mouth was too damned dry.

"Thank you. I hope you have fun on the hunt with your aunt." She whirled around and went toward the kitchen and the stairs. I looked out the window and saw how the snow was swirling down again, and how the day was turning that winter afternoon shade of blue, tempered by the gray of the sky and the softness of the snow. The color spoke of the fading day and the coming night, of a temperature that was dropping. It was beautiful, but it did nothing to ease the pain in my heart.

JACKSON KEATS
FALL 1927

SNOW WAS SPINNING IN THE WIND on the hill the day he met Sophia again, the world white and cold and clean. Six inches or more had fallen, light and fluffy. He wore his big wooden snowshoes; it was good to pack a base for a trail. He worried that perhaps Sophia would decide not to come—she would not be used to so much snow—but he waited and soon saw her emerging from the side of the hill.

She wore no hat but had a small pair of mittens on her hands. He had noticed the wool jacket when she found him by the rock—fitted and pretty, meant more for a cold city street than the woods and most likely borrowed from someone in the hotel. Jackson had realized she brought nothing with her. That would mean she did not have the time to pack a bag or even to grab a coat. What had happened?

Today she smiled as she crossed over to him, and Snowy Day bounded over to greet her. Jackson regretted that there would be no sitting together among the dead straw-like grasses, and with the snow gathering on her fair head he would not want to keep her long.

"Are you cold?" he asked. He pulled his knitted hat from his head. "Here, take my hat, Sophia. You'll catch cold." He worried the hat might be dirty, though he had washed it last spring, when the winter was over.

"I am fine, Jackson," she said, petting Snow's head with her mittened hand. "It is not so cold as I had thought."

"All right." He kept the hat off, not wanting to be warm if she was not.

They stood awkwardly for a moment, not knowing where to begin. Finally Sophia said, "I have some money, Jackson. I have gotten paid for my work. You'll need money for the ticket to Seward. Money for a boat to Sitka. And money to bring Peter back."

Jackson said, "I have some furs I will try to sell, Sophia. I don't want to take your money."

"My money is not worth anything to me, without Peter," she said.

"Oh, Sophia," he said, the words spilling out before he could stop them. "What has become of us? What happened on that island that was once our home?"

She looked at him, snow on her lashes, and did not say anything, only looked.

"I know," Jackson said. "I know you tried to tell me. I will never forget how I did not listen." He looked down at the fronts of his snowshoes, standing between him and her. He had not meant to say anything of that sort. He had meant to stay focused on Peter, on his rescue, the thing on which they were both aligned.

"Jackson," she said. "I will tell you before you go. I have decided that. You will not like it and you might hate me all over again—"

"I never hated you, Sophia! Never!" He looked at her and their eyes met, her blue and his black-brown. "I doubted you, yes, but I never hated you, Sophia. It is the opposite of that."

Her eyes narrowed, as if a cold wind had blown past.

"There will be time, yes—I will get Peter and bring him here and there will be time, to sort this out, will there not?" *We are both here,* he wanted to say. *So like how we had dreamed!*

She looked past him and did not answer. He felt his hopes falling.

"Can you not forgive me?" He thought she had. He had hoped she had.

Now she looked at him again. "I do forgive you, Jackson. You must know I am no longer the Sophia I used to be. There are things that have happened that I will tell you, some other day."

"Have you no love left for me?"

She smiled a little, and he felt his heart leap again.

"There will only ever be you," she said.

He felt on the edge of a cliff. He could jump to his death or jump to great joy. What did she mean by those words? There was a voice inside of him, to be cautious, to be slow.

He said, "It is the same for me, Sophia. Only you. I realize I no longer know what that means. There is time. We must first bring Peter here, then perhaps we can sort things out between us, yes?"

Despite her smile, her lack of a responding yes fell heavy upon him. She will see, he whispered inside himself. He will bring Peter here, and she will see that they could have their life.

"I will bring the furs to the hotel—soon," he said. "I will have to find a good time, when the manager might not see me. I don't know if he is still unhappy with me or not."

"I can try to find out," Sophia said. "Nellie June knows everything. I will see how much money is needed for the ticket. And I will insist you take my money, Jackson. It is for Peter. It should be used to bring him here."

He nodded, slowly. He would not disagree with her. "I can go soon," he said.

She smiled—broadly this time. "Thank you, Jackson. To be with Peter again, to know that he is safe—."

Safe? Again he wanted to ask. Before he left, though—she had said before he left, she would tell him.

"I would have to take Snowy Day with me." The thought had just struck him. He could not leave his good friend.

"Would that be possible?" she asked.

"Yes—I have seen dogs on the train."

"I will check for you, to be sure."

He nodded. It felt like there was so much to do.

"We will pick a day, for you to leave."

"Yes."

"Are you certain, Jackson?"

He held her eyes. "Yes."

She stepped past his snowshoes and tipped her face up toward his and kissed him again, and this time he kissed her back, pulling her close and lifting her up as the snow swirled all around.

SOPHIA PETERSEN
FALL 1927

"WHY ARE YOU CRYING, SOPHIA?"

"I miss our mother."

"I do, too."

"I know."

"Why are you sleeping on the floor?"

I pulled myself up on my pile of bedding. I had woken to Peter's round little face as he sat cross legged staring at me. I had been weeping in my sleep.

"I do not know," I told him, brushing his straight blond hair from his face. It needed cutting; later I would try to do that myself with Mama's sewing shears. It would come out too short, with his bangs a bit crooked, but when he smiled his little gap-toothed smile to prove to me he liked it, I was well rewarded for my effort.

That was after we sat together in the semi-dark, the gray, grainy light of another dreary day struggling its way in through the window.

"Are you afraid?" he asked. The words squeezed on my heart. Yes, yes, I was afraid. I knew I mustn't ever let him know.

"I felt like sleeping in this room," I said.

He wasn't convinced. "Are you afraid of the bear?"

The day before that morning we had seen big tracks on the beach. I had warned Peter not to run along the beach by himself.

"We need to be careful about the bear, you remember that, right?" I said, evading what he really wanted to know.

"Is the bear why you are sleeping here?"

Peter was stubborn, like me. I knew he would not give up. "No, the bear is not the reason," I said.

"Then why?"

"Because I want to hear the house better," I said. "I am now the one who has to protect us, Peter."

He thought about that, and I wept inside at the uncertainty—and fear—my words had brushed upon his face. After a time he nodded and said, "I will sleep here, too, and listen to the house too."

"All right, Peter." And for months we played camp in the night-time, the house dark and quiet and he and I bundled in our blankets on the floor, listening to the wind rattle against the house, to the rain pattering on the roof, and the muffled rhythm of the waves upon the shore. I never knew what I would do if Father Mikhail chose to visit in the nighttime, but I had put all my faith into my belief that Father Mikhail would not harm Peter or wish to cause him distress. He sees Peter as an extension of himself, and I know that when Peter grows older he will look like him, only with our mother's fair hair and light blue eyes.

This evening Nellie June and I walked by the river after dinner, in the beautiful snow that was falling all over everything, only lightly now, seemingly longing to stop. The river was quiet, as if it wanted to listen to the little flakes fall onto its surface. I asked her about a train ticket, how much it would cost, to go to Seward and back.

"You can get a pass—all the workers can, even us laundry girls," Nellie June said. "I don't pay a thing to go back and forth to the village to see my family."

"Oh!" I said. I knew I would not be able to use a pass for Jackson. For myself someday, maybe—myself and Peter.

"You'll have to wait until I get back," Nellie June said. "Mrs. Johnson wouldn't like having both of us gone at once."

"Of course," I said. "I do not know when I would go." I could not think of a way to ask about taking a dog.

"Hey—maybe sometime we should go there together," she said. "When we get more help in the laundry, I mean. Wouldn't that be a hoot?"

"Yes," I said, and I wished it could be so. I have never done anything such as that, going on a journey with a friend for no other reason than fun.

"So, no sweetheart back home?" Nellie June asked. She has asked me this before. While she was never satisfied with my simple "No," she was always happy to tell me about the young man in the village she sees when she goes home to visit, and how they slip beneath the train trestle on the silty edge of the river to kiss.

"Not in a long time," I said this second time of questioning. I had been thinking of Jackson all day—the feel of him close, his beautiful lips on mine—and did not mind the thought of thinking of him some more. I also needed to find out if he would be all right, to return to the hotel.

"Oh—tell me," she said. "Who was he?"

"Just a boy from the village." Of course Jackson was never that. He was always that boy, the fisherman's son, the boy with the wild dark hair and the dark dark eyes.

"Was he handsome?"

"Yes."

"Describe him for me!"

"Oh, well, he looks something like your Jackson Keats."

"Really?" she said. "So, he's handsome!"

I smiled at the idea that Nellie June thought Jackson handsome. "But younger, and without the beard," I added. "And a sweet, sweet smile."

"Hmm, all right, yes. Our Jackson does not smile much, as I'm sure you've noticed."

"Yes. Is he still unwelcome here, at the hotel?"

Nellie June raised her brows and glanced up at the sky, twisting her lips as she thought. "I almost forgot about that. It's been a while. I don't think anyone cares anymore."

"Oh—that is good," I said, and added, to continue our discussion, "The boy from the village smiled often, not like your Jackson. He was always trying to impress me, by skipping rocks over the water, or doing cartwheels over the sand. And of course, by telling me about every big fish he ever caught."

Nellie June laughed at that. "A universal trait of the male species, I'd wager," she said, and we laughed some more.

I caught myself, and wondered how I could laugh, at anything. Was it a sign that I had given up, that nothing mattered, or a sign that something in me was healing. How was that possible? I was damaged beyond repair, stained and soiled beyond redemption. When I am around Nellie June—and Harry, too—people who don't really know me—I feel I become who they see me to be, and it is in those few moments, here and there, that I forget who I really am. Then when I am with Jackson, like today on the hill of the dead horses, I remember who I was—it is like Jackson holds my old self inside of him and the sound of his voice, the smell of his skin, the sight of him and the feel of him pour the old Sophia into me, like water into an empty jar.

CHAPTER ELEVEN

EMILY WELLS
EARLY WINTER 1974

THREE WEEKS LATER I WAS BOARDING the southbound train to travel to Anchorage to get the windows and to restock our now bare-bones food supply. The snow Raymie had predicted had come, and the world was startlingly white. Thomas and I piled snow up against the cabin to act as the insulated skirting we did not have, and we spent most of the quickly abbreviating days getting firewood with a chainsaw and a little plastic toboggan while wearing our new—and very awkward feeling—snowshoes that were tossed off the train in a big box one day with the rest of our mail and other supplies we had ordered. Thomas laughed at that, and he laughed a lot in that last, good stretch of time we had together.

Thomas had managed to throw onto the train a letter for his lawyer about the song. Or songs; we had no way of knowing what others they were using.

Thomas wanted to forget about it. I reminded him we would have to make our living somehow someday. "If they need songs so bad they have to steal them, Em, they can have them," he'd said. "I'm done with that whole scene."

"For God's sake they already stole the band, Thomas—we can't let them take your songs."

When he remembered that they were my songs, too, and his mother's, he wrote the letter, while I remembered that night in the apartment, how his stack of song lyrics and notes appeared to have been the only thing—besides me—that was touched.

In Anchorage I stayed at the same hotel I had stayed in before, followed the same routine, and soon was back on the train heading home. It was a quiet ride and I chatted with Harry about his plans for the holidays. It was November already and the holidays weren't far off.

"I have a nephew of sorts," he said. "Well, he was taken in by my aunt of sorts so I don't know for certain what that makes me, other than the fact that he's grown used to me and calls me Uncle Harry."

"That sounds nice, Harry. Where does he live?"

"In Seward with his wife and three children. They run the roadhouse my sort-of aunt ran until she left us."

"Your sort-of aunt," I said, laughing. "I think you mentioned her before. She ran the Deadhorse Roadhouse, didn't she?"

"Yep. The one and only Cora Allen."

"Well, I hope you have a wonderful time with your sort-of nephew."

"Peter," Harry said. "His name is Peter. He was an orphan in a small religious community in the Southeast part of the state. We were still a territory then, and old Cora knew anyone who was anybody, so she pulled him out of there and gave him a better life."

"What was so bad with where he was?" I asked it lightly, not anticipating his response.

"There were people in the community who had done his family great harm," Harry said, and went no further. I had wanted to tell him of my and Thomas' holiday plans, how Raymie would take us with him to the lake where Monique and Raoul and the rest of the hippies lived for a big Thanksgiving, then Raymie would spend Christmas Eve and Christmas with us, and on New Years' Eve we would go with Raymie back to the lake and Monique and Raoul's. The mood, though, had shifted, and I felt a great sadness seeping out of Harry, as if through his very pores.

I looked for signs of Raymie when we passed his stop, and I could see his trail in the snow leading off into the woods. I had sent him a message about the windows while I was in Anchorage, via a service called "Bush Pipeline" that aired messages to people off the phone system over a far-reaching country-western radio station.

WHEN THE TRAIN GOT TO FINDLAY, I searched for Thomas. There was nothing but a smooth unmarked slate of clean snow from the snowstorm that had started the night I'd left. It was clear and bright now, the storm having blown on its way, and the snow was glaringly white and the sky an endless blue. A Thomas Findlay sort of blue, I thought, as if the sky had captured the color of his eyes.

Where was he? Most likely trying to break a trail through the new snow, I reasoned, and smiled at the thought of him struggling on those big clumsy snowshoes. I would have to wait for him; that was the only thing to do; he would be bringing my own pair of snowshoes and I could not imagine trying to make my way through the snow without them, awkward as they were.

"You'll be all right?" Harry asked as he helped me grab the gear from the baggage car when we saw no sign of Thomas.

I nodded. "I'm sure he's just having trouble in the snow."

"All right now," Harry said, patting my shoulder. "You two take care and we'll see you next time."

"Bye, Harry," I said, and I stood stupefied by the pile of windows and food while the train slipped away into the silence of the day.

I stood steady by the tracks for a while, pacing when the cold started seeping through my boots and my impractical Afghan sheepskin coat. A half hour passed, and another. I was going to have to start moving, and hopefully I would meet Thomas on the trail.

I took my bag with me and left all the rest as I started trudging through the new snow. I was up to my knees in it, past the tops of my tall boots. I stopped and listened. The day was still and silent. I heard nothing—anywhere. "Thomas!" I yelled. There was something frightening in the sound of my voice, swallowed by the thickness of the trees. "Thomas!" I could feel panic rising in me and tried my best to beat it back. He was drunk. He'd forgotten what day it was and didn't hear the train (he was chainsawing; he had fallen asleep; he was passed out). I tried to hurry though it was hard. My efforts warmed me some, but I was cold.

It took hours, literally hours, for me to get through the snow to the cabin. I felt the silence of it when I saw it, the stillness of it, saw that there was no smoke spilling from the chimney, and I knew at once that Thomas wasn't there. Had he gone to Raymie's? Had Raymie taken him back to Monique and Raoul's? Had they both forgotten what day it was?

No, no, no, that was all impossible, unless somehow Thomas thought I was staying in town until the Saturday train, though he had no reason the think that. I floundered the rest of the way. There were boot prints near the door and my heart leapt as I pulled on the wooden handle. I could forgive him, whatever it was. As long as he was okay, everything would be all right.

The cabin was empty, quiet, and cold. Everything in the cabin was frozen: the water in the water jugs, the water in the tea kettle, the half cup of tea left in a mug on the table. The shirt Thomas had worn the day I left was draped across the top of a chair, and his big chunky sweater with the red snowflakes was tossed across the other chair. My mind spun. I turned and looked out the open door. There were tracks in the snow, around the cabin: Thomas', and he had been here since whenever the snow had stopped. I found relief in that, briefly and before I realized that if he'd left the cabin, to go to someplace like Raymie's, I would have seen his tracks, there would have been a trail telling me where he had gone—

There was. I hadn't seen it at first. A trail going up the hill, boot prints on top of snowshoe prints. I threw my bag into the cabin and ran in his footsteps as fast as I could up that godforsaken hill and there he was, sitting in a camp chair by the edge, but not sitting, slumped, his hair gold in the receding sun, one arm, free of his blue down jacket, hanging down, his white hand in the white snow.

"Thomas!" I yelled, screamed, I don't know which, I only felt the ripping in my throat as whatever sound I was making tore its way into the frozen air. I ran and stumbled, stumbled and ran and stopped just short of the back of the chair. "Thomas?" I said. "Thomas?" I didn't want to touch him; I didn't want to feel that cold skin. I wanted him to turn around and say, "Hi Em! Oh, shit I missed the train!" And smile, and move, and beg my forgiveness with kisses and hugs.

I had to be dreaming. It had to be a mistake, a terrible mistake. I saw the needle, still in his arm.

I screamed, and I was the scream, there was nothing of me for that moment except the scream that flew out into the air above us and spread itself across the hills.

Next I found myself grabbing him and jostling him, saying, "Thomas, Thomas, wake up! Thomas please wake up!" Then I realized how cold he was, how stiff he was, and I threw up into the snow and fell to my knees and howled.

"What's happened?"

A voice—how? Who?

"What has happened?"

A figure was coming across the hill, swiftly on snowshoes. Coming toward me. The figure from the hill, the man I had seen. The trapper? An animal ran beside him, like a wolf.

"No!" I screamed. "Get away! Get away!" I did not think. I only felt. I was alone. Thomas was dead. A strange man was running toward me, and I could scream and scream and no one would hear me—

I turned and started to flounder forward.

"No!" the man cried. "Stop! You must stop!"

And I was falling through the air, taking the snow from the edge with me. It was like being inside a whirlwind of white.

HARRY HARBOUR
EARLY WINTER 1974

I HAD A BAD FEELING, LEAVING EMILY Wells by the tracks that day, no sign of her Thomas anywhere, the snow all smooth and white and silent. It was that old feeling, that only time had helped me subdue—time and repeatedly passing by this spot, again and again until the wound became a thick, hard scar. A feeling that something was terribly, terribly wrong.

I don't believe, as the old saying goes, that time heals all wounds. It sure as hell doesn't. Under those scars the wound is always there, pushing, wanting to break its way out. Findlay is one big wound that time keeps trying to erase—for me, for the people who once lived and worked there, for the memories of the people who died there. Yet Findlay—its story and its woods and hills and wild beauty—carries on.

EARLY WINTER 1927

"ARE YOU GOING TO BE A great Gloomy Gus this entire time? What is wrong with you, Harry?" Cora said, the hotel barely behind us and the miles and miles of wild country in front of us.

We were both on snowshoes pulling sleds and wearing white canvas parkas with fur ruffs over our wool coats, like the Indigenous people farther north wore, only theirs would have been made of animal skins. We wore wool pants and heavy boots with thick knitted socks. There was a big flurry when we left the hotel; all the staff and the overnight guests came out to see us off, and we had to pose for pictures and the whole shebang. I searched for Sonja in the little gathering and did not spot her. I was hoping that at least she'd get to see me like this.

Once the hotel was out of sight and sound, all that was left was the wind, which blew crisply over the hills that November day. Despite the leather shells and thick wool liners of my mittens, my fingers grew cold as I pulled my sled along, following Cora's trail. The days of snow had ushered in the freezing temperatures.

Occasionally, Cora would stop and pull her binoculars out of the big front pocket of her parka, scanning the hills and the valleys between. There were herds—branches of a much larger herd—that came through this area and which moved in their own time at their own speed. My first year at the hotel one such herd crossed the river just upstream from the hotel; I had never seen anything like it—that great moving mass of roughly a hundred animals traveling as a unit—one massive moving harmonious family—across the river and onward into the same hills where Cora and I were now as we made our way to the high tundra, though we had no way of knowing if any herd was anywhere nearby. There could be smaller branches, too—a half dozen here, three of four over there, two or three like we saw that day on the hill. We knew it was possible we might not see them at all on this trip, but Cora Allen rarely got skunked.

Moving along in the wild quiet afforded me plenty of time to think and to become ever more aware of the growing pain in my heart. The days were short and we had to make the most of the light. Eventually Cora stopped and announced it was time for some tea and pemmican—spiced jerky and dried berries pounded into dust and mixed with melted animal fat—a concoction I sometimes liked and sometimes hated. Cora's pemmican was always pretty good though; she added a touch of sugar, and she was careful with the fat. While I blew warm air into my mittens to thaw my fingers Cora quickly built a small fire with a stash of spruce boughs and small slices of wood from her sled, filled her enamel coffeepot with snow and put it on the fire when it was ready.

"Come get those fingers warm, Harry," she said, and I squatted down near the fire.

"How much farther today, Cora?" I asked.

She tipped her head in the direction we'd been traveling. "We're heading for that pass over there," she said.

I tried to sort out what area she meant. It was all hills and valleys.

"When it's about dark we'll stop and set up camp. We should be able to find a spot out of the wind." She threw some tea into the pot on the fire and put a big spoon of sugar each into two enamel camp cups. A few minutes later we were sipping hot sweet tea, slightly smokey from the fire.

"You going to tell me what's on your mind, Harry?"

"I don't think so," was my flat repose.

"Well, I think I've got it figured out somewhat anyway," she said. "Harry—do yourself a favor and leave the hotel behind for a few days, all right? Look around you. You're out in some of the most beautiful country on earth. Soak it in, Harry. It will feed your soul like nothing else."

I nodded though I didn't think so.

We made camp a few hours later near a patch of trees like an island in the snow. We built another fire and heated some beans and brown bread Cora had made ahead of time and I had to admit they tasted pretty darn good. The stars came out in the deep sky above us, and Cora made more tea and we rinsed out the dishes in a pot of melted snow. I noticed she didn't talk as much, out here in the wild, and she was less agitated than usual. She told me a few stories of hunts she had been on in the past, and it wasn't with her usual gusto. It was as if she slid into a kind of harmony with her surroundings, and for the first time I could really see how she managed all those times being out in the wild on her own.

She didn't bring up the hotel again, and that night I slept about as well as I ever had, and certainly as I had since Sonja Antonov's arrival. The wind buffeted the tent, and the cold kissed the end of my nose as it stuck out of the warmth of my sleeping bag. The universe had shrunk and expanded at the same time: it was the cold on the end of my nose and the warmth in the sleeping bag, the walls of the tent that kept out the wind; it was the wind itself, blowing across the endless miles of wild country to find us here, and it was the big bowl of deep sky and bright stars above us. And somewhere out there, in these miles of hills, were the caribou, the herd like a big, breathing organism resting on the land—thousands of them in that main herd we were unlikely to see, with smaller groups and herds scattered here and there. We would find them or we wouldn't. I decided it didn't matter. What mattered was being here.

THE CARIBOU FOUND US, SOMEWHERE IN the hours of our second night, when we were about halfway through the pass. It was all like a dream. I thought it was a dream, thought I was dreaming of the train, that the train was coming and that someone was breathing loudly somewhere beside me only I couldn't see who it was. When I finally opened my eyes I thought, it must be the wind, though my mind was beginning to put things together that it wasn't any wind. Cora's eyes caught mine in the dark. She put her fingers to her lips and stared at me about as seriously as I've ever seen her. I began to understand. A herd was passing through—a smaller herd and not the big herd of thousands, maybe a hundred or so. They were moving like a river through this valley and going past our tent the way water goes around a rock. The ground hummed with the touch of hundreds of hooves, singing an ancient song. The walls of the tent trembled, and everywhere there was breathing and grunting and snorting and I theorized we'd be lucky not to get trampled. Regardless, I was feeling pretty lucky. I was feeling like the luckiest human on the planet, to be out there under the stars in wild Alaska, in the middle of a moving caribou herd.

JACKSON KEATS
EARLY WINTER 1974

SHE WENT OVER THE HILL AND disappeared. The woman. Jackson's snowshoes crossed and he nearly fell. He had to see if she was all right. He had to keep running. River Blue ran beside him. They both stopped when they reached the dead man in the chair.

He was so young. Jackson felt the loss of this person he didn't know and remembered hearing him sing once when he came to the hill and the couple was beside their campfire far below. Jackson was surprised at the beauty of the voice; it was the kindness he heard within it, and it stirred in him memories of being young and believing in his father, believing in the village, and believing in Father Mikhail. A time when he would see Sophia Petersen every day of the school week. When he would go home, and his father would be there to greet him, and he would say, "Something warm for you to drink, Jackson? The damp of the day most surely chills the bones."

He would give Jackson a cup of tea, made from the mint leaves they grew the previous summer, and he would put honey in it for him if they had any. From their front window, where the table was, they could see the ocean, and they would talk about the waves, or the wind, or the color of the water.

Jackson would go back there if he could. He would go back there and he would say, "Papa. Papa." Then what? "Do not become a bad man. Do not become a follower of those who would do harm to others."

Oh, Papa. Even now Jackson would let himself dream of that home he had so wanted: his father, Sophia, himself, and Peter all living together in that house with the window that looked over the sea, the sounds of laughter bouncing off the corners and echoing up the stairs.

This man with the kind voice who sat in this chair and the woman who flew off over the hill—they had such dreams as those. Jackson could feel it.

"We will be back," Jackson said to the dead man in the chair, and he and River Blue turned to descend the side of the hill. It was too late for the man, perhaps not for the young lady.

"We need to find her, River Blue, and see if she is all right," he said, the big gray dog following him.

There was a day that kept pushing at him, like an open wound beneath a mask of scar. He pushed it back, thinking of the young woman—this young woman, here, now—who needed his help. It was hard, as if the past reached its fingers through the web of time and recreated a series of events to torment him.

They hurried along the base of the hill. Soon they could see where she went down and where she landed in the snow. There were places on the snowy face of the hill that had caught her, perhaps arrested her fall for a moment or two, then sent her on her way. Those places may have been enough to save her. He studied the impression her body left in the snow, like a child's unsuccessful attempt at a snow angel. There was red blood on the white snow near where her head would have been.

"We must find her," he told River Blue. Where was she going? Her trail ran shakily along the streambed; perhaps she was going to the railroad tracks to find help. Or perhaps her head was injured, and she did not know what she was doing. The trail in the snow zigged and zagged erratically. Jackson increased his pace.

She made good time, despite possible injury and lack of snowshoes. Like an animal in flight. She was afraid of him, Jackson realized and understood. He had much to explain to her, should he have the chance.

There was a train coming. He heard it: miles off, coming from the north. He must reach the young lady before she reached the tracks. "Come, River."

Time moved forward, Jackson kept running, the train grew closer. He heard the whistle blow as it approached the start of the long swooping bend to the north that curved along the river and which would bring the train straight to Findlay. Soon. The freight trains moved fast. In this time all the trains moved fast, compared to the one that Jackson rode that long ago day when he arrived in this country. The creation of the diesel locomotives began the decline of the hotel; perhaps it would have struggled on, however, if not for the fire. Jackson did not know. He was sad for the deaths of the woman and the girls and the dog, lost in the fire, but he was not sorry the hotel was gone. At that point it was a shadow of its former self, and the sight of it always filled him with pain.

Jackson and River broke through the trees as the train was on the final approach to Findlay. He saw the young woman stumble and fall as she ran down the tracks. She righted herself and began to wave frantically at the train. The light of the day had faded to a blue gray wash, shapes now dim and indiscernible. The train would not be able to stop in time if she did not move from the tracks. If they even saw her.

Jackson hurried out of his snowshoes and said, "Stay," to his dog, then he ran toward the young woman with everything he had.

The train whistle blew, and Jackson heard the scream of the brakes; they saw her there, in the far beam of the headlight. She continued to stand on the tracks, continued to wave at the train. She looked over her shoulder and saw Jackson right before he crashed into her and sent them both flying into the snow at the side of the rails. She yelled and screamed and kicked at him as he pinned her down and held her.

"They cannot stop!" he yelled above the screaming and the rumbling of the train. "The train cannot stop quickly! You would have been hit. I am not trying to hurt you; I wish you no harm. No harm!"

She pulled in deep breaths, her chest heaving.

"They are stopping," he said. "We can get you help. They will help."

"I saw you," she said when at last she could speak. Jackson knew she was not talking about this day on the hill, but that evening in the fall, when he'd looked down upon the camp and she had seen him there.

"I know," he said. "I did not mean to frighten you. I did not know what to do."

She was going to begin the questions, Jackson could sense. The train had halted and he heard running footsteps coming toward them.

"Have you hurt your head?" he asked. He could see some blood on her forehead, half hidden by her hair.

"I don't think so," she said. "I hit a branch, I think, when I fell."

"You are very lucky," Jackson said.

A man took shape from out of the darkness. "All right here? Are you both all right?"

Jackson pulled himself into a crouching position. "The young lady—she needs assistance."

"What's happened?" The man knelt by the woman. "Are you hurt?"

She began to sob and could not respond. Jackson said, "I don't think she is badly hurt, but she had a fall. It's her husband. He has died, on the hill of the dead horses, about a mile from the tracks."

"Accident?"

Jackson nodded. "I think he has done something to himself. Some accident."

"You're Jackson Keats, aren't you?

"Yes."

"Well I'll be damned. Harry Harbour's old friend."

"Yes."

"All right. Let's see what we can do here, about this situation." More figures were coming down the side of the train. Jackson stood and began to walk back to River Blue while the train men talked to the young lady.

He was planning to slip off into the woods when one of the train men yelled, "Hey! Mr. Keats! Emily here would like for you to walk her back home and wait with her until the troopers arrive. You all right with that?"

Jackson stepped back toward the circle of light surrounding the small gathering beside the train. The young lady was standing now, and she looked at him through the dark. "Yes," Jackson said.

SOPHIA PETERSEN
EARLY WINTER 1927

THERE IS A STORY I DID not know, until my last day on the island. A story my mother did not tell me, one which came to me as a strong fist slammed into my stomach and as strong hands that wrapped themselves around my neck and I thought, This is how I die. Now they want me dead.

I did not understand the story at first, the bits that came flying out at me like shards of glass from the mouth of my attacker. It started, of course, with these words:

"Whore! Whore! Whore!" A hit between each exclamation of the word.

I did not believe what Father Mikhail had told me, that my mother had signed over our home to the church. She would have told me of that, though I was slowly realizing she did not tell me everything.

I did all I could to avoid Father Mikhail, yet he would find me. I walked Peter to school every day, then roamed the forest and the beaches until it was time to go back to the school and pick him up. In the non-school times Peter was with me, always, unless he was invited to the homes of friends which I could not deny him. I had learned to finish the sewing ahead of time and deliver it to the church before Father Mikhail could have a chance to return for it.

"Here is the sewing," I would tell Mrs. Nicholai, whose wide wild eyes recoiled at the sight of me. "He does not need to come to get it."

I was telling her something. And I knew there was a secret understanding between us. She knew, and she wanted to protect him from himself.

Often on days when there was no school Peter and I stayed in the woods, sleeping beneath such shelter as we could build with sticks and branches. Peter loved those days and believed we did it for the fun of it, because we had no parents and could do as we chose, though sometimes he cried for his mother or complained of the cold and wanted to go home to a nice warm bed. I could not explain to him, the fear I now felt in my own home. How every sound—the creak of the wind on the old boards, a small creature scurrying past—sent such fear through me. Peter and I continued to sleep on the floor beneath the big front window, close to the wall so I could hear all sounds and not be seen, the table in the kitchen pushed up against the door. Always there remained the question, what would I do, if Father Mikhail came at such a time?

Or the one he sent to beat me that first time, who came again that last night, who waited for me inside the house, hidden.

Peter had been invited by a friend to stay over. It was not anything to do with Mrs. Nicholai, but a real friend. I said it would be all right. I was not going to let anyone rob Peter of a normal life. I knew that Father Mikhail was in Juneau for a conference. It had been two years since the first beating. I did not feel I had to worry.

Regardless, I did not like to be in the house without Peter, so I visited Mr. Wassily until it was near dark. I hurried home as darkness came. As soon as I walked in the door I was tossed against the wall.

I bent over and tried to protect my stomach. I did not and do not know how I feel about this child inside of me; I have only known to protect it, that it is innocent of what Father Mikhail has done to me. Then my hair was grabbed, and my head yanked back, and my flaying arms were kicked by booted feet. "If you knew! If you knew! If you knew what you carried you would not want to live!"

Despite the pain, despite my fear that I would be killed, I began to think. What is he saying, and why?

There was a cut in my forehead, near the hairline, and blood ran down my face and into my eyes. It all began to feel like a dream, and I had turned into a broken rag doll being tossed and tumbled and kicked and punched. Time became thick like heavy syrup and still I tried to think. What was I missing? Despite my efforts to hide my sickness from Father Mikhail, he had caught me one morning, vomiting into the bushes by the house. He looked at me and walked away, saying nothing, and a chill ran through me. What could he expect? I had done well, the past two years since the first rape, evading and escaping, yet there were times he would catch me. Peter's schooling became my undoing, along with his visits with his friends, because I could not take those things away from him. No matter how many ways I found to walk out of the village, they were not enough. Father Mikhail would lie in wait for me, like a wolf. What could he expect?

I could not refuse him. He claimed ownership of our home, and there was no one to challenge him. The only money Peter and I had now was the money from the sewing, and there would never be enough for us to use to run away, though I dreamed of that always. Me and Peter. Away.

Amid the horror of the beating, I felt myself rising above it, as if my soul left my body so I could observe and I could think. What was so terrible about this child inside of me? Why was this child different from Peter, of whom Father Mikhail was so obviously fond?

I remembered. It came to me as if sent, a whisper of knowledge from deep in the past. My mother, perhaps, reaching out from beyond her lonely grave to tell me what she should have. I do not know. I remembered: a rare thing, a photograph of the members of the church, gathered to celebrate the arrival of Father Mikhail. He stood in the center of the gathering, a young, handsome man in his holy garb. My mother and her family were in that group, my mother so lovely at only fifteen, her smile so bright and beautiful, her face turned toward the handsome priest whose hand rested upon her shoulder.

"I loved somebody once."

"The young fisherman, Mama?"

She would not say yes, she would not say no. The young fisherman did exist; his name was Percy Petrovitch, and he was indeed lost to the sea with several other men of the village, including Ilian

Nicholai's father. I remember going with my mother to put flowers on his grave, his being among the bodies that the wind blew to shore.

"Everything would have been all right," she said once, "if he had lived."

Because he was my father, I had always believed. At that moment, when this man that I had known my entire life was doing his best to kill the baby inside of me, I realized what my mother meant. He would have been a father to me, that young blond-haired boy, barely older than my mother. But my father was not who he was.

"Abomination!" my would-be murderer proclaimed. "You carry an abomination inside you!"

And then I knew. Father Mikhail was my father. And now he was the father of the baby I carried. My abomination.

In these moments of happiness with Jackson, I sharply remember this in sudden thrusts, as if a knife slips through my body, slicing and destroying. We have leapt over a sea of obstacles, Jackson and I, but there are monsters in the water that I have not shown him. The truth of my family, and of his.

It has been too many days since we have seen each other, Jackson and I, and perhaps that is a blessing as I can delay telling him that truth. With Nellie June gone, I have only had time for the laundry in the daylight hours and could not make an excuse with Mrs. Johnson to leave. Once when I came up out of the door to the basement on the side of the hotel, he was there nearby. My heart jolted with life at the sight of him.

"I have been busy in the laundry," I said as he came closer.

"It is all right," Jackson said. "I have managed to talk with Mrs. Grant, and she will buy some furs."

"Thank you, Jackson."

"Do not—" he began and paused. "Do not thank me, Sophia."

His look was such that I would not argue. I knew Mrs. Johnson planned to take a day to stay home with her child when her husband was not able to, and I told Jackson I would meet him at the end of that day.

"I have snowshoed a trail for you, up to the hill of the dead horses," he said. "It will make it easier for you to get there."

I opened my mouth to thank him; his face told me not to, and I stopped the words. I would let him have what it was he needed from that, and when the chance arrived, I knew I would fly on my feet up to the hill to meet him there.

CHAPTER TWELVE

EMILY WELLS
EARLY WINTER 1974

"THE SCAR ON YOUR FACE," I said. In the light of the fire I could see it there, the slight curve of a haphazard slash, from his left eye to the corner of his mouth, so thick his dense beard could not shield it from view, and that one wounded eye, not quite right. He had built a fire near where Thomas remained in the chair as we waited for help. We needed to leave him as he was, Jackson—that was his name, Jackson—explained; the death would need investigating, even though the cause was obvious. So he built the fire and brought up blankets and the camping chairs from by the table that Thomas and I had sat in together only days ago, and with River Blue between us we kept vigil on this quiet hill of death.

He touched his face. "It is a long story."

Most stories are, aren't they? When you peel back the layers, lift the covers, peer around the corners. All of us walk around with the stories of our lives trailing along behind and circling around us, always there in everything we do, every thought we think and decision made and action taken. We are an accumulation of our stories, of our parents' stories, and they of theirs and so it goes, our other DNA.

"I don't think we're going anywhere," I said. I felt remarkably clear; it must have been the shock. I felt as sharp and bright as the dark, starry sky above us. While the days to come would be thick with a haze of confusion and sorrow, that night I was there in the moment.

"The story ends on this hill," he said.

Of course it would. This bloody hill. "It has something to do with the"—even in my grief I recognized the word "skeleton" would be insensitive; how could I ever think of Thomas as that, as nothing but bones?—"the grave," I managed to say. I focused back on the now. Perhaps the night could last forever, the three of us on the hill, Thomas gone yet not, frozen in the moment that was his last.

"Yes."

"Someone who meant something to you. That's why you were protecting the grave."

"Yes."

"I'm—I'm sorry. We didn't know, we—"

"It's all right. Do not worry about that. Sophia was kind and she would forgive you."

"Sophia."

He nodded. "Sophia Petersen."

"Someone you loved?"

"Yes."

"Like I love Thomas?"

"Yes."

"Someone you still love."

"Yes."

"How did she die?"

He looked past Thomas to the edge of the hill. "She fell," he said. "Like I did."

"Yes." He paused, then said, "Only she jumped, because my father had beat her and was about to stab her with a knife."

"Oh my God."

"Yes."

"Oh my God."

"Do you want me to continue?"

I had to think. Then I heard Thomas' voice, *Hell yeah—family dysfunction. How many people know that story?* and I said, "Yes."

"All right." He waited, then tipped his face toward the stars.

"I did not always love Sophia, though I had known her nearly all my life. We were from the same village, you see, in the Southeast part of the state. The place where it rains almost daily, though sometimes in the winter it snows. We were both outcasts of sorts, and I think that is what brought us together: my father was a simple fisherman, who fell in love with a girl from the village. The village was Russian Orthodox, you see, and very strict. The priest was a man called Father Mikhail, who was young when my father was, and new to the village. In order for my father to marry this girl that he loved, he had to convert or he would not have her parents' approval and the blessing of the church. My father had been orphaned at a young age and longed for nothing more than belonging. He converted wholeheartedly and won his bride. When my sister was born, when I was two years old, she and my mother both died in the childbirth. That happened more in those days than it does now. While growing up, I worried my father resented my presence, because some would say they could see my mother in my face, and as at times my father was very strict with me. Yet there were moments of kindness and closeness. I never felt my father to be anything except a good man, even when we disagreed.

"My father stayed with the church, despite—or perhaps because of—his terrible loss. My father depended on the kindness of the women of the village to help with me when I was young, and Father Mikhail made certain we were treated well. But everything comes with a price, does it not? Perhaps my father did not know what his price would be; perhaps. Even if he did foresee it, he would have determined that what he gained—and me by extension—was worth the sacrifice of his soul.

"Now Sophia, she was the daughter of a whore. Or so I was always told. She and her mother lived in the wind on an unkind rise above the beach several miles from the village; their house, built by Sophia's grandfather, was roomy enough but the walls leaked when the wind blew and the roof leaked when it rained—and the wind was often blowing, and the sky was always raining. Who Sophia's father was no one claimed to know for certain; there was a boy from the village who had loved Sophia's mother and drowned at sea, but some said the timing was not right for him to have been the father. There had also been a young fisherman from Petersburg passing through, who Sophia's mother had been seen with, whose boat left our harbor in short order and was never seen again. He became the likely contender when Sophia's mother could no longer conceal her condition. Was it rape, or desire? Whatever occurred, the child was conceived out of wedlock, and that meant sin. Sophia's mother was shunned and doomed to live her life on the outskirts of the village.

"As he had done with my father and me, Father Mikhail watched over Sophia and her mother. They were allowed to come to church on Sunday and were allowed to purchase what they needed from the shops. If anyone turned them down or was unkind to them, Father Mikhail would set it to rights. They were not treated badly; however, they were avoided. Except, of course, by Father Mikhail.

"Now this Sophia and I—when we began to know each other as children, we became friends. Though maybe we did not like each other so much at first—that is the way with children, is it not? When we became older, we became different kinds of friends. We fell in love, like in the way the sea loves the sand and the stars love the sky, and talks grew between us of how we would someday marry. By that point Sophia had a younger brother, Peter, though no one was concerned who Peter's father was. Was it the Petersburg fisherman, back again, was it rape or was it not? Surely the village must have talked, though I think they felt that since Sophia's mother was a known whore, what difference did one more child born of sin make? Once purity is gone, it is lost forever.

"Then Sophia's mother fell sick and died. I think, now is the time that we can marry. Sophia needs me; Peter needs a home, and my father and I had a house full of empty space for far too long. We could be a family—Sophia, Peter, my father and me. It was something I longed for as much as my father had, when he was young and orphaned. Sophia's mother could not be buried in the cemetery. Sophia could not forgive that and was enraged by it. She ground her teeth in anger and kicked the walls of her house. Peter grew frightened. One day Sophia was beaten and she blamed Father Mikhail for this and for worse, far worse—she said her mother had been his slave nearly all her life, and that he had done unspeakable things to this woman who could not be buried in the cemetery. In the next thing that happened, a young man named Ilian Nicholai confessed to the assault against Sophia. He was properly punished, forgiven, and sent away. Yet Sophia's story did not change. Sophia would not change. Even though I begged her to confess her lie and seek forgiveness and allow us to be married—to *be*, to let us be who we were meant to be, together, Sophia would not relent. She would not let it rest. We became like the waves pounding the shore or the wind bending the trees. There is only so much that the shore or the trees can stand. Only so much before things begin to break. We broke. Because, in the beginning, I had stood by Sophia against Father Mikhail, my relationship with the village was broken as well; at my father's urging I too was sent away, and that is how I came here. Sophia, unrelentingly unrepentant, remained behind, and in essence belonged to Father Mikhail, and the history of what once was, played itself out once again. Like her mother, Sophia became pregnant with Father Mikhail's child. Unlike with her mother, Father Mikhail decided the child must never be born. Father Mikhail had committed a great sin, you see, for Sophia was his own child. Sophia was beaten within an inch of her life and by some miracle she managed to flee, and the village believed she drowned. By another miracle—which is more coincidence than miracle—Sophia came here, and so we were reunited, unhappily at first but after a short time we began to find each other again.

"Then my father arrived. He was not here to see me. He was here to find Sophia, and to kill the child within her, because I mistakenly said in a letter to him, before I knew she was really here, that I thought I had seen her."

He looked away from me. I saw such pain on his face. He fell quiet and in that quiet I heard the howling silence that was screaming into the void where Thomas' voice once rang.

"How did you feel about the baby?" I asked, to get him talking again.

"I did not know about it. Sophia did not tell me, only until she lay dying. I would have accepted such a child."

"Oh. I'm sorry."

"It is all right. I continue. I am almost to the end. Sophia and I, in those last days, met here, on this hill, on days when she could be free from the hotel laundry where she worked. We made plans to rescue Peter, to bring him here. Winter was in its early stages, and there was snow on the ground. As I approached the hill that one day, I saw her in the snow on the ground and a man stood over her, beating her. Kicking her, in her stomach. I was wearing snowshoes as I ran, and I tackled that man to the ground. He had a knife, and it slashed across my face, and there is the scar you see.

"Sophia yelled, 'Leave him! Leave him alone!'

"He started to stab me again, in my side, and our eyes met, and we recognized one another. He threw me off of him and ran for Sophia. My feet and my snowshoes were tangled and twisted and I was blinded by pain. My dog, Snowy Day, who had bit at my father's legs, stood beside me and I grabbed onto him and he tried to pull me up. Sophia was running through the snow, staggering, my father after her. She was going toward the steep edge of the front of the hill. I called to her.

"I knew what she was doing. I said, 'No, Sophia, no! No! No!'

"She lurched forward, my father stumbling toward her. She reached the edge and turned to face him. He lifted his knife. Then she turned her back to him and fell into the wind, and at that same moment a shot rang out from somewhere behind me and struck my father and he dropped down into the snow."

"What?" The words were unexpected. "Someone shot your father?" I knew this wasn't the important part—the important part was Sophia, tumbling through the air to the bottom of the hill, but I wasn't entirely sure I had heard it right.

"Yes," he said. "My father was shot dead."

"By who?"

"The hotel boy."

"The hotel boy?"

"Harry. Harry who worked at the hotel. Harry who works on the train now, as a conductor."

"Oh my God," was all I could manage to say.

And so we passed that most awful night.

HARRY HARBOUR
EARLY WINTER 1974

IN THE END, I GUESS YOU could say it was Jackson's story, well, his to tell at any rate. He'd been there, in Sophia's life, long before the rest of us, and he stayed, in the quiet of those hills, long after the rest of us moved on. Do you ever really move on, though, after something like that? I never did, hence the fact that I ride past the place of my undoing as many times in a week as I can. I hope Cora did, before she died. None of it was her fault, after all. She didn't want anything except a good caribou hunt and look what she got. I'll bet she never guessed in a million years I'd cause her so much trouble. I'd have thought it would be the opposite, and I'm pretty sure she thought so, too.

Trouble or not, and setting that line between right and wrong aside, sometimes you know what's got to be done in a certain situation and you just do it, regardless of the consequences.

That's what she always told me, in the years that followed: "You saw what needed to be done, Harry, and you did it."

And I'd say, "Cora, you did the same." That's how we got through the burden of the secret we carried with us through the years. Purely guilty people, I don't know how they manage. It was hard enough doing the wrong thing for the right reason. Hard enough.

EARLY WINTER 1927

WHEN CORA AND I WOKE THAT morning, on that caribou hunt all those years ago, it was dark and the air was bitter cold. Cora was as angry as anyone that we'd been skunked, even though for a small stretch of time we were within arm's reach of more caribou than we could ever want. That moment, when they surrounded our tent on their way through our camp under the light of the moon, was more magical a moment than I had ever known. And I'd felt closer to God than I'd ever thought possible. We'd risen as soon as it began to get light, packed up camp and headed after them. A herd on the move is not an easy thing to catch, however. We tried; God knows we tried.

After a day and a half of not getting them properly in our sights Cora said, "We'd best head home, Harry. We'll get so far out there we'll never make it back."

I didn't argue. We were well out on the high tundra at that point, with nothing except endless white miles in front of us. And even though I thought I might impress Sonja with a sled full of meat, after my religious experience of being in a tent in the middle of a herd I was more reluctant than ever about killing any of them. It took us several days of steady snowshoeing in the weighted whiteness of that massive world, and after a while of it even Cora found her quiet. I'd often wondered what she did, in the woods all alone, and I'd figured she must talk to herself or talk to the birds as I couldn't imagine her as silent. She was quiet on that trip, especially on the journey home. Could be she just ran out of things to talk about that she'd thought I'd be interested in, though that never stopped her before.

On that last morning, however, her tongue worked again. We were sitting beside the morning fire drinking bad boiled coffee when she said, "Your girl gained some weight since I last saw her, Harry."

I nearly dropped my mug and managed to burn my fingers in the process. "What? My girl?"

"Sonja, you know—Sonja Antonov—though I really doubt there's any such person."

I clenched my jaw and tried not say anything sharp, and I missed the quiet Cora of the day before. "Why—why would you say something like that, Cora?"

She looked at me, lifted her foot and kicked a log deeper into the fire. "About the girl's weight or about who she really is?"

"Well both, I suppose."

"You don't fool me, Harry. I know you've been trying to sort out the puzzle yourself for the last month and a half. I know that, despite the fact I haven't been here most of that time. Because I know you, and because I know something about human nature, and because I could see straight away we didn't know what that girl's story was and probably didn't know who she was. She's not a good liar and not a good faker, Harry. Do you know what I think about it?"

"What, Cora?"

"I think it's none of our business."

"You're the one bringing it up," I said.

"Just because something is none of your business doesn't mean you're not curious about it. I've been imagining all kinds of things, and it all comes down to this in my thinking: she's afraid of someone."

I nodded. "Yeah—I think so too. I saw it the first day she arrived. She's scared to death of Jackson, and I can't figure out why."

I said it even though I knew better now as she certainly wasn't afraid of him when she held him. Cora's coffee mug was on its way to her lips when she stopped and stared across the fire at me with a look that only said I had managed to severely disappoint her.

"Harry," she said, "I do so hate to tell you this, but there's something you should know. She's not afraid of Jackson Keats—far from it. She's in love with him."

It took me a moment to respond. Had that been so obvious all along? "I know that," I said quietly. "I only said she was afraid of him because when she first arrived here, it seemed like she was. Guess I was wishing it was so."

"You can't change the truth of something by saying it's different from what it is," Cora said, "though it's been tried many times, by folks both big and small."

I nodded, looked into the fading fire then up past our camp to the glow of the coming dawn and I heard in my head the sound of all those hooves around us, like blood flowing through the veins of the earth.

"Before you lose the plot, Harry, it's also pretty obvious that something bad happened between them and that love's been stretched to its limits," she said, her patience for a proper response from me dead and gone. "I wouldn't lose hope. Sometimes when love gets bent like that you can't put it back into shape. So bide your time and see what happens; either way you've got to let this one play itself out."

I nodded and took a pull of my coffee that somehow tasted better now. "I suppose you're right."

"I suppose I am," she said. We sat quiet for a few minutes. I could sense how my new found stoicism had her on edge.

"Why don't you come back to Anchorage with me, see your

folks for a while?" she asked. "Or better yet, come all the way to Seward. I could use your input on the roadhouse."

I nodded. "Might do that," I said. I stood and began the process of breaking camp.

It was afternoon when I felt the earth tipping down toward the river. We went up hills and down those same hills only to climb up the next one and do it all over again. The spruce and birch were coming back, and we began to see things like fox tracks and weasel tracks in the snow. I'd let most of my earlier talk with Cora slip from my shoulders like a coat that didn't feel right and kept focused on things playing themselves out. Stories are full of surprises, aren't they? Little did I know I was headed toward the surprise of my life. I had Cora's 30.06 strapped across my chest and realized I was finally used to the feel of it. Maybe Cora would make a man out of me after all, dead caribou or no.

We'd just come down one hill and were making our way up the next when I realized we were getting close to the hotel and were actually on our way up the backside of the hill I'd taken Sonja and Nellie June to, the "hill of the dead horses" as I would always think of it now. As I flashed on the moment when Sonja lingered too close to the edge, we crested the rim and there she was, Sonja, falling and stumbling toward that same very edge. A dark-haired man—Jackson?—was rushing toward her, something in his hand that glinted in the last of the sun. Was he going to stab her? Before my brain could attempt to answer I saw another man on his back in the snow, and even from the distance and in the bad light I could see it was Jackson there, and I could see the blood all over his face. He was yelling as he struggled to lurch himself up and forward, Snowy Day stoically beside him.

No, Sophia, no! No! No!

I felt Cora's arm across my chest, like the arms of a railroad crossing, saying effectively, *Stop*. I didn't even know I was beginning to move and was pulling the rifle up over my head.

In a flash Sophia—I knew in that moment that's who she really was— reached the edge of the hill and turned and faced the man who was coming at her with the knife. She was bent over slightly and held her stomach with one arm, holding out the other as if she could stop him. The man raised his arm high, she straightened and turned, and with a sideways step away from Cora I lifted the rifle and fired.

"Holy God, Harry," was all Cora managed to say.

I'd just shot a man in the back.

And when he fell, Sophia was no longer there. I began to run, but I knew that she was gone.

JACKSON KEATS
EARLY WINTER 1927

WHILE THE HOTEL BOY STOOD OPEN mouthed near the treacherous edge of the hill, seeking a way down, his aunt knelt in the snow near the body of Jackson's father, to see if anything could be done. Jackson knew there was nothing; he knew his father had died, and during those few moments Jackson managed to make his way past them both and rush to Sophia, holding onto brittle brush and rocks and spindly trees until he slid through the snow beside her and gently brushed the snow from her face.

She breathed with a jagged sound, and there was blood in her mouth, and he sensed she would not last long. Up above he heard the shouts of Harry and his aunt and knew his lack of answer would bring them down.

"Jackson."

"I am here, Sophia."

"It is not raining."

"No, it is not."

"I would have liked that, to learn to live with the snow instead of the rain."

"How are you, Sophia? What do you feel?"

"Nothing. I feel nothing Jackson. I should, shouldn't I?"

"I do not know." Carefully he moved her arm so he could hold her hand. With his other he pressed his scarf against his face, to keep his blood from falling onto her.

"Your father—is he coming?"

"No. You are safe now, Sophia."

Her lips struggled into a small, shaky smile. Then her eyes looked wildly around and Jackson said, "Look at me, Sophia; only look at me. There is help coming; Harry—Harry is here and is climbing down the hill and his crazy aunt is right behind him. We have help, Sophia. Help."

"What was that noise? Right as I jumped. There was a sound so loud."

"It was nothing."

"Your father—oh, look at you! Your face! Did he hurt you, too, my Jackson?"

"I will be all right, Sophia."

"Is he coming? The knife, Jackson, the knife—"

"He is not coming now. Your friend Harry stopped him."

"Harry? Harry is wonderful."

"Yes, Sophia."

"Please tell him I am sorry."

"You have no need to be sorry, Sophia."

"I am sorry I did not tell him my name."

"I will tell him, Sophia."

"Will you tell him about me?"

"Yes."

"Peter must be safe."

"He will be safe."

"You must promise me Jackson."

"I promise, Sophia."

"If I am dead, he will be safe."

"The village already thinks you are dead, Sophia."

"Your father will tell them."

"He will not say a word."

"Won't he?"

"No, Sophia, he will not be going home."

"Oh," she said. "The noise. Harry."

"Yes."

"I am sorry, Jackson! Your father!"

"He chose to hurt you, Sophia. He chose what was wrong over what was right."

"Peter," she said again. "Peter's secret must be safe! Father Mikhail will not seek to harm him, as long as the secret is safe. You see, Peter is his son. His son! No one must know."

Had Jackson known that, somewhere inside? "The secret is safe, Sophia."

"Good, good." She closed her eyes, opened them again. "Do not tell Peter what has happened to me. Oh please. Or that he is Father Mikhail's son. I do not want him to know what happened! His life would be ruined, always!"

"I will make sure Peter has a normal life, Sophia. I will figure it out, somehow."

She looked up at the sky. "It is a wonderful feeling, to fly."

"Sophia—"

"Do not blame the hill, Jackson. I love the hill! When I am dead bury me here, Jackson, please—where I can watch the trains and the hotel and all the goings on and you can come visit me, you and Snowy Day."

"Sophia, I—"

"I know I am dying, Jackson."

"Sophia!" He pressed her hand to his lips.

"It is all right. How could I have lived?"

"With me," Jackson said. "I would not leave you ever again. I am so sorry that I ever did!"

"The baby is Father Mikhail's!"

"I know. I know that he is Peter's father." But she had not meant that, had she?

She shook her head. "This baby. Inside of me. Why they wanted

it dead. Your father, and Father Mikhail. I was going to tell you—
truly I was."

Jackson looked at the blood spreading across her skirt.

"As is Peter," she said.

"I know."

"As am I."

The air stopped in his lungs. "Oh—Sophia. No."

"Yes."

"It does not matter. It would not make a difference, not to me,
Sophia—"

"Jackson, when you fly in the wind, nothing matters." She
began to blink, and her breathing became rapid. "The beach," she
whispered.

"I remember."

"We are there again, aren't we?"

"Yes."

And then she was still.

THERE WAS NO TIME FOR HIS PAIN. Harry cried out at the sight of
her and his aunt said, "Hold onto yourself, Harry, there's not time
for that now. We're going to lose the light in a few short hours, and
we have to decide what to do here."

"I'll go to the hotel. They'll call it in," Harry said, his mitten
between his teeth as he talked so he would not scream.

"Harry, you're in for a rough road now, I need you to understand that," the aunt said.

The hotel boy nodded. Jackson said, "No. No. We cannot tell
anyone what has happened." His hand still gripped Sophia's. His
father was dead on the hill. Jackson had been cut lose, as if he too
walked off the edge of the earth and flew through the sky. "There
is a story that must not be told. There are terrible things Sophia's
brother Peter must not know. If we tell this part of the story, it will
all have to be revealed and Peter's life will be ruined, and I do not
know what the priest will do to him."

"What priest?" the aunt asked.

"He is Peter's father. He may cause him harm. He fears the truth."

"The man on the hill?"

"The man on the hill is my father."

The hotel boy fell to his knees in the snow. "Your father?" he wailed. "Oh God! Why? What was happening? What was he doing?"

Jackson shook his head.

"I thought he was trying to kill her!"

"Harry," the aunt said. "Harry, keep calm."

"He did not care about her life," Jackson said. "I do not blame you, Harry." He looked at Harry then back at Sophia. "He killed her. Even if she had survived this fall, I do not think she would have survived the beating." They were silent for a moment, save for Harry's stifled sobs.

"Jackson," Cora said. "I am so very sorry. We have to sort this out and decide on a course of action. We need to report your father's and Sonja—Sophia's—deaths right away or not report them at all. I don't know how that's all going to look for Harry, shooting a man in the back, but he's a good boy and I know he'll accept the consequences."

"No," Jackson said. "He should not have to. I would have killed my father myself, if I had brought my gun today. He came to— to harm Sophia. It was him, him all along. My own father." He breathed past a choking feeling in his throat and repositioned his scarf against his wound where pain throbbed thunderously. He added, "There is another life to consider. Peter. If these deaths become known, it will stir up things that should be left quiet. It was her wish—her dying wish. I must do this for her, protect Peter."

"I'm not afraid of any priest," Cora said. "I am afraid for Harry. This is a tangled mess, and hard to prove things either way."

"I will take my father home with me, and bury him," Jackson said.

"What about Sophia?" the aunt asked, and Harry let out a noise. "She told me, just before. She wants to be buried on this hill."

The aunt looked hard at Jackson for a moment, then looked up the steep face of the hill. The hotel boy moaned and gasped as if for air. Her eyes turned to him, then she looked back at Jackson. "If we're going to do this, they can never, ever be found," Cora said. "Not in our lifetimes."

Jackson nodded.

"Once we do one single thing to cover this up, we can't turn back."

"I know this."

"We'd best get busy then," Cora said. "Harry, go back up top and empty out one of the sleds and bring it down. Grab the first aid kit so we can tend to Jackson's wound. Are you doing all right?" Cora asked Jackson as Harry rose to leave.

He did not reply.

"I mean, your wound. Are you doing all right with it?"

"I will survive," he said, knowing there were ways in which he would not.

HARRY AND HIS AUNT HAD BOTH a shovel and an ax, and they picked a spot on the hill where the view was wonderful and which was not too near where Jackson's father had died and Sophia had jumped. They brought Sophia on one of the two sleds up to the spot and kept her close while they worked, chopping through the frozen ground until they found the softer layers underneath. Jackson knew he was now bound to the hotel boy and his crazy aunt for the remainder of their lives; Harry who had tried to save Sophia, and Cora who was now trying to save all who were left. There were candle lamps with the camping gear, and they worked by their light and by the light of a cold November moon. Cora said a prayer of sorts as Jackson and Harry lowered Sophia into the dark quiet grave, and it was done.

TOMORROW, IN THE THIN GRAY LIGHT of dawn, when Jackson and Snowy Day arrived home, Jackson would tie the sled carrying his father to a nearby tree and leave his morbid load outside. The cabin would not be warm when they would enter, but the air would hold the faint remains of yesterday's fire. Yesterday. Jackson would look at his cot and remember waking there. He had been his old self, only yesterday, the person he had been before the trouble in the village. He had recognized how he was that old self, and the stirrings of happiness had swirled inside him. It was like a dream; the person, a ghost who would now look at him in this new day through the veil of one day gone.

SOPHIA PETERSEN
EARLY WINTER 1927

I DON'T KNOW WHY I WRITE, EXCEPT that it is all I can do while I hide and wait. He is here, he is here, he is here. Oh heaven help me now.

I must tell Jackson, and I must trust him and he must trust me.

I saw him with my own eyes, stepping off the train. Like Jackson yet not, Jackson must favor his mother, I have always thought, with his dark dancing eyes and the dimples in his cheeks when he smiles. Even so, I am sure others will see the resemblance—the thick dark hair now laced with silver, his broad shoulders and strong hands. He carried a small bag and pushed past the others on the platform to enter the hotel. My wits came back to me in time to slip around the corner and press myself against the wall. I had to act quickly.

I hoped perhaps he has come only to visit Jackson; I have learned that is not so. Mrs. Grant caught me sneaking back into the basement and asked, "Sonja, do you know a Sophia Petersen?" I shook my head and hoped my face did not betray the lie.

She said a man had gotten off the train looking for a young lady by that name. He had also told her he was Jackson's father, and she told me how she assured him Jackson lived near the hotel some-where though she didn't know exactly where, and that if Harry was here, she would have had him show the man the way.

I excused myself as quickly as I could, and came here to the laundry to hide, stopping in my room only for my journal. Today is the day Mrs. Johnson is at home with her sick child. I have done the work that needed doing.

Someone may take Jackson's father to my room, if he describes me to others; someone might say, "Oh, you mean Sonja. She must be in her room; follow me."

And I would be caught, there in that little box.

I have torn pages from my book and written three hasty letters: one to Mrs. Johnson, that I will leave here in the laundry, saying how very sorry I am that I must leave; one for Jackson, telling him what has happened, in case I do not see him today on the hill of the dead horses like we had planned; and one for Harry, who I will ask to deliver Jackson's letter for me in the event that I have gone. Harry continues on the hunting, and I will leave the letters in his room. I also asked him to tell Nellie June goodbye on my behalf; I did not write to her as I did not know what to say. I have lied to them all.

If I could ask Jackson to come get his father and take him back to his cabin, that would be the best; I could wait until morning and leave on the train. For now, I must find my way out of the hotel and go to meet Jackson.

All I have ever wanted. I do not know how to finish that sentence, because it changes and shifts with the course of life. When I lost my grandfather, all I wanted was for him to return; when my mother was dying, all I wanted was to be able to save her. When I realized I loved Jackson, all I wanted was to be with him; after my mother died, all I wanted was for me and Peter to be safe from Father Mikhail. I have wanted so many things since that earlier time. I wanted to die, after that first rape; I wanted to walk out into the ocean and vanish into the sea. If not for Peter, I think I would have done so, the shame I felt burned painfully inside of me. But when I was beaten for the second time and went out on the water in the little boat, I felt how I wanted only to simply survive, to make it to another day, and in the days since, I lived for the hope of someday to see Peter again. Then with Jackson, on the hill, the second time we met there. How I kissed him again, and how he pulled me up against him and kissed me back, and I felt again all the good things for him, all the wanting him and loving him and longing for him. I do not know now if I could leave him behind, after he brings Peter here. At the same time I do not know how I could look him in the face, once I tell him everything that has happened to me. But I want to try.

To be free, that is also something I have wanted, to do as I choose. I choose. But even in the womb I was not meant to be, and everything was already determined for me. Can one change such determinations by simply choosing to?

I will try. For Jackson and for Peter. And for myself.

I must go. I will slip into my room for my coat and pray I can leave the hotel unseen.

CHAPTER THIRTEEN

EMILY WELLS
EARLY WINTER 1974

RAYMIE ARRIVED A FEW HOURS AFTER the Alaska State Trooper helicopter made its abrasive appearance on the hill, the spinning blades slicing and beating the air. Jackson and I had been interviewed separately, the scene was extensively photographed, and when it became time to begin the process of removing Thomas from the hill I turned away and felt my face contract as I struggled not to wail. I closed my eyes and counted as I breathed. I opened my eyes and there was Raymie, cresting the hill. I floundered though the snow toward him and fell forward into his arms. He said nothing, simply held me, and I listened to the sounds of Thomas' departure from his beloved hill and let Raymie be my eyes. We stayed like that until the sound of the helicopter faded and left only the wind, which seemed to whisper hussshhhh as it blew past.

I could hear Jackson moving through the snow toward us. "I am Jackson Keats," he said to Raymie.

Raymie said nothing at first, then finally gasped, "What happened here?"

"I will tell you," Jackson said. "But she has been outside all night. Let us warm up the cabin, and see if she will rest, before she goes on the train."

I could feel Raymie nodding. He said, softly, "Come on, Emily, let's go down, okay? Let's get you warm. I'm here; I'll stay. I'll go with you, on the train. Oh my God."

I let him help me down the side of the hill, and he and Jackson built a fire in the cabin and put me in a chair up close to the stove and tried to stop my shaking with cups of hot tea. I dozed intermittently, each time waking bloody and raw with a start. River Blue sat stoically beside me, and in those moments of waking my eyes would search for his, my hand finding the warmth of his fur.

Somehow, when it was time, I went through the motions of stuffing fresh clothes into my bag, finding Thomas' wallet and taking that, too, in case the troopers needed anything in there.

I realized that someone had been in the cabin searching the small space, and when I asked, Jackson said, "The troopers sent a man in here, to see if they could find anything connected to what happened. I will put these things away for you."

"I'll do it," I said, and my eyes blurred as I started to grab Thomas' clothes and put them back in his duffle.

Raymie placed his hand on my shoulder. "We have to get down to the tracks, Emily, so we can get to Anchorage."

After a long moment I nodded and dropped the things that were in my hand. A tee shirt and a belt. I almost picked them back up, wanting to take everything with me, as Raymie gently guided me to the door.

Jackson went with us down to the tracks, all of us on snowshoes, which Raymie had strapped to my boots as if I were a child. My windows and packages were where Harry had helped me put them, and Jackson pulled the pile away from the tracks while Raymie stood close as we waited.

I knew I was cold though I couldn't really feel it, and it was dark by the time the train came, the bright headlight piercing the night. Raymie flagged it down then returned to my side as the train hissed and screeched to a stop.

"Oh, my dear Emily," Harry said as he and Raymie got me onto the train. "Come. I have a nice place for you to sit."

I looked fleetingly back at Jackson, a shadow in the dusk. I felt his eyes on me and I lifted my hand. Harry looked, too, and I wondered what silent messages passed between them as I remembered the story Jackson had told, a faraway dream that didn't seem real.

Harry led us to the back of the car where no one else was sitting, and we sat with our backs to the other passengers, and Harry brought us hot tea from the dining car and sat across from us when he could. I thought again of the story Jackson told, the two of them young men, a beautiful girl, a knife, and a gun. As quickly as it surfaced it fell away, and in the following days, as I tumbled down into the deep hole of grief and loss, it would repeat the process of surfacing and sinking, like a drowning person, and would never fully engage in my thoughts.

In Anchorage, we waited in the depot for Harry to get his car—something from the 50s, that on another day would have made me laugh—and he drove us to the hotel and spoke with the desk clerk. Raymie, with his arm tight around my shoulders, took the key Harry gave him and got me settled in the room where I crawled into bed with everything on except my boots. I turned toward the wall, only partially listening while Harry came and went and Raymie fell asleep in the big lounge chair beside the bed.

I felt like the bed was a raft, and I was floating through the dark in a great flood that had washed everything away. Among the many things I thought about in that river of night was a day when Thomas and I were splitting wood. It was bitterly cold, and to our delight we found that the wood split easier, and Thomas made a big show of lifting the splitting maul and bringing it down on the wood, each piece becoming two as the maul tore through its center.

We had smoked some pot Raymie had left with us, and we laughed ridiculously at the wood succumbing so easily to Thomas' touch. As I'd watched him my mind took a sharp turn to the tree we had killed, sawed into pieces and now were tearing through its middle.

"Think about it, Thomas," I'd said, trying to explain. "What if someone did that you?"

He did think about it, then bent down and kissed me, his cold nose on the side of mine.

"I hope it would be quick," he'd said, and we went back to laughing in the cold.

I am the wood, I thought that night in the hotel. I am the wood.

Our first day in Anchorage Raymie took me to the trooper station, where the trooper who spoke to us explained that Thomas would be autopsied. I wasn't family, at least not in the eyes of the law, and that meant I couldn't see him. I gave the troopers the contact information for Thomas' parents. I should wait to call them, the trooper said; the news would be delivered by Sacramento police officers, which was protocol. I couldn't even think about that— Thomas' poor mother. I should be the one to tell her. It would be possible that Thomas' father would find out first, given that he was a Sacramento police officer, and that felt unfair. I remember thinking all that, even though I was still on that raft in the flood. We went back to the hotel, and I crawled back into the bed and the rest of that day and another night passed as I tried not to think about Thomas being autopsied and what that might entail. There were people I should call and things I had to take care of, I knew that, but I could barely move.

"Emily, you have to eat," Raymie said the next morning. I had slept and light came in through the windows. "And you have messages, down at the front desk. Thomas' mother called you. And some other people—I can't remember who."

I sat up in the bed. "I'm going to have to go back there. To Findlay."

Raymie said, "You don't have to do anything, Emily, though I think you'll feel like you should."

"I'm going to have to leave the cabin."

"It will be there for you, whenever you come back."

I knew I could never live there, without Thomas.

I let Raymie order breakfast, and I got a little of it down. I talked to Thomas' mother, whose words were barely discernible amid her sobs. We managed to determine that she would have to be the one to make the arrangements to have Thomas' body shipped home, whenever they were done with the autopsy. I would come back as soon as I could.

I called my parents from the phone in the room, and I had to have Raymie tell them what happened. Those were dense days, where so little and yet so much occurred.

Harry came by to see us, and I decided to go back to Findlay on the Saturday train to pack up my and Thomas' things and close up the cabin, then return to Anchorage on the Sunday train and fly out to Sacramento. We had a late lunch with Harry in the hotel restaurant. I didn't want to, but I had to get out of that room that smelled so thickly of grief. The Anchorage day was bright and sharp—white snow and blue sky. It was ten below zero, Harry told me.

Someone had left a newspaper at the table next to us; I reached over for it and looked at it numbly. With a jolt I saw, in the lower right corner of the front page, Thomas' face. I made some kind of a noise—not quite a shriek and more than a gasp—and dropped the paper to the floor.

"Emily! What is it?" Raymie's hand wrapped around mine. I put my free hand to my mouth and breathed.

"I'm all right," I said after a minute. I felt like I had fallen through a hole in the ice, and now was suddenly back in the air. "The paper."

Raymie leaned over and picked it up. He spread it down on the table, and the three of us looked.

Singer Thomas Findlay Found Dead in Alaska

Beneath the headline was a column of type and a photo of Thomas, smiling at the camera as if the sight of it were a pleasant surprise. I did not read the story as Raymie and Harry took it in; I stared instead at the photograph, wondering if I could remember the day—was I there? —wondering how many days I had already forgotten.

"I didn't know that about Thomas, Emily," Harry said, and a cloud of both confusion and realization crossed Raymie's face.

"I was just—" Raymie began, and I knew he was remembering the night by the fire. He looked at me, a question in his eyes.

"We were starting over," I said. I looked quickly away, the grief rising. "God, we didn't make it very long, did we?"

Harry and Raymie both reached for me. I struggled against the wave of sorrow and swallowed it down. I had to do something. There was something I had to do.

That night, our last in the hotel room, I dug Jimmy's phone number out of my bag and called it every hour until he picked up.

"Emily! My God! What happened? It's all over the news down here. Oh God."

"You can't have the songs," I said. Raymie stirred in the chair and looked at me when the words began to fly out of my mouth. "None of them. You can't have a single one—not a one of them, Jimmy, and you have to pull 'Window.' It's even on the radio up here!"

"Emily, Emily, wait wait wait wait wait. Let's not talk about this right now. Thomas' lawyer contacted mine and let's let them handle it, okay? We can figure something out. Thomas' songs shouldn't disappear, Emily. They shouldn't."

"The songs are mine now, Jimmy, mine and Thomas' mother's! And I'm telling you no, right now, stop!"

"Emily, Emily, hush, hush—hush little lamb, I know you must be in such pain—"

He kept talking, his voice fading from my ear as I let the receiver fall to the floor. It was him. It was Jimmy. How had I not realized?

Shh . . . hush little lamb. Hush.

Raymie was on alert now, up out of the chair and standing near. He picked up the phone and looked at me questioningly. I grabbed it from his hand.

"Emily? Are you there?" Jimmy said.

"It was *you*," I said, calmer than I would have ever thought possible. "It was you, Jimmy! 'Hush little lamb.' Oh my God it was you!"

"I don't know what you're talking about—"

I hung up the phone. Raymie reached for my hand, and we stood there, breathing.

HARRY HARBOUR
EARLY WINTER 1974

"WHAT I DON'T UNDERSTAND, IS IF she was leaving, why did Sonja get on the train to Fairbanks? That would only take her farther away from getting home. She wanted to go to Seward, not Fairbanks!"

Nellie June hounded me for years after the incident on the hill, some instinct within her telling her that Sonja Antonov's abrupt departure didn't make sense. We'd gotten lucky, when all that awful happened, that Nellie June was already down in the village for her visit with her family. Otherwise, I'm not sure what we would have done, except maybe what we should have done to begin with: told the truth and dealt with the consequences. Cora kept saying we were also doing it for Peter, and hence for Sophia, but I knew too well she was trying her best to protect me and keep me from prison.

I'd said previously that this was Jackson's story. Maybe it's simply Sophia's—my story, Jackson's story, and also Cora's story from that awful day all revolved around Sophia and the harm that was done to her. The story went on long after she died, a sort of extended denouement, and it even reached its boney hand into the here and now and inserted itself into the story of Thomas Findlay and Emily Wells for one sharp, glaring moment before slipping back into the darkness of the past where I spend a lot of my time, remembering.

EARLY WINTER 1927

THAT NIGHT, AFTER WE'D BURIED SOPHIA and loaded Jackson's father onto the sled, Cora said, "Harry, you have to return to the hotel. Soon."

She said to Jackson, "Jackson, you rest up then head home, if you can do that in the dark and if you feel you're okay to make that journey."

Jackson nodded across the fire from us, pale and wounded and silent. We'd gone down the back of the hill and built a fire in the shadows. Cora made some strong tea and loaded it with sugar and passed out chunks of pemmican, though Jackson's face, now crudely stitched with Cora's thick thread, was cut so bad I didn't know how he would manage after Cora refused to let him refuse the tea and the food. We'd put a gauze patch over his eye and hoped for the best.

"Let the tea cool some and suck it in on your good side," she told him. "Pinch off bits of the pemmican and do the same. You need your strength to make it home." She turned to me. "Drink your tea, Harry. You've got to head out soon."

She'd already told me what I had to do. I had to go into Sophia's room, dress in her clothes, sleep in her bed, pack her things and somehow that morning get on the train and pretend to be her. Before that I had to sneak into Jackson's father's room with the key we took from his pants pocket, grab his gear and hide it in my room for us to take to Jackson at some other time. I had a note from Jackson to leave on the front desk, saying his father was going to stay with him for a while and that he no longer needed the room. I didn't see how any of this could work. The only thing that made it even a possibility was the fact that Nellie June was gone.

"What are *you* going to do, Cora?" I asked. I felt like a child that night, wanting nothing more than for her to make it all go away.

"I'll be out here. Remember, when you get to Fairbanks, find somewhere to sleep without attracting attention and in the morning get rid of Sophia's clothes and her bag. Get on the south-bound looking like someone besides yourself and get off at that stop between the Indian River and the hotel. You can do this, Harry."

I nodded though I was full of doubt. A lot of the train staff knew me. I had that ticket to Fairbanks Cora had shoved at me on that day my life took the turn that led me here. I also had some things from my theatre days that I'd brought with me to the hotel for laughs and when the staff thought we might do a play or two: a pair of round tinted glasses, a fake mustache and beard, a few wide brimmed hats, and the blond wig I wore when I was Viola. No one in their right mind would have ever imagined the reason I would wear that again.

Reluctantly, I set off through the dark woods. Clouds were moving in for which Cora was glad and grateful: we needed new snow, to bury our tracks and cover the grave on the hill.

It was well past midnight by the time I made it to the hotel. My keys were in my pocket like they always were, along with the key we'd found in Jackson's father's pants. I slipped into the empty lobby and left the letter from Jackson on the desk. I saw the guest-book sitting there. I already knew which room Jackson's father was supposed to stay in; the number was on the key, but I realized I didn't know his name. I had killed him, and I didn't even know what name his mother had given him. I looked in the guestbook and found it. Ewan Keats. The sight and sound of it sent a panic through me and I fought the urge to throw up my guts. He had been alive mere hours ago, had signed his name in this guestbook then at some point, he must have seen Sophia leave the hotel and followed after her. If only he hadn't.

The room was on the main floor. I pulled up the hood of my parka and adjusted my scarf to partially cover my face. All was quiet, and I slipped down the hallway unseen, the key to the room ready. I braced myself for what I might find, what traces of the man I killed might there be, scattered across the space, and found some small relief when I saw the room was untouched except for a small bag placed unceremoniously on the floor by the bed. I grabbed it and slipped back into the hall, walking quickly down the remainder of the hallway to my room where I shoved the bag deep under my bed. I packed my things as quickly as I could—the costume stuff and that damned ticket—and I almost missed it, a little package of letters on the floor that had been pushed through the crack at the bottom of the door. My heart almost stopped. The top letter said, *Harry*. Somehow, I knew who it was from, that it was from Sophia, who I had called Sonja those last few months, unknowing. Did she hate that, the sound of that name? I pulled the first letter from the bundle and read it quickly, knowing I must keep moving.

I looked for words it did not say: *Harry, I never told you . . . Harry, this is the truth about me, and the truth of how I feel for you.* No, it was none of that. It was very simply this:

My dear friend Harry—

If you are reading this it means that I have left the hotel and missed seeing you before I did so, as at this moment you are away on the hunting. My leaving is very unexpected, and I hate to do it without a goodbye. Perhaps we'll meet again. You have been very kind to me, and I will always be grateful.

I have some favors to ask if I may please, and if you would be so kind. I have composed a letter to Mrs. Johnson explaining as best I could my departure. I do not mean to cause her inconvenience by the lack of notice; for reasons I cannot explain, it cannot be helped. I left the letter for her in the laundry. Would you be so kind as to make certain she had received it? I did not write to Nellie June. Please tell her how much I enjoyed her friendship and her company.

I am leaving with you a letter for Jackson Keats. I implore you to please see that he receives it. I do not have a stamp so am unable to slip it into the mail. There are things I did not tell you about my life before coming here, Harry, and Jackson is someone I knew from before and his presence here was very

*unexpected for me. Years ago we did not part as friends, but
in this short time I have been here we have become friends
again, and he is very dear to me. As are you, Harry. If at all
possible, in the future, I will let you know where I am—*

Yours truly and in gratitude,
Sonja Antonov

I choked on the sobs that rose in my throat, then imagined
Cora slapping me across the face and put the letters in my bag. As I
left my room and walked back down the hall, past the room Ewan
Keats never stayed in, I wondered if that was where he had seen
Sophia, in the hallway, delivering those letters. Where he chose to
follow her. If only I was still in the bunkhouse. But I wasn't, and
nothing I could wish for was going to change anything. And I had
to keep moving.

I put the key to Ewan Keats' room on the front desk beside
the letter from Jackson about his father staying with him. Then I
crossed through the dark and silent hotel and made the trip down
the back stairs, past the work kitchen and down the hallway and
into the little box of a room Sophia shared with Nellie June. I stood
for the longest time in the dark with my back against the door. I'd
made it that far in our crazy plot. What would Shakespeare have
thought? Were we evil murderers or bumbling fools? The only
thing I knew was that life had turned tragic, in the course of one
wrong minute.

There was some other story, I reminded myself, that had been
playing itself out for what must have been a long time, the last of
which had been happening right under my nose. Jackson did not
say much and was as confused as anybody why his father would
want to harm Sophia. I had seen enough, however, as Sophia lay
dying and Jackson gripped her bloody hand in his, to know that
they had experienced a lifetime together before this ending they
found here. The backstory that followed each of them here to
Findlay.

After a long time, I let myself sit down on Sophia's little cot. I opened the collection of Shakespeare beside her bed to the scrap of cloth she'd been using as a bookmark: *All's Well That Ends Well.* My heart clenched at the irony of that, Shakespearean in itself. I started to sob. It was when I stretched out to try to sleep, that I found her journal.

IN THE MORNING, I HAD BECOME HER; I wore the Viola wig and the thin skirt and the baggy sweater Sophia had arrived in. I carried the tattered bag into which I put everything of hers I could find in the room. A small bundle of money. A blue bandana handkerchief. The journal, which I had read instead of sleeping, her voice in its pages haunting the halls of my heart. I kept moving. I had a job to do and I was doing it for her, and for Peter. I would get Sonja Antonov on that train, and she would disappear, folded into the pages of this time and this place, someone who had been here briefly, and then was gone.

A day later, when I got off at the flag stop right before Findlay, all mustached and disguised, after the train moved on Cora came out of the woods, a pile of bloody meat and an antlered caribou head on her sled.

JACKSON KEATS
EARLY WINTER 1927

JACKSON BURIED HIS FATHER ON A small rise in the landscape out of view of his cabin. He had to tend to it right away before the ground froze deeper, though he was exhausted from grief, exposure, and loss of blood from the great wound across his face and the glancing stab wound near his ribs. He was quite certain his father did not know who had grabbed ahold of him when he made the first slash with the knife. Before the second strike the two men had locked eyes and they recognized each other. Perhaps that was why the second thrust of his father's knife was not so fierce as the first. So Jackson wanted to believe. Or perhaps his father saw that Sophia was escaping and would have to deal with Jackson later.

He did not know. And he did not know there could be a day when he could bury both Sophia and his father, only hours and miles apart.

Before he left the hill, he said to Cora Allen, "I must get Peter." It was not the first time he said it, and the woman gave him once again the same reply: "Jackson, you can't. Now listen to me. You spiriting Peter off into the night after your father comes to see you and never returns to the village—well, that's going to be a bit too much for those people there. They'll start wondering, putting pieces together even though one's a rock and one's an onion and one's an apple. They'll start seeing that all those things are round, even though they're as different as night and day. Three people vanished from their village, three people with threads running from one to the other."

"I promised," Jackson said.

"You promised to take care of the boy. What was it Sophia was so desperate to protect him from? Besides that God-forsaken priest. The truth of what had happened to her in that village, and the truth of who he was, that's what. Now we made a plan, and we need to stick to it or else we're all in a heap of trouble, and Peter's life won't stand a chance of a decent way forward."

Jackson nodded, slowly and reluctantly, shards of pain from the wound on his face shooting through him like lightning.

"I promise you I will get that boy, and he'll be safe with me and well cared for. Let some time pass. I'll let you know how that turns out. Later on if you think it's the right thing—for the boy, Jackson, not necessarily for you—he can come be with you or you with him, whichever seems to be best. In the meantime, those hotel people and those village people need to think your father decided to stay on with you. Eventually you can drop the idea at the hotel that your father went home or just went somewhere—that you walked your way down to the village and you put him on the train there, or he caught a ride on one of the steamer boats. That way people will stop wondering why your father doesn't venture out to the hotel with you.

"These are awful secrets we're keeping, Jackson, and always remember why we agreed to carry this awful burden. And I'll tell you one dammed thing—that father of yours, and that priest—had secrets far worse than this, and they are the reason we are here, right now, and that beautiful young girl is dead in the ground and my Harry will not live another normal day in his entire life."

Jackson had given a final nod. He knew the woman was right. He would do his part.

After a night of pain and darkness, he composed a letter to Father Mikhail in his father's handwriting, which he knew well and could so imitate:

Hello my friend:

I have decided to stay on here with my son in this won- drous land in order to salvage what is left of my relation- ship with him, and to convince him that everything that was done was done out of love for God and love for all involved. You can rest assured that he will not trouble you ever again, and that Sophia is nowhere to be seen, as we had already expected. I am beholden to you my friend and I well know it; if I decide to stay here, I will bequeath to the church both my property and my boat as well as the belongings I left behind; they are no use to me here. Here there is gold in the streams the same as there is fish in the sea; I shall not want.

In Christ,
Ewan

Now Jackson sat outside in the fresh layer of snow, at the end of another long and painful day, with Snowy Day warm against him. An impossible sun had broken through the clouds and Jackson felt its touch on his great wound. He would have to make some story, he knew, for the thick scar he would carry into the future. Something simple, plain: a falling tree, a kick on the ax he had used to fell it, sending it back into him.

So many things he would have to remember now. Now that he had lost everything and everyone again.

A little chick-a dee came out of nowhere and landed on the tip of his boot. Snowy Day glanced at it but gave it no mind as it looked about at this strange growth on the snow it had perched itself upon. The sun caught on its feathers, and Jackson thought how fine that must feel to the little creature, how fine this day must seem with the warm sun and the clean fresh snow and this nice little place to perch upon. He wondered if the bird knew happiness, or if it only knew moments of splendor verses moments of fear and flight, moments of hunger verses moments of the perfect berry in its bill.

Happiness. All his life Jackson had been close to perfect happiness, that feeling he could touch when memory blessed him with fragments of his life when he had a mother, but all his life these wonderful things were transient, fleeting, like the little bird that rested momentarily on the rounded toe of his blood-stained boot. Those two years in which he had both a mother and a father; the day he first kissed Sophia on the hill above the cemetery, and he had felt lifted into the sky. Then in the wind on the beach, when they became like husband and wife. And here, now in this new place, when he realized she could love him again, and the future broke open in front of him, full of hope and possibility. However, his life was like a wave upon the shore, almost reaching his waiting toes, then pulling back to the sea. Or like this little bird, who graced him with this brief moment of a visit, and with a flutter now was gone…and he still lived, on the other side of that window separating him from what was once possible, but forever gone.

SOPHIA PETERSEN
EARLY WINTER 1927

Dear Jackson,

Hopefully I will see you today, soon, but I have decided to start this letter in case I do not. I am hiding, here, down in the laundry listening for sounds. You see, Jackson, I must not let him see me, and it is not only because he would tell Father Mikhail that I am here.

I have not been able to tell you this because I do not know how. I only tell you now because I will have to try to leave tomorrow on the train, and if he is seeking to know what has become of me, you must know what I know of your father.

It was never Ilian Nicholai who beat me, Jackson. It was your father. The first time, he simply knocked on the door. It was after I demanded Father Mikhail move my mother to the cemetery or I would tell everyone what she told me. He had caught me alone when Peter was not at home. So yes, I did lie, Jackson, in the church about the beating—I did and I didn't. Because I knew Father Mikhail had ordered your father to do it, just as I knew, later, that Ilian had been made to confess to a beating he had no part of. I could not tell you that your own father would do such a thing. I could not. Even now it pains me to do so. Even though your father beat me that second time, and far worse than the first, I could not tell you something that would hurt you so badly. Now I must.

I fear he is here to beat me again. Not for what is past but for the future. I carry three secrets with me. The first two are that Father Mikhail is both my and Peter's father. The third— I am afraid to write it, to make it more real in that way—is that I carry a child inside of me, and that child is fathered by Father Mikhail.

You see how awful that is. I know why they want this baby, and possibly me, dead. I and this child are an abomination. It would have been best, had I died in the water. But I believed that somehow, I could watch out for Peter from afar, and that eventually he and I would outlive Father Mikhail and your father and could be reunited. There was also that animal instinct to survive. The body is strong, even when the mind is not. It wants to breathe the air. It wants to stay warm. It wants food for its belly. It wants to see the sunrise of another day.

It wants its child to survive.

So I pulled myself out of the water the night I left the island and stowed myself away on the boat that would take me from those shores.

I did not expect to find you here. I had always thought your father had you closer and fast under his thumb—his own reason to want me dead.

I suppose it could be worse. Centuries ago it would have been much easier for them. They could simply have burned me as a witch.

I don't know where I will go. I hope we have a chance to discuss it when we meet, though if you are reading this it means we did not meet on our hill. I beg you—it is important your father believes me dead. Peter must be kept safe from the secret of his creation. Though Father Mikhail dotes on him, if Peter's existence becomes a threat to him or the church, he will not be safe. And so Jackson I am trusting you now to not only believe me, but to keep these secrets buried deep inside your soul. I am so sorry that you now must share my burden. Telling you is the only way I know to explain the urgency and the danger. On her deathbed, when my mother told me, I wanted nothing more than not to know. How different things would be, if she had taken her secret with her! She feared for me, had she left me in ignorance.

I do not know where I will go. To ask you to raise with me a child of such sin is something I do not think I can do. But if you are willing—if you are willing—

If only I could explain all this to you face to face. I fear I may not have that chance.

If I do not see you, please know, Jackson, that I am always yours—

Sophia

Chapter Fourteen

Emily Wells
Spring 1970

"Good morning."

The light slanted in through the tall windows of Thomas' hotel room. I had left the curtains open for all that was left of the night, so I could watch the lights blinking outside. His manager, Jimmy, went with me in the taxi and helped me get Thomas up to his room before he went back to the club to watch the rest of the band finish what was left of the show. "You'll be all right with him?" Jimmy had asked before he left. "Call an ambulance, you know, if anything gets weird."

"I can watch him," I'd said. I knew what to look for. Alcohol poisoning. Jimmy looked at me like there was something I didn't know. "I'm almost a nurse," I reassured as he hovered by the door.

"So you said." And then he was gone, and I sat in the chair by the bed, watching the city lights swirling in the dark beyond the window. My city. Sacramento. Thomas Findlay had come to my city— was from my city—and I was the girl that drew the lucky straw.

He winced when he opened his eyes—eyes the color of a bright blue sky—and his gaze found and registered on me as my voice fell into his ears.

"Good morning," he said in return. Then, with a smile: "Who are you?"

"I'm Emily."

"Emily?"

"I'm the one you fell beside."

EARLY WINTER 1974

WIND AND MORE SNOW HAD COME through while Raymie and I were in Anchorage, and the hill was clean and swept as if nothing had happened there. I felt I marred it with my footsteps as I drug a camp chair across the top of it to the edge where Thomas had spent his last moments. Was it day, was it night, or something in between? Maybe he was watching the sunset, the mountains that frosty pink, the sky a painful shade of pale, pastel blue. How could I leave, I wondered, but how could I stay? I would go mad, I was certain, in the cabin by myself. I would struggle to survive.

I sat and wept, the cold not caring. The only thing I understood, really, about what Thomas was doing—about what happened to him—was that he needed to be elevated in this world, to be distant and above the traumas of his childhood, his feelings of unworthiness. He was a bird that needed the sky. Hadn't I always, really, felt that I couldn't keep him? I was of this earth, two feet on the ground. Even during the wildest times we'd had together, I would always come to my senses before things went too far in our daily lives. Take the bottle from Thomas' hand, help him to bed. Make sure nothing was left burning, leave the hall light on in case he had to stumble to the bathroom. A glass of water and some aspirin handy.

There was a little secret pocket in his duffle, which I'd found when I was going through his things deciding what to take and what to leave behind. An extra needle, but no additional heroin. One dose. Why did he bring it? Was it a constant test for himself, or a break-glass-in-case-of-emergency sort of thing? There was no evidence anything had happened after I'd left. He had seemed happy. Maybe he was celebrating. Maybe he wanted to get rid of it and couldn't stand the thought of throwing it out. One shot's worth. Probably his old, usual dose. He didn't know his body was no longer equipped to handle the dose he used to take. It could be as simple as that. Was as simple as that. One last dose, one last flight, a perfect chance to see his beautiful world in an old new way.

The pain tangled my heart, coming in waves so overwhelming there were moments when I thought I, too, would die. I closed my eyes. *Thomas, I'm here. I'm here. Where are you?* Then I remembered the coming sunset, and opened my eyes so not to miss it, hoping, praying, it could tell me something.

"EMILY, COME. IT'S GETTING TOO COLD." Somehow Raymie had joined me on the hill, so quietly my numbed brain failed to register his presence except as a muffled sound behind me. The sunset was over, and night was pouring its blue-black shades over the hills and over the long winding ribbon in the landscape where the river and the rails twisted along, over the now fading forms of the Alaska Range. Fading. Vanishing.

I cried out, doubling forward in the chair as if I'd been hit.

"Emily!" Raymie's arms circled around me, banding me together. "Emily. Emily."

"I'm leaving him behind, aren't I? I'm leaving him behind!" I choked between sobs. "He's going to fade—he's going to disappear!"

"Emily no, no. That won't happen. That won't ever happen. You'll carry him with you, long after you leave this place. You will. You will."

"I don't know how to do this, Raymie! I don't know how!"

"You will, Emily, you'll find a way. You will. You'll get there. Just hang on, hang on. Hang on, Emily."

"Raymie you don't know, you don't know!"

He stepped back a little and knelt in the snow beside the chair so he could look at me. "I do Emily, I do know. Listen," he said. "Listen. I don't go home much because my little sister died. There was a party—mostly my friends—and she OD'd. I'd left her there because I was hot for some chick. I left my little sister at a fucking party, and someone gave her some pills and she'd already had too much to drink, and she died. My parents keep saying they forgive me, but I can't—I can't forgive myself for that, though I learned—not how to accept it, but how to live with it, and to keep her, always, with me. I learned that. You will, too, Emily—you will."

I looked at him, into his eyes, and saw at once that we were the same, we were the ones left behind in the swamp of guilt and grief. "Oh, God, Raymie—oh, look at us, look at us."

I cried into the front of his coat, tears turning to ice, and after a time he nudged me into moving and we went back down to the cabin.

I returned to the hill the following afternoon before we were to head to the train. Jackson showed up in the morning, and he and Raymie hauled up the windows from the tracks and stashed them on a sheet of leftover plywood underneath the cabin, then boarded-over the Visqueen windows. I went through my and Thomas' things. In the end all I decided to take were Thomas' guitar, a few changes of clothes for myself, an old doorknob from the hotel, and the shirt Thomas had worn the day I'd left for town that held the smell of him woven inside its threads. Raymie looked at me questioningly as I brought my few things out to the sled, but Jackson nodded as if he understood painful departures and lost dreams and the meaning of what we keep and what we leave behind.

Jackson had brought me Sophia's journal, and a letter she had written him, wanting to make sure I understood the story he had told me was true. He slipped them to me when Raymie was off at the stream getting water. I read them both when Jackson and

Raymie made the trek to the tracks for the windows and was able to discreetly return them. I hadn't needed to read them. I hadn't thought Jackson's story was anything less than true.

Hill of the dead horses. Oh, how I longed to tell Thomas.

ON THAT HILL, WHEN I WENT UP FOR THE LAST TIME, I tried to sing Thomas a song, to let the hill and the wind lift my voice up to wherever it was he had gone. I chose a Jackson Browne song called "From Silver Lake" that we both loved, a song about someone beautiful and loved who was here and then gone—

I didn't get far. It wasn't because I started crying; it was because I had nothing to give to the words, to give to the music, my voice hollow, empty. *What have you done to me,* I thought, kneeling into the cold white snow, empty and clean, a reflection of the strange feeling of blankness that had found me. We make tracks on the ground, in the snow, and then we're gone, vanished. *You left me with unopened boxes, Thomas, a stack of unopened boxes that will turn into empty boxes full of nothing.* That is what I felt then. In time, I would find that those boxes were full and layered with the golden treasures of the time we had spent together on this earth.

I leaned back into the snow and looked at the fathomless sky. The wind moved softly across the hill, cold and pure and clean. How far, I wondered, had that wind traveled to find me on this hill, to move past me as if I wasn't even there?

I thought of Jackson, and the journal and the letter he had kept with him, for how many years? And Harry, riding the train over and over and over.

I had a sudden flash of the little green house, my hand reaching across the table to hold Thomas', and he looked up at me, ragged and wrecked, and smiled.

I started singing again, lying on my back in the snow, my voice weak and fluttering, chasing Thomas into the sky.

HARRY HARBOUR
EARLY WINTER 1974

NIGHT TRAINS. WE HAVE THEM, IN this time of the diesel engine, freights that travel in the dark of cold winter nights, a thunderous rumble of noise breaking that pristine stillness, a great beam of light, piercing the blackness for a few moments, then gone.

Lately I've been thinking that's what a life is, a train going through the night, making all kinds of noise and sometimes hurting things that get in its way, yet lighting things up for a brief, glorious time.

What part of my life was like a light in the night? I guess I don't really know. It certainly wasn't when I shot and killed Jackson Keats' murderous father. If I had it to do over again, would I pull that trigger? I don't know. For years I had said yes, yes I would; he had already as good as killed her, with those murderous kicks to her stomach, slamming her organs, slamming the baby she carried. Though I did not know that for certain, and though my shot was an effort to save her, it would not stand if the man who murdered Sophia had lived. But I don't know, given now the gift of hindsight in this old age of mine. I didn't grieve for him, not after some time had passed. I grieved for Sophia, I grieved for the life I had to leave behind from that moment on; I never married of course—how could I—and I grieved the disappointment that was to my parents. I grieved, too, the lifelong pain that was leveled onto Jackson that awful day as he lost his father in two different ways: the man he believed his father was, and the man who ran after Sophia with a bloody knife.

Jackson was there the evening the train stopped and picked up young Emily after she'd returned for the final time to gather her things and close up the life she and Thomas Findlay had briefly lived in this place that carried his name. I saw Jackson standing back a little, a shadow by the skeletal outlines of the alders in the dark, just out of reach of the light of the train. Word on the railroad was he'd saved her, down on the tracks, another addition to the legend that was Jackson Keats.

"My dear," I said as I helped Emily up the stairs. She faltered as if her knees were going out from under her. I grabbed onto her and lifted her up. "You're all right," I whispered. "You're all right, my dear, let's get you settled in." She moved her mouth to try to speak. I knew what she was going to say and headed her off: "It will be here, Emily, whenever you decide to come back and join us again. And we'll look forward to that day."

That settled her and she took a step, and young Raymie, done loading up the baggage car, hopped up behind her and got her the rest of the way onto the train. That's when I saw Jackson. Our eyes met, even through all that dark, and I felt that bond between us, still there. The bond of our secret, and the bond of our secret watch over the grave of the young woman we both loved, and the more visible watch over the brother she'd left behind, Peter.

"All set, Harry?" Maxwell, the young baggage fellow, asked. He had his radio mike up to his mouth, ready to give the go ahead to the engineer. I glanced at him then looked back at Jackson, but he was gone.

"Yep," I said to Max. "Let's go." I pulled up the step and soon felt the train begin to move. The night was full of stars. I imagined Jackson and his dog walking off into the woods, the sky brilliant and swirling.

I stayed standing by the door through the short ride to Raymie's stop, trying not to observe the tearful goodbye between him and Emily. As tragic a story as this was—and, mind you, I'm not discounting the impact of this horrible tragedy on all those who loved Thomas Findlay—I'd been part of a more tragic tale. It was a tale that took two lives by violent means (three, if you count Sophia's unborn child), that left one man orphaned and in essence widowed, and that made a murderer out of a goofy kid from Anchorage who fell in love with a majestic wilderness hotel and the young woman who came there looking for sanctuary and safety only to find her past waiting to greet her. What would my teenaged Shakespeare-loving self have thought, if he could have looked ahead somehow and saw what was going to unfold on the stage of his life? *We know what we are, but know not what we may be.* Perhaps that, though I would say this, with the benefit of long years behind me: *We are such stuff as dreams are made on and our little life is rounded with a sleep.* Shakespeare saw past the stage, past his stories playing out, into the stars. All the world's a stage—and more than we will ever imagine.

I placed my hand on the young man's shoulder as Raymie stopped on his way down the steps, looking back toward the interior of the train.

"I'll keep an eye on her," I said.

With great reluctance Raymie stepped off onto the snow, into the night, and the look on his face in the light from the train jolted me with stab of déjà vu: my younger self, hopelessly in love with someone I would never have. I put my fingers to my forehead in a two-fingered salute, which was answered by an expression of confusion, and the train moved forward into the night.

I gave Emily some time. We made a few more stops in the next few miles and picked up a few more passengers while at the village (thankfully not Nellie June). After these newest riders were settled, and after the brief bursts of lights from houses faded away, did I finally sit myself across from Emily Wells and take her hands in my own.

"Can I get you anything?" I asked. "Some hot tea maybe?"

She shook her head, her watery eyes looking downward at our feet. After a moment she lifted those eyes and looked into mine and said, "Harry."

The way she said it, and the way she looked into my eyes, like she saw me.

"Yes, that's my name," I said. "How can I help, Emily?" She looked to the side, as if someone was sitting next to her, then looked back at me.

"Hill of the dead horses," she said, words that both stabbed and startled. "Jackson stayed with me on the hill—we had to stay with Thomas you know, that first night, while we waited for the troopers to come. We built a fire and talked. I asked about his scar, and he told me a story."

My heart lost rhythm for a beat or two before I found my voice and replied, "I imagine he did."

"I sort of shoved it aside, when I saw you afterward—I was—overwhelmed with everything."

"As of course you would be."

She squeezed my hands. "Oh, Harry. That's quite a story, isn't it?"

"You could call it that," I said, and added softly, "I'm really sorry for what you're going through, Emily."

"I'm sorry about Sophia," she said quietly.

It jolted me, after all these years, to hear her name spoken by someone other than Peter or Cora. It took me a moment before I could talk again. "I'm sorry I didn't tell you about that," I said.

"You tried to warn us, didn't you, about building in those hills."

"I didn't do a very good job though, did I?"

"We found the grave," she said. "We weren't sure what to do."

Well, the past has a way of catching up with a person, doesn't it? And I've read enough great pieces of writing to know that truth doesn't like to stay silent.

"How could you tell me—or anyone—that story?" she said.

"I couldn't," I said. "It wasn't my story to tell."

"Oh," Emily said, "I think it was your story, Harry, as much as anyone's. You had a starring role. Don't you think?"

A flash, then—the cold air, the crisp snow. Cora's arm, the gun already over my head as I pulled the strap away from across my chest.

I couldn't answer Emily's question, one way or another, so I said nothing.

"I'll keep the story a secret, Harry, I promise," Emily said. "I won't tell anyone about the grave."

"Thank you, Emily." It was a strange relief to have what I'd feared would happen, happen, and perhaps without the consequences I'd envisioned.

"Jackson showed me the journal," Emily said. "Sophia was lucky to have you, Harry. To have a friend like you," and those words soared through me like a bird across an empty sky.

"Thank you," I said. "I hope so."

I guess, if it all came out, if I went to jail at this point in my life it wouldn't be so bad. I'd miss riding the rails, though, miss the people I'd had the privilege to meet over the years—those different waves of folks going back and forth across the state or those who tried and sometimes failed—or sometimes simply changed their minds—to carve a life for themselves in the woods that bordered the tracks, the train their lifeline, their connection. As for Peter, if old Uncle Harry got arrested the whole thing would come spilling out, and it was a story Sophia didn't ever want him to know. Sometimes I think he should. I'll have to look at those letters again—one from me and one from Cora—that we put in an envelope with my will for Peter to read. Our confession, you might say, for keeping something so important from him for all those years. With Cora gone it was solely my decision now if Peter should ever see them, and one year after another goes by and I still can't decide.

"What happened to Father Mikhail?" Emily asked. "Do you know?"

I thought for a minute before answering. "Hmm—not really," I said. That was the truth. "I do know Mrs. Nicholai—from the journal, you might remember, Ilian's mother—went to the territory government in Juneau and made a complaint about him and asked for an investigation into the disappearance of her son. She wanted the priest gone and she wanted Ilian found. I only know that because Cora had friends in the government and Cora was good at getting things out of people, and Cora in part was after the same thing: to get that priest out of the village and out of power. Before too long we heard he'd left; where he went no one seems to know."

I stopped there because the rest is pure conjecture, though not totally unfounded. There's something Jackson told us, when he came to Seward to reunite with Peter after Peter moved in with us at the roadhouse, about how Father Mikhail might have been seen fleeing the island on the fishing boat owned by Ilian's brothers, Dimitri and Alexei, and how those brothers might have decided to let him swim the greater part of the way to Juneau, and how he might be swimming still.

We were silent for a time, looking out the black of the window, and I imagined each of us was thinking about the fate of Father Mikhail and what might have been a proper and fitting end for him. The whistle blew and I had to get back to work. As I stood I asked, "So, my dear, where are you headed now?"

It took her some time to respond. As I waited, I thought about the two of us, there on that night train moving through the dark, and how our lives had been running beside each other without our knowing, because of course how could we have ever envisioned that our stories would intersect in such a way as they did?

"I guess I'll be gone," she said. "But I think I'll always be here."

I nodded. That was something I knew.

JACKSON KEATS
EARLY WINTER 1927

THE DAYS AFTER THE DEATHS ON the hill grew darker and colder with each passing one. Jackson spent the hours of light collecting firewood for the stove and hunting for food. His root cellar was full of cabbages, potatoes, and turnips from his garden, and he would kill ptarmigan and caribou as he needed. There was no joy in anything, only survival. Except for Snowy Day, who faithfully helped Jackson move forward.

One morning Jackson lingered in the warmth of the cabin

drinking hot tea. Outside it was well below zero; he would wait an hour or so to let the temperature struggle to rise before going outside to cut more firewood. He watched from his window as the light slowly spread across the hills, gray and pink and yellow. He had only been to the hotel once since the day on the hill. It was to put the letter to Father Mikhail he had written as if from his father into the mail. He went at night so as not to be seen. The wound on his face remained too horrible to look at, and too difficult to explain. He waited and was able to slip the letter onto the front desk. If there was any mail for him, it would have to wait. But there would not be any mail for him; the two people in this world who might have written him were gone and lived now only in the past. Or maybe, he hoped, maybe something carried on somewhere else, some other world beyond physical reach. He has seen Sophia in his dreams, and it is as if she says to him, *Jackson, I am all right, I am all right.* He would wake up and look for her, in the dark corners of the cabin.

Jackson could remember how, in his early days in Findlay, the wild world around him breathed life into his soul and how he had felt flickers of happiness, despite all that had happened and all he had lost when he'd left the village and Sophia behind. He must wait for that to come to him again, like the light of a winter dawn, faint and fluttering at first, then slowly spreading until he could see the world once more.

Jackson rose from the table to feed the fire, Snowy Day loathe to move from his spot in front of the black cast iron stove. "It is all right, Snow," he said. "You are not in my way." Jackson opened the door and shoved a piece of wood onto the flames. Snowy Day yawned and rested his head upon his paws.

Jackson returned to the table. When he looked out the window again, a figure on snowshoes stood a short distance away, looking at the cabin, a familiar bag in his hand: his father's bag, that had been left at the hotel.

Jackson rose and opened the door. "Come in where it is warm," he said. "Leave the bag outside." He closed the door and waited. It was the hotel boy, Harry.

There was the shuffling sound of removing snowshoes. A moment later Harry knocked, even though Jackson had already invited him in.

"Come inside, Harry," Jackson said, and the boy entered. "Hang your coat behind the stove and come sit."

Harry did so, and soon all that separated them was Jackson's small square table.

Harry said nothing at first, and Jackson saw how Harry's eyes grazed across his wounded face. The boy had aged in the span of weeks; Jackson saw how he was now more man than boy when just a mere month ago it was the opposite.

"What is it, Harry?" he asked, not to be unkind but to quell the anxiety that was growing within him.

"How's your wound, Jackson?" Harry asked in response.

"It is healing," Jackson said. "I removed the stitches some weeks ago."

"And the eye?"

"It hurts, and I cannot see everything that I once could."

Harry nodded solemnly. After a moment of quiet he said, reaching into his pocket, "I brought you some things. Thought I might see you at the hotel, though I suppose it's good you've stayed clear. But here—this is for you."

It was a letter, neatly folded with his name written across the outer side. Sophia's handwriting. Her beautiful handwriting. How?

"She'd left it," Harry said quickly, "in my room that day. She left me a note asking me to give it to you. She had seen your father get off the train and didn't know what was going to happen."

All Jackson could do was give a brief nod. His heart thundered and he knew his hands were now shaking.

Harry reached again into the pocket of his coat and placed a small little blue book, the blue bandana Jackson had given Sophia in a different world, and a roll of money onto the table. "These were hers; I found them in her room."

Jackson stared at the items. After a time, he shoved the small roll of bills back toward Harry.

"What should I do with it?" Harry asked. "I don't want it, Jackson. She worked hard for that money. We shouldn't throw it away."

Jackson glowered at first, then his face softened. "You are right," he said. "Of course. We must get it to Peter. Is that something you can do, Harry?"

Harry nodded. "Cora's going to the village next month with a friend of hers who works for the governor. She's going to see if she—if we—can do something for the boy."

Jackson took a deep breath and nodded. He understood why he was not the one who could go, though he did not like it. The village must forget about him, and his father. He stared at the table.

"Cora thinks the territory can get the church to unseat that priest there," Harry said.

Jackson looked up quickly.

"There's been some complaints about him, from the village. A woman reported to the governor's office that the priest forced her son to confess to something he did not do, and now her son is missing. She asked for an investigation, Cora heard."

"Mrs. Nicholai!" Jackson said. He felt a rush of excitement. If only Sophia could know this, that someone else has finally stood up to Father Mikhail. And Mrs. Nicholai—the most unlikely of people.

"Cora wants to get the boy away from the village," Harry went on, "and take care of him. She's got ample resources, Cora does, and a nice roadhouse in Seward. And since the complaint about the priest—and some nudging from Cora—the governor's office discovered Peter and his orphaned status, and the territory is probably going to put him in a home for children in Seward. Cora's pretty sure she'll be able to sweep him out of there and take him home with her."

"I should take care of Peter," Jackson said. "He knows me. He would be happy, to see me again."

Harry nodded. "I know, Jackson; I know," he said. "I think there'll be a time when that can happen."

Jackson, in that moment, had no hope for that, could not imagine how in a little more than a year he would see Peter again, and he would remain connected to the boy for the rest of his life. At that time the idea of such a possibility was for Jackson like the great white mountains of the Alaska Range: there for him to see, but far beyond his reach.

"Please," Jackson said. "Let me know what happens with Peter."

"I promise you," Harry said. Jackson felt Harry holding back tears. "I am always so sorry about your father, Jackson."

Jackson shook his head. "Do not worry about that, Harry. You saw what my father did to her. You see here in front of you what he did to me. I will never understand it. If you had not shot him, I would have killed him with my own hands." Jackson did not think his words made Harry feel better, so he added, "It was my fault he came. I had told him in a letter, after I saw Sophia that day of her arrival, that I thought I saw her. I gave him the idea, that maybe she was here."

Harry stared at him a moment before quietly saying, "Don't blame yourself for that, Jackson. You can't control what someone else decides to do."

"Save Peter, Harry. Let us try to give him a good life."

Harry nodded and stood, touched the blue book he'd placed on the table. "This is her journal. I found it in her room. I—well, I read it. I know I shouldn't have; it was like it—like it was calling to me."

Jackson tentatively touched the little blue book, as if it was something living, sitting there before him. "It is all right," he said. "I do not think Sophia would have minded that, Harry. She knew what you did to save her—and me, as well, Harry, on that day. She knew before she died. Also before she died, she said to tell you she was sorry you did not know her name was Sophia."

"Oh," Harry said, then swallowed hard and took a deep breath. "Well, the journal won't make you feel any better about your father, but—." Harry paused, biting his lips as he searched for words. "I think she loved you very much."

Jackson continued to stare at the letter and the little book waiting there for him, and Harry said goodbye and walked back out into the winter day. Jackson sat unmoving until Snowy Day came up beside him, his wet nose on Jackson's hand, and Jackson picked up the little blue book. That was where he would begin.

CHAPTER FIFTEEN

EMILY WELLS
EARLY WINTER 1974

She is my window
To everything in me I cannot see,
A world where I don't stumble and fall,
Where I am who I'm supposed to be.

Window window window,
Window—yes, she is.
My window window window
Window—yes, she is.
To everything in me
That I cannot see.

Through that glass that is her vision
I stand tall amongst the trees.
My feet have roots deep in the ground,
Someone strong is who she sees.

As if another takes my place
When I exist through her gentle glass—
My pieces are not broken and my
Possibilities are vast.

Window window window,
Window—yes she is.
My window window window
Window—yes she is.
My window to everything in me
That I could never see.

That song lived in my head, during the beginning of my life without Thomas, and I realized, on that last train ride when I left Findlay, in those quiet moments when I found myself alone with the reflection of my face in a dark window, a silent companion sitting beside me, that Thomas was my window as well. I had lived the last four years of my life as the person he saw me to be. I loved being that person, both his savior and his love. *This is my love, Emily Wells.* I didn't know who I was now.

I was twenty-five years old. The road had vanished from in front of me. I could not even begin to think about Jimmy, my now-known rapist, except in regard to Thomas' songs: I would take those from him, and for that, I would make him pay. But the only thing that mattered to me, in that dark time, was that Thomas was gone, and I remained.

Harry came and went as I sat through that last train ride when I'd left Findlay behind, and we talked about the events that brought our lives together as opportunity allowed. I tried to picture him, a young man out hunting, sees something awful happening to someone he loves, and in a flash he shoots his gun and changes his life.

"It's not the easiest thing to live with," he said, sitting back down across from me between stops.

"I imagine not," I said. "But at the same time, Harry, he killed Sophia."

"Yes, he did." He paused a moment, rubbing his hands absently. "Cora and I, we were able to save her brother. We gave him a good life, I think."

"Your almost-nephew." Of course.

"Yes. The territory government became aware of Peter's situation, and he was placed in a children's home in Seward. He wasn't there long, though, before Cora managed to convince somebody that she'd be fit to raise him."

"That's wonderful, Harry." I hesitated before asking, "Is he happy?"

"I believe so," Harry said. "He never gave us any trouble, and there were even times of great crazy fun. I think, though, there was always a bit of a sadness there, in him—you could see it sometimes. After he got married to this wonderful young woman and began his own family, that sadness began to dry up like a puddle in the sun."

I smiled, it felt like for the first time since I lost Thomas. The idea that Sophia's little brother came into some happiness was a wonderful thing.

"Does he—does he know what happened?"

"No. As far as he believes, his sister drowned a long time ago, when Sophia fled the village."

Harry and I looked at each other in silence before he added, "We could never decide if it was the right thing or not, for Peter to learn there was an awful secret we had kept from him all these years, and I still don't know. A can of worms, it is."

"Yes."

"He's more than a grown man now—goodness, he's in his fifties already—and he could bring flowers to her, and give her a proper goodbye, if he knew," Harry said. "Sophia deserved to be remembered for who she really was: fierce and brave, and she did everything she could to protect him. Did Jackson tell you Peter goes up there sometimes to see him? More often when he was younger. And Jackson has gone to Seward a time or two, to see Peter over the years, though overall Jackson remains reclusive."

"No," I said, and I felt yet another smile. "He didn't tell me that."

Maybe happiness had no place in what we were going through that night, but like stubborn grass happiness finds a way to fight its way out of the darkest of places into the air and the sun. Peter's story contained hope, something I wasn't ready for that night but someday would be. The train whistle blew, announcing another stop, and Harry squeezed my shoulder as he stood.

"Be right back," he said.

HARRY RETURNED AFTER THE TRAIN STARTED moving again, bringing me a cup of tea he insisted I drink. Dear Harry. He quietly gave me his address and asked me to write, and I would, and I would keep writing until one day in 1985 I would receive a letter from Peter Petersen, the so-called nephew, which read:

Dear Miss Wells,

It is with much sadness I write to inform you that dear Uncle Harry passed peacefully in his sleep—perchance to dream, and with his beloved Shakespeare at last—at home with my wife and I in Seward where he has lived these last few years. I know well of the friendship between the two of you and the bond that connected you. I have been to your cabin several times since you left Alaska while visiting my sister's grave on the hill with Jackson, and we thought you would like to know it still stands. Jackson, too, continues on, though the day is quickly coming when I will have to try to convince him to come live with me in Seward so my wife and I can look after him, though we ourselves are getting on in our years. I doubt Jackson would leave Findlay. He told me to send you his regards.

Obviously, I know the two stories of what happened on

your hill, and how they became intertwined. Jackson had told me the first story when I was fifteen and he thought I was old enough, and indeed knowing the truth, and knowing where my sister really was, helped to heal some old wounds. Uncle Harry and Cora long believed that they had protected me from that awful reality, and I let them have whatever peace that brought them—a small price for all they did for me. Uncle Harry, however, a short week before his passing, made a worthy production of revealing the truth to me— though he was somewhat deflated to learn Jackson had beat him to it long ago.

I hope that you, too, have found healing in your life. If you ever wish to sell your Alaskan property please let me, or my eventual heirs, know.

With best wishes,
Peter Petersen

After reading the letter I would feel my grief for Thomas resurface and reverberate through me and mix with my grief for Harry, and for Alaska, and for everything I—we, all of us—had lost.

THAT NIGHT ON THE TRAIN, HARRY ASKED ME, "So, my dear, where are you headed now?"

For the longest time, the words hung in the air unanswered. I knew I was soon to be getting on a plane and flying home to Sacramento where my mother, father, and sisters would wrap me in their love, but where I was really going, I had no idea.

I didn't know—could not see beyond the thick wall of no future that I faced then every day—that one day I would finish my nursing degree, and that someday I would notice that the little green house had come up for sale, and that the money from Thomas' songs would give me more than enough to buy it. That someday—a decade down the road from that night I sat with Harry on the train that moved steadily on through the dark woods—there would be a knock on the door of that little green house, and I would open it and there he'd be—Raymie Weatherell, the poet.

"Hey," he'd say, and I'd smile and say, "Hey."

But at the time of Harry's question, I only knew that I was on a train moving through the darkness of a long night.

ACKNOWLEDGEMENTS

MY DEEPEST THANKS TO NORTHERN SUSITNA Valley historian Kenneth L. Marsh, who urged me to use the Curry setting and whose book, *Lavish Silence* (Trapper Creek Museum/Sluice Box Productions, 2003), was indispensable in the writing of this one. Huge thanks as well to former longtime Curry resident and family friend Dan Mawhinney, whose photos and knowledge of the land were invaluable as were his thoughts and advice. Thanks, too, to my brother Jonathan Durr for his archeological knowledge of the Curry area and to Bill Barstow for helping me navigate maps and building plans. And many thanks to my writing group friends Sondra Porter, Barbara Mannix, Ruth Wood, Kathy Trump, Kate McKelvey, Wendy Battino, and Corinne Smith, who were there from start to finish with feedback and support, and who make the writing process a less lonely endeavor.

I am also deeply indebted to all at Epicenter Press, including Phil Garrett, Jennifer McCord, and Laurie Evans Dinneen, for choosing this novel to publish and add to their wonderful collection of books about Alaska and the Pacific Northwest. I am forever grateful to Peggy Shumaker, Carla Helfferich, and Ron Spatz for the roles they have played over the years in helping my work find the published page.

Alaska Digital Archives (https://vilda.alaska.edu), John's Alaska Railroad Page (alaskarails.org), and Alaska's Lost Ski Areas Project (alsap.org) were websites I went to again and again to study old photographs of Curry and read the written memories, particularly those of Charlie Rainwater and the memoir by Ralph Omholt (*Curry Alaska 1955-1958: A Strange Moment in Time*) both of which appear on John's Alaska Railroad Page. Other sources I am indebted to include *Alaska Nellie* by Nellie Neal Lawing (2010), and *Shem Pete's Alaska* by James Kari and James A. Fall (University of Alaska Press, 2003). For information on the history of the Russian Orthodox Church in Alaska, I visited the Library of Congress' website as well as the NPS History website, among others. *The Anchorage Daily News* article, "People on the Peninsula, the Old Believer tour guide" by Tegan Hanlon (July 22, 2018) provided both a historical and modern-day perspective on Russian Orthodoxy in Alaska. My thanks and gratitude to all these sources.

The Jackson Browne songs mentioned in the novel, "Jamaica Say You Will" and "From Silver Lake," are from his 1972 album, *Saturate Before Using* (Atlantic Recording Corp), music that has resonated with me and inspired me for decades. The Shakespeare quotes scattered through this book are from the plays *Romeo and Juliet, The Tempest, As You Like It,* and *Hamlet,* and the William Wordsworth quote is from the poem, "The Tables Turned," published in 1798 in *Lyrical Ballads.*

Thanks always and forever to my late mother, Carol L. Durr, and to my family, Chris and Jen especially, for their love and support and to Henry and Jasper, who brighten my world and inspire me in more ways than I can say. And to Jack and Lola, always by my side.

Photo by William Barstow

SARAH BIRDSALL HAS LIVED IN ALASKA most of her life, with many of her formative years spent in remote parts of the state. She is the author of the award-winning novels *The Red Mitten* (McRoy & Blackburn, 2006), and *Wild Rivers, Wild Rose* (University of Alaska Press, 2020), the latter of which was the 2021 WILLA Literary Award Winner in Historical Fiction. Her short fiction has appeared in the *Alaska Quarterly Review*, *Alaska Women Speak*, and *Cirque*. She is a Rasmuson Foundation award recipient. A former award-winning journalist, she has an MFA in creative writing from the University of Alaska Anchorage and lives in her hometown of Talkeetna, Alaska.

www.ingramcontent.com/pod-product-compliance
Ingram Content Group UK Ltd.
Pitfield, Milton Keynes, MK11 3LW, UK
UKHW041434150325
456118UK00012B/29